WAKING
MAYA

WAKING
MAYA

W.J.Goldie

To order additional copies of this book, contact:
Xlibris Corporation
1-888-795-4274
www.Xlibris.com
Orders@Xlibris.com
20653

For Meghan

To my friend
Drew, with
good cheer!
Best always,
WJ Goldie
3-27-04

CHAPTER 1

Maya Burke's father showed up exactly two weeks after her twenty-second birthday in a most unexpected way: up through the earth. Well, it wasn't exactly *him*, but rather something that belonged to him. To Maya it represented her first real experience of her father, except perhaps for a few glimpses she'd had of him through the milky vision of a newborn, back when he shared the house in Plainfield with her mother, long before he disappeared and the visions of him began to grow in her mind with wild abandon.

Her cat, Livingston, was there, too, wrapped tightly in a plastic bundle at her feet, his life force gone, the vet's prognosis finally realized. Maya was already missing her steadfast companion, that warm presence on her stomach when she lay down, the fur that shimmered like a halo in the flickering light of the TV. Her thought: The Lord giveth and the Lord taketh away.

Or some such nonsense.

The sky, slate gray and heavy, seemed to be pressing down on her. She felt so small, so inconsequential, so *squished*, as she scanned the yard from end to end, from the house clear out to the woods, in search of the perfect spot.

There.

Just beyond the old oak tree. She took the shovel and strode over to the area, and drawing a deep breath, touched the tip to the ground. She stepped down with all her weight. The metal edge bit hard into the rubber sole of her tennis shoe but she didn't care. Pain seemed to be appropriate at a time like this.

She lifted and tossed the pyramids of dirt out of the hole until she had scattered enough earth on the grass to really enrage her mother. When she stopped to catch her breath, her back was moist with perspiration.

She peered down into the hole.

"Deeper," she ordered herself, and so she bent over and stabbed the metal tip down again and resumed digging.

Dink.

What was this?

Treasure?

Dink.

"Hmm," she said, wrinkling her brow, forming that upside-down "U" between her eyes, the expression that her mother had warned would be the birth of early wrinkles. It was just like Muriel to criticize something she couldn't change. What was she supposed to do? Anyway, the lines were barely noticeable.

She fell to her knees and brushed loose dirt from a hard, flat surface lodged securely in the ground, as tingles of excitement buzzed through her. When she couldn't lift the object out, she dashed over to the tool shed and ripped a hand spade from the wall.

Breathlessly she began to dig again, this time more carefully, scraping a narrow gully around the flat surface until a metal box began to take shape, like an ancient temple rising out of the dirt, an archeologist's dream.

As she brushed the last of the earth from the top of the box, etchings became visible, intricate grid-like patterns cut lightly into the silvery metal, abstract web-like designs interlaced one upon the other, receding back to infinity. At either end were carved images of the earth and sun.

Finally the box came loose. Gently she lifted it out—it was surprisingly light—and placed it on the ground. Holding her breath she pulled up the metal clasp and opened it.

The treasure: a leather-bound notebook.

Buried in the ground.

In *her* backyard.

Transfixed, she practically fell into the hole. She collected herself and opened the book.

A white page, a handwritten sentence. An impossibility.

"Oh, my God," she said.

There, sitting on her lap, a crucial piece of a puzzle she had long tried to solve fell into place. It began with a single scrawled sentence which seemed to be reaching forward from the past to seize her. Right there, in black and white:

To my dear daughter, Maya, with love from your father.

She exhaled—finally.

"This isn't happening," she said. "This can't be happening."

She ran her hand over the page. Yes, it was real. She glanced at the inside cover, saw that he had written out his name: David Orr. Muriel hadn't even told her that much.

She shook her head as if to wake up from a dream. Her next thought: maybe magic does exist in the universe. Maybe God does. And maybe that God answers prayers, even those that live deep within, unknown even to the mind.

Until this day Maya had known almost nothing of her father, had seen no evidence of his existence, no artifact, no memento, nothing, save one old photo she had dug out of a basement drawer at the age of five, which she had stupidly given to Muriel. That was the first and last she'd seen of him. Miraculously, she remembered the blurry image. He was with Muriel in a park. That was it.

Her father had been erased from their lives like someone in a witness protection plan, spirited away to parts unknown, assigned a new identity, all evidence of his former life destroyed. For all she knew this was true—until now. Now, she held the real truth in her hands.

She ran her fingers across a sea of blue-ruled pages on which he had written extensively about exactly the kinds of matters she hungered to know. The answers to her questions lay right in her hands: his life of two decades ago, what he did, what had happened. Why he left. It was all there. There could be no better birthday present.

This is who I am, she thought.

She looked closer now, saw that the text was shorter than she had first thought, for the intense handwriting stopped abruptly after only fifteen pages. An ocean of empty white followed, and she felt a loss for what those pages might have held. But never mind, she was grateful for what she had. It was a lot, and a fountain of hope welled up inside her.

Sitting there, beneath the heavy Maryland sky, in the shifting winds of late summer that made the trees sing like the ocean surf, Maya hugged the slender volume in her arms. She would savor it beyond her wildest dreams.

But not yet. For that she needed calmness, receptivity, which she could not have until the feline body at her feet, wrapped in an improvised plastic burial shroud stained with tears, was laid to rest.

In death, as in life, Livingston brought her hope. His exit was an entrance of a kind, then, bringing her father to her. This knowing moved through her like a warm salve. Looking down, she thought: one into the earth, one out. Maybe life was like that—an even exchange through a revolving door, a zero sum game.

Now she turned her gaze to the large lawn and wondered, How? How had she managed to find this lucky spot beneath the creaking branches of the old oak? Why here?

She hadn't exactly *found* it; more like it had found her. She had unplugged her pinball machine of a brain for just a few moments and let her feet carry her on a path of their own choosing, freely, as a leaf zigzags down to the ground. By releasing. By trusting.

And strange as it may sound, she felt as though she had watched this process unfold from a distance, as if a part of her had broken free and was looking on from beside her. When the shovel tip had hit metal this witness part of her had watched it all.

Suddenly overwhelming emotions engulfed her, not about Livingston but somehow related to this stroke of luck. Her face darkened. She began to tremble.

No. Not now.

So predictable, the arrival of this pall, this dread, this blackness that had so often owned her. And here it was again—even after a positive event—the usual aftershock of a strong emotional reaction, that nauseous sensation that had been stamped into her far back in the dim mists of childhood, when her mother would slap her across the face or jerk her around like a stingy vending machine, screaming at the girl at the top of her voice, blaming her for things she hadn't done and often didn't even understand. At these times Maya would disappear inside herself, into her mind, terrified, hating herself for displeasing Muriel yet not knowing how to make it better. The echoes of Muriel's shrieks still lived on inside her, and so she had grown up watchful, wary, untrusting.

But this was *good* news! Why should she succumb to the darkness for this? She was older now, Muriel didn't pull her strings anymore; she had learned to control herself, to weather the storms, to outlast them.

She would do what she had learned, what the books had taught her: Detach. The mind was the enemy at such times. Separate from it and its unneeded warnings. Let them fall where they will; don't follow. Focus on the body, the moment. The breath. Breathe slowly, intentionally.

One, two, in, out . . . expand the abdomen . . . slower . . . slower . . .

After a minute of this the grip of the anger and sadness began to weaken. Her mind calmed, settled, emptied, despite what it wanted to do: to rage. She stared out at the woods, opened herself to the beauty of the trees that bent like hula-skirted maidens in the wind.

Look at them. Be them.

Feel the wind brush against the skin. Devour the fragrant air.

As if by magic, her attention shifted from the well-worn track of her childhood fears to her senses, to the now. Her shakiness subsided, then disappeared altogether. When she gazed up, the sky seemed brighter. Soon, though, a few random thoughts crept in again. Wistfully, she surveyed the property, wishing it was the way it used to be.

When Muriel had married Maya's father twenty-three years ago, her sixty-acre property of expansive plains and rolling hills that girded Plainfield's northern border was fallow. The moment Muriel had inherited the land from her parents—it had been in the Burke family for generations—it ceased to be a farm. In an instant, Muriel had put a halt to an agricultural legacy. And though she had said many times she would plant, the fields had always remained open and empty.

Over the years the neighboring farms sold out to the developers, one by one, and Plainfield gradually became a well-coifed suburb, its rural character sliding slowly and absolutely into oblivion. Muriel was the last to sell out. Within weeks workmen were hammering away at the skeletons of rancher and split level homes, filling up all that open space. To the ten-year-old Maya, who had flung herself into many happy hours ranging over the grassy fields in search of Indian arrowheads or playing hide and seek with friends in the tall grass, the arrival of these cookie-cutter homes spelled the end of childhood.

When the earth movers had gone, when all the streets were straight and uniform and clean, Muriel's spread had shrunk to only two acres. But with the sale of the land went her money worries, too.

Muriel had had the old Burke farmhouse knocked down and a new house built, just like the others only twice as big, a tract mansion, Maya called it. The sole survivor of the rickety farmhouse that had been in Muriel's family a hundred and fifty years was a lonely section of splintered fence at the back of the yard, hidden beneath a tree branch that reached over from the woods. It was strange, Maya had often thought, that this one little artifact had escaped Muriel's campaign to obliterate the past. She would never raise the subject, though, for fear that Muriel would eliminate it, too.

As for David Orr, Muriel never spoke of him. Not then, and not now. That part of her life remained buried. Maya had long ago learned not to ask about her father. It was hopeless. There was nothing she could do about it.

Maya put David Orr's journal back in its box and sealed the lid. She picked up the bundle containing poor Livingston and gently placed him in the hole.

"Don't be afraid," she whispered. "There's only freedom where you're going."

Then she took up the shovel and began to fill in the hole, each toss of dirt feeling heavier than the last. As the soil slapped against the plastic with an ugly splattering sound, her eyes filled with tears. She finished as fast as she could.

Wiping her face dry she pushed a tiny wooden marker into the ground: *Livingston, Trusted Companion.* Muriel or the lawn guy would probably remove it, but at least Maya would have tried.

She hung the tools back up in the shed and headed for the house, just as Josh was pulling into the driveway. She called out to him to wait. He nodded and waved to her.

She wanted more than anything to stay home, to be alone, to read her father's writings. To understand the past. *Her* past. She needed to fill in the blanks; there were so many. The pull was intense but Josh was there and she couldn't just send him off, especially since he had said how badly he wanted to go out. She looked over at the journal. What could be more important than this?

She pulled a sweatshirt over her overalls and flipped her long auburn hair out from her neck. Standing at the bedroom mirror, she smiled, pleased at how brightly her teeth contrasted against skin which had tanned almost to the color of coffee during the summer. She had full wide lips, long-lashed brown eyes, and a face that shouted out whatever emotion she was feeling, making any attempt to deceive nearly impossible. She tied her hair into a ponytail and pressed out her chest. She had a slender athletic body, and long, strong legs.

She couldn't help but see the dramatic changes in herself over the last few years. The gawkiness that had plagued her in her teens had miraculously transformed into five-feet-eight-inch stateliness, which had brought with it the attention of men. This was okay. She was getting used to it. Her slender physique had begun to blossom in her late teens, proportioning itself better and better with each passing year. Her beauty was earthy and neutral, and

not entirely feminine. She never used makeup; Muriel's gift bottles
of perfumes and oils gathered dust in a bathroom cabinet.

*   *   *

Josh Rosenberg waited patiently in his rusty old Mustang,
absent-mindedly tapping his foot to one of the songs that
perpetually played in his head, and flipping through *Guitar Player*
magazine. He was in his usual uniform: black jeans, white T-shirt,
black leather jacket and work boots with untied laces that spilled
out like Medusan locks.

Maya hopped into the car, and Josh smiled his broad,
incandescent smile and flipped back his black hair, which
immediately fell back over his eyes. Maya shook her head and had
to laugh to herself. Josh could be so affected. He was cool *and* a
caricature of cool at the same time. What she had liked best about
him was that he was exactly the opposite of the conservative, khaki-
wearing guys she had been going out with when she met him, the
ones who never had an original thought.

He turned to check traffic, and his motion caused the tattoo at
the back of his neck to move. A half dozen loop earrings jiggled on
his right earlobe.

They had passed each other in the hallways of Plainfield High
but did not meet until years later, just before Maya's college
graduation. Josh's band was playing a dorm party, and Maya and
Josh had walked out to the parking lot at the exact same instant.
They started up a conversation that ended up running so long
that the drummer had to pull Josh in by the arm to finish the set.
But not before they had made a plan to meet. Maya was surprised
at how such a punked-out guy could be so down-to-earth and
accessible.

That was six months ago. She liked him. He was fun. He was
spontaneous. He had opened her up. She stayed at his place
sometimes—Muriel had completely dropped the reigns on Maya
during sophomore year—but was it a relationship? What *was* a
relationship? She didn't know.

They rolled down the windows and cruised the quiet streets of Plainfield in silence, the full moon hovering like a Ping Pong ball in the darkening sky, the September breeze flowing like warm water across their faces.

The Orion Cafe was packed with the usual students from the art institute across the street who poured clear out onto the sidewalk tables. Josh disappeared inside while Maya pounced on an open table. He returned with two café lattes.

"Thanks," she said, reaching out for one.

She turned and watched the passing traffic of Harlow Street, trying to contain the growing frustration at not being at home reading her father's journal. What was wrong with her? Why was she out at a time like this? But here she was, and that was that.

"I found something."

"Really?" he said, sipping his latte. "What?"

"A journal."

"A what?"

"A book," she said. "A book my father wrote."

"Your father?" he said, surprised. "I thought he died."

"What?" she said, taken by surprise. "Where exactly did you hear that?"

"You said it, didn't you?"

All she could do was level a hard stare at him, and simmer with anger. "That's really an insensitive thing to say."

"Sorry."

"*Sorry?*" She shook her head.

"Hey, cool down. I didn't mean anything."

"I just wanted to tell you about this great thing that happened and now I'm regretting even bringing it up."

"I said I'm sorry. Honest. Come on, tell me."

She turned away. Something was wrong, she could feel it, beyond the usual stupid arguments they had. It was hanging in the air, plain as day. Only she didn't know what it was.

They drank in silence for a time, their eyes wandering around, settling on anything but each other. Finally, she could stand it no longer. Life was too short for angry silences.

"Oh, hell," she said. "I'm being a bitch. I'm sorry. I've been rattled lately."

"All right," he said.

"So, can I tell you about this journal?"

"Sure."

"Well, he wrote it to me. I mean, *directly* to me. As in, 'To my daughter.' Isn't that amazing? He obviously wanted to communicate something really important to me."

"And what was that?"

"I don't know. I didn't get very far."

"Why not?"

"You showed up."

"Oh yeah, blame it on Josh," he said. Then: "Maybe you shouldn't read it."

She laughed. "Yeah, maybe I'll just toss it out. Can't be anything important in it."

"No. I'm serious."

Again she felt broadsided, and became agitated. It was just like Josh to be contrary, to take the wind out of her sails, to be combative simply to elicit a reaction. And just when she was working up some excitement about something.

She played with a sugar packet, staring at him, wondering what she had ever seen in him. This was ground she had covered many times. Of course he was attractive but was that all? Was she that shallow? What exactly did they have in common? Anything?

Now, more than ever she wished she'd stayed home.

"Wait, wait," he said. "You don't know what I mean. Hear me out."

Then, suddenly, he changed. The other Josh emerged, the one that made her feel good, the intense warm Josh, not the casual hipster, the guy who played with his hair. The smirk was gone, melted seamlessly into a knowing smile, and she saw what it was that had excited her about him.

This Josh was connected to something deep, something untamed, a passion of real power. He was the guy whose guitar could turn a room full of strangers into a single pulsing being. He knew how to channel some kind of primal energy force. She was drawn to people like that, even though she also envied them. *She* wanted to hold that power in her hands, feel it pass through her to others, be that connected. And the fact that Josh didn't give a damn about ninety-nine percent of life made it that much harder to stomach.

"Livingston died," she blurted out.

"Who?"

"My cat."

"Ah," he said, nodding. "That's why you're so funky."

She shook her head. "I feel sad about him, of course, but mainly I feel this, this—I don't know how to describe it—this existential pressure. This may sound crazy but it feels like I have to figure out my purpose in life. Is that corny, or what? I'm having a purpose attack. Jesus. It's all I can think about. It's like this high command inside my head has ordered me to get moving, or else. Or else what? I'm about to burst with all this. What's the purpose of my life? You know what? I don't care! How about that?"

He said, "Maybe your purpose is to live and be happy."

"Easy for you to say. You're a musician. You have a calling. What about me?"

"You really don't know, do you?"

"No."

"Do you want to?"

His directness gave her pause. Strange—this was not exactly a Josh conversation.

"Go ahead," she said. "Tell me."

He put his cup down, leaned forward and said, "It's not a matter of looking inside, as you are always so gung-ho to do, because you know what you'll find in there? The past, what's already happened, what's done and gone. Journals in your backyard that take you backwards when what you want to do is go forward—"

"Josh, it was written by my father. Can you seriously be telling me not to read it?"

"I'm not saying that, Maya. Just listen to me."

She waited, her arms crossed.

He said, "You don't discover what to do with your life. It's not something you find. It doesn't exist. It's not *located* anywhere."

He ran his fingers over the dragon tattoo on his forearm. She had known no other than the illustrated Josh, though others had of course existed; he wasn't born with mythical creatures on his arms. She had always been awed by the absolute certainty possessed by the tattooed. She'd wished she could feel that much commitment about something, but she never had.

"You make it up as you go," he said.

"Excuse me?"

"You make it up as you go."

"That's it? That's the whole fount of wisdom?"

He nodded, undaunted. "No signposts, no guides, just what you decide, here and now."

Here was the yawning canyon between them. She saw life as something lived in the service of some higher principle beyond oneself, even if it was just a belief in something like God, or gardening, or building aircraft carriers, whereas he lived for the here-and-now with little thought of the whys and hows of life. The uncomfortable truth, though, was that given the choice, she would have chosen his way. People like Josh always seemed content.

"I understand what you're saying, Josh, but don't you ever wonder if there's a greater point to life?"

He shrugged, emotionally checking out. They had been here before.

"Well, there's got to be more to life than Plainfield," she said, a little too forcefully. "I can tell you that." Then she caught his look of annoyance.

"I know," she said. "Blah, blah, blah. You don't care about any of this, so go ahead and make a face. I don't care, I'm used to it."

"I'm not making a face," he said. "It's just . . ."

"Just what?"

She looked at him and suddenly she understood. This was what he had wanted to talk about. She had not let him. Instead she had blathered on and on about herself and her meaningless life. Perfect. Just perfect.

What a fool I am, she thought.

She waited for him to say something, but he just sat there, silent. Time droned on. A few feet away, a car backing into a parking space bumped into the car in front of it. An ambulance screamed by, leaving a wake of noise that bounced through the buildings. Two girls sauntered down the sidewalk in full-body black leotards so tight that everyone turned to watch.

Finally, Josh spoke. She held her breath. She *knew*. Knew what he was about to say.

"I'm not saying we should break up," he said.

She drew a quick breath. Her skin felt hot and prickly. She had suddenly become mute, docile, obedient—not the spirited Maya that people knew but more her mother's girl. The wimp.

The old programming had kicked in. She desperately wanted to fight, yell, kick the table over. Anything but give in. She swallowed, feeling sick in her stomach.

She said, "You want to see other people."

"No," he said. "I just want some time."

She laughed derisively. "What do you mean? You've got plenty of that now. I don't keep any tabs on you."

"I know," he said. "I can't explain it. It's not the same thing."

She shook her head. "Then I don't understand."

He sat there, just staring down, miserably.

"Can you tell me what's going on?" she asked.

"Let's not do this."

"Do what?"

Still he said nothing.

"Are we breaking up, or what?" she said.

"I need time on my own, that's all."

"Okay, then. If that's the best you can do, can you take me home now?"

"Sure," he said, reaching for his keys.

She stared out the window the whole drive back, a familiar agony welling up inside that took real strength to keep down. *You're bad*, it said. This was incorrect, yet there it was. She wasn't bad. If anything, Josh was.

What a day. First Livingston and now this. She did not—would not—cry until she was alone in the safety of her room. The tears would not be for Josh, either. No. They would fall for the whole unexpressed backlog of frustration inside of her. After awhile she would not remember why she hurt. It would be just one big howl, a floating mass unattached to anything real. When it was over she would feel better. That was how it worked.

She walked from the car without a word. He called out but she did not turn or answer. Why should she? As she reached the door she was surprised when a hint of lightness crept into her step.

She did not cry that night, after all.

Later, clean and warm in bed, leaning on the pillows against the headboard, she felt her bond with Josh begin to withdraw in favor of one she knew would be stronger, the bond of blood. She reached under the bed for her father's journal.

She did not know it then, but the slender volume she held in her hands would be the doorway she had always longed for, a passage into a world that held the answers to the questions which had haunted her for her entire life.

CHAPTER 2

She looked around the room and noticed, perhaps for the first time, that the pale yellow light flowing from the bedside lamp illuminated a child's room. The desk, chest of drawers, table and bookshelves, now a decade old in white and powder blue, were purchased by Muriel for a pre-teenager. On a shelf that rode just below the ceiling, a row of stuffed animals stared blankly downwards, their faces frozen in empty smiles, their fur rimmed with dust, the comfort they once gave long gone.

She wondered: Was this room *ever* hers? A strange feeling had been building in her for some time, that her room was really Muriel's—or at least *her* idea of Maya. Maya had never claimed it for herself. She couldn't have. If she had tried, Muriel would have blocked her. Somehow. From the beginning the girl had yielded. It just hadn't been so obvious before.

She heard the front door shut. She quickly slid the journal under the bed and switched off the light.

Footsteps sounded in the hallway, then whispers and soft laughter. Maya heard the deep tones of a man's voice playing off of Muriel's high-pitched flirtatiousness. The whispers turned to giggles, there was a burst of laughter followed by a loud "Shhhh!" and then all sounds disappeared into Muriel's room with a click of the door.

The door opened a minute later, then Maya's door opened, too. *She never knocks.* Maya looked up at the figure of Muriel in silhouette, backlit by the hall light, her face hidden in shadow.

"Sweetheart?"

The word flowed into the room on a blast of liquor-laced air. Looking up at the tall figure of her mother, Maya felt her stomach tighten.

"Hi, Mom."

"How's it going?" Muriel said, slurring the words.

Maya's internal radar spun wildly but could not determine her mother's emotional state, at least not yet.

"Fine," Maya said.

"That's good, *really* good." Muriel let out a long yawn. "What was I saying? Oh, yeah. I try. I do. Honest. You can't fault me for that, right?"

Maya started to panic. What was this about? Why the apology? She mentally clicked back through the previous hours and days, searching for the topic of this conversation. She found nothing. She'd hardly even seen Muriel lately.

"It's fine, Mom, really," she said finally in as warm a voice as she could muster.

"Really?"

"Yep. Honest."

"Oh, good," Muriel said, happily. "Oh, by the way, Henry is over. You know Henry. I introduced you, right?"

"Uh-huh," Maya said, though she'd never met the man.

There was a long pause. Muriel said, "Still there?"

"Yep," Maya said, sliding slowly under the blankets.

"Whatever you may think, I do love you," Muriel said into the darkness. "That's all I wanted to say. Goodnight, kiddo." She shut the door and left.

Lying in the dark, Maya exhaled a sigh of relief. She had no idea what that was about, but then she hardly ever did. First Josh and his stupid break-up and now Muriel apologizing for non-existent events. Why did life have to be so confusing?

Sometimes she just wanted to run away from it all, sprint down the road and never look back. Maybe catch a plane somewhere. That would be efficient. She had always felt at odds with the world. She emanated an *otherness* that she was certain repelled people. What were you supposed to do about that? Get a personality transplant? Go off to see if you had a home tribe somewhere?

Then there were the practical issues in front of her. She hadn't done much about them, either. Now that she had finished college it was time to work, but the idea of getting some job she would probably hate was distressing. She hoped her attitude would change—maybe she could force it to—because if it didn't she'd be stuck for God-knows-how-long with people ducking their heads into her room in the middle of the night apologizing for events that had never occurred and asking questions that had no answers. And that just could not happen.

She turned her thoughts back to her father's journal, and her worries began to dissolve. This was a special night, after all, one to be savored, possibly forever. She walked over to the window, lifted it open, slid the screen all the way up until it snapped into place with a twang. Then she leaned out of the third-floor window and stretched her arms out as if lording over all the land.

Space!

Above her, the orb of the moon hung as bright as a headlight, drenching the woods in soft light. The trees rustled gently in the wind, as if to get her attention. *Look! Over here!*

Mystery filled the night. The world was an empty cup waiting to be filled, its secrets within reach. She inhaled deeply, felt her lungs fill to capacity. The peacefulness of one a.m. caressed her. Time had dissolved, she was floating. Muriel and Josh and everything else had disappeared like a stale old dream in the light of morning.

She felt herself slip out of her body, float out of the window, drift up into the sky like a bird that understood the night, an eagle, gliding on rivers of wind, peering down at the world and its sleep-walkers, swooping earthward in spirals that grew ever wider, high above the twinkling lights that pierced the clouds like fallen stars . . .

She smiled. She'd done it, released the day, her life, Muriel, Josh, all of it.

She pulled herself back, down, to earth, to the house, to the room, to her body—and accidentally caught her nightshirt on a nail sticking out of the windowsill, ripping the fabric up to her bellybutton. She laughed. No matter. The shirt was threadbare, disintegrating. Too bad, though, it was a favorite, with its Yin Yang symbol stenciled on the front.

She mused on the Yin Yang for a moment, the black and white teardrops caught in a circular embrace. Why were they endlessly moving in circles, chasing each other's tail? Would they ever catch up? What about the seeds inside? Would they grow larger and take over their hosts? What then? The questions brought up an endless stream of new questions, which is exactly what she liked about it. It led directly into mystery.

She liked the image so much that she had carefully painted one on the back of her tennis shoes, stretched to abstraction, designed to go undetected by all but the most perceptive of observers. If she ever met a guy who spotted her Yin Yang, well, it would all be over. But what was the chance of that?

She pressed her ear to the door. The house was quiet. Muriel was probably in for the night with this Henry person, or whatever his name was.

She settled back against the pillows and opened the book. The first thing she noticed was the handwriting: not pretty. A jumbled mess of script and printing almost as tortured as her own.

Proof! She *was* his. She could not write a sentence from one end to the other without all sorts of interference taking place, as if her hand and brain were not synched up like everyone else's. At times her handwriting could become so intense she would poke the pen right through the paper. Her sixth-grade teacher had suggested she take up engraving. The rambling letters she wrote to her uncle Buddy felt like Braille. Though her writing had eased up over the years, still she struggled. Once she had learned to type on a keyboard, everything changed.

Now, for the first time, she viewed her poor handwriting not so much as a liability as an inevitability. An inheritance.

She slid her fingertips across the page as a sightless reader would, absorbing all the little ridges and valleys.

Then she began to read.

Maya, you must believe that I love you with all my heart.
That is the first order of business. Whatever has happened or will
happen, this much is true—I am your father and always will

be. I know there is much you will want to know. In due time, my love.

I do not know what your mother has told you. You may feel anger toward me. If so, you are justified. But I am hoping that your hunger to know will triumph above all else, that you will be open to what I have to tell you.

There is no way I can properly explain why I left. Why I had to leave. My reasons, which are—were—compelling, cannot match the disappointment you must feel in not knowing me. Maybe, maybe, this can change. My reasons for doing what I did will soon become clear to you.

She lay the book down in her lap as intense emotions exploded in her like land mines—confusion, longing, loss. Every step across the page seemed to contain one. *Breathe*, she told herself. She read on.

To tell you my story, I must speak of a greater story, of matters not specific to me or you but shared by all people. Here's a small fact about me: it is difficult for me to separate myself from my work. For better or worse, I am that which I do.

It is early evening as I write to you in my study. Your mother cares for you down the hall. You are a lovely runt of one, ruddy-cheeked and alert. When I look at you I am filled with awe. It's odd. After all my searching, it is only through you that I begin to feel the presence of a divinity. For that, I am already in your debt.

My window looks out on the farm. A white picket fence snakes out into the distance. Though I was an athlete in my youth, I now resort to taking long walks for exercise, which I do in the fields.

My heart breaks as I write this, my "future" daughter. But never mind that. What must be, must be. I am—was—a researcher, at the university and elsewhere, and this is where it begins.

Through my work I have stumbled—and that is the right word—onto observations of a phenomenon of the most unexpected and fantastical nature, having to do with the way that change comes about. By change I mean in all ways, from the small to the large, from the personal to the societal. In the course of my work I have become certain of some things. I cannot give the details here, but I know what I say to be true. It is this: that a sweeping cultural change will occur in the coming years, one which will alter all the ways of the world.

At this moment, Maya, the world is poised at the dawn of a period of tremendous upheaval and transformation, unseen in many centuries. Monumental forces are churning, even now, as I write to you.

I tell you this because discord always accompanies change. All of the world's peoples will begin to feel it. You, dear daughter, must endeavor to see whatever confusion occurs in the coming years as the precursor, not the destination, of the change. As the storm strikes, look beyond its violence to the nourishment of the rain, for that is its greater purpose.

She stopped, looked up. The world seemed to be set on pause. The ticking of the nightstand clock sounded like the cracks of a sledgehammer. Her mind was hard at work, trying to wrap itself around his words, attempting to understand.

Here was the first communication she'd ever had from her father, and she was confused. What was this change of his? Twenty years had passed, at least from her point of view, and the world was still spinning pretty much as it always had been. Even if something *had* changed, how could she separate it from the normal course of change? She frowned. She felt deflated, disappointed in him. He wasn't as impressive as she had hoped.

Then an idea occurred to her, something which should have been obvious from the start. One of his predictions had actually come about.

She had found the journal.

His burying it had presupposed her discovering it, right? How could he have known, or even thought, that she would find it? It was a prediction, too, just like the rest of what she'd read, her finding an object buried in a random part of the yard and years in the future.

Or maybe it was just coincidence.

She thought back to the way she had selected Livingston's burial place. It was an inner, an intuitive process. She had *opened* herself, hadn't she, but to what? Could something unusual have happened? She had prompted her intuition and awaited a response from within, an invitation, a direction telling her where to dig.

Maybe she'd received one.

From him?

That's insane, she told herself. She should have her head examined for such thoughts. Get a grip. But thinking back, it did feel that way.

Suddenly shivers were crawling all over her neck and arms, and she wheeled around, looking for something.

"Hello?" she said to no one in particular.

She swore she felt another presence there in the room, watching her. Panicked, she vaulted out of bed and charged into the living room like a frightened gazelle, switching on every light until the room was as bright as an operating room. She turned on the television, too, but muted it for fear of waking Muriel.

The perfect anesthesia was on channel sixty-eight. The benign, colorful maps of the weather channel, the high and low pressure systems, the temperature figures, the weather lady's soothing voice; all worked to slow her racing mind. A low pressure front was approaching Boston, threatening storms. Rain was good. Rain wasn't scary.

Her mind slowed but it did not stop. What it had seized upon with pit bull tenacity, despite the distracting potential of precipitation in New England, was the significance of the *finding* of the journal, beyond the fact of the information it held.

In Maya's world, every thought, every action, every event, no matter how inconsequential, held meaning. Taken together, the events of one's life added up to an infinitely complex, mysterious and meaning-laden master plan. Nothing was random. If the batteries in her CD player died on a particular song, then hearing that song at that moment likely would have been detrimental in some way. Maybe the lyrics would have led her to a poor decision or the radio she would have switched on instead would have offered her a better perspective. If she took a wrong turn in the car, then the street she had happened upon probably held something for her. And on and on it went.

And if she found a decades-old journal in her backyard, then there was a reason it had happened at that exact moment and no other.

Lacking an understanding of how all the events of one's life meshed together to create this meta-symphony of meaning, one's existence made about as much sense as the back of an embroidery, a mishmash of threads going every which way with no rhyme or reason. If, on the other hand, you understood the bigger picture, or at least pieces of it, then you got to see the perfectly stitched scene on the other side, which, she theorized, amounted to some kind of higher truth or mystical experience.

She put a lot of stock in synchronicities, those seemingly chance occurrences that carry within them profound meaning—being in the right place at the right time, intuitively knowing of an event before it occurs, and so on. Synchronicities were clues that hinted at how the meta-symphony worked. The mysterious and perfect universe didn't have to be drawn out if you had synchronicities to work with—then the universe was actively communicating, sending information back to you from its perspective of total knowing, as if saying *Hint!* Within the synchronistic event hid a glimpse of the big picture.

She was certain that the finding of the journal represented a synchronicity of monumental importance. She fully believed that the journal would change her life. She *knew* it.

This knowing was familiar. Since Maya was a child she'd had an intuitive ability that bordered on precognition, though it was spotty and often disappeared for weeks and months at a time. Her prescient visuals would appear in her mind accompanied by a unique feeling, a kind of chill that ran through her body. Almost always this information was borne out sooner or later as events in her life.

She went into the kitchen, scooped some Rocky Road ice cream into a dish. She ate while wandering around, until she was satisfied that everything was all right, that whatever weirdness had occurred was now finished. Then she made her way back to her room and continued reading.

> *I taught in the field of psycho-social dynamics to further an understanding of the behaviors of large masses of people on global events. My focus was on religious, cultural and political movements. Why do some gain enough momentum to change the world while others weaken and fade? What are the mechanics?*
>
> *I didn't stay long at the university, though. Eventually I signed on with the government. There I—*

Here several lines had been struck out with a heavy black marker.

> *—cannot be more specific about this. Suffice it to say that recently I left a project of great importance.*
>
> *My purpose here is to give you a little something in the hours before I go, a primer of the old man's work, if you will. I know I cannot be there for you, my dear, but here is a bit of what I am—or was. Just a pittance, I'm afraid.*
>
> *There is a bank in Calhoun called First Street Federal. There you will find a safe deposit box in your name. Take the key from the back of this book—*

Excitedly she flipped to the back cover where a slit had been cut. She slid a finger in and pulled out a flat key.

> *—go there and remove the contents of the box.*

*　　*　　*

Calhoun was fifteen minutes down Rural Route 32, past some of the oldest homes in the area, two-hundred-year-old stone mansions built along the river like fortresses constructed to greet eternity. The countryside was lush and thickly wooded, and the drive down the winding road pleasant.

Calhoun had managed to retain its small town flavor through strict zoning laws that controlled new development. Its business district of five bustling blocks formed almost a perfect representation of the America of the nineteen-fifties, with its granite-fronted buildings, soda shops, art deco flourishes, and antique lamp posts that reached over the sidewalks like the branches of weeping willows. The town contrasted sharply with nearby Owings Mills and Reisterstown, suburbs which had experienced building booms that had grown them to the size of small cities.

Maya swerved her little red Corolla into an angled parking spot in front of the bank. She was still sleepy from staying up half the night with her mind chugging away with the implications of what was happening, wondering what secrets the bank would hold. Surprisingly, Josh had not been on her mind at all. Maybe she needed time away from him, too.

She had brought the journal with her, safely tucked away in the backpack she carried everywhere she went.

. . . in the hours before I go.

What had he meant by this? Go where?

The morning was a perfect seventy degrees, the sun hidden behind a solid overcast. The gong of the clock in the square struck loudly as she pulled open the heavy door of the bank.

Walking through the lobby, for the first time she began to worry. What was in the safe deposit box? Was it illegal? Would the clerk push a secret button under his desk when she made her request? Would a soundless alarm bring the police rushing in?

Who exactly was David Orr?

Never mind, she told herself. She had to do this. There was no choice, really, at least not if she wanted to understand the past.

She stood in front of a desk where a clerk was filing some

papers in a drawer. He did not look up or acknowledge her. The wait was torturous.

She sighed.

"I know you're there, young lady," the clerk said curtly.

"Sorry."

Finally, after two more minutes, the man said, "Yes?" Still not looking up.

"I need to get into a safe deposit box, please."

The man, mid-fifties and balding, with a single tuft of hair swept up over his pinkish head and a sneer permanently etched on his face, finally peered up at her. Immediately, as if that motion was hard-wired to another, his eyes jerked toward a glass-walled office near the front of the bank and into the laser-beam stare of a silver-haired man in a neatly tailored suit.

Suddenly the clerk snapped to attention as if he'd been smacked on the back of the legs with a paddle. He turned to Maya and forced a smile.

"Sorry to keep you waiting," he said, straightening his tie. "Your name?"

"Maya Burke."

"Just a moment." He shuffled through a drawer, pulled out a small card.

"ID?" he said, his voice now convincingly pleasant.

She handed over her driver's license.

He placed it on the desk. Holding the card he had pulled from the drawer, he registered a look of surprise. "This is rather unusual."

Maya froze. She waited—waited for the man to reach under the desk and push the secret button.

He didn't. Instead he said, "This box hasn't been used in about twenty years."

"Yes," she said.

"It's not a problem. It's been prepaid for thirty."

Thirty years?

"We've been out of town."

"So you have," he said. "Sign here, then."

She took the card. Gracing the line above where she quickly scrawled her name was the signature of one David Orr. It was almost unreadable, just like hers. She smiled to herself.

"This way," the clerk said, rising.

He led her into a walk-in vault where a bank of safe deposit boxes lined the walls from floor to ceiling, and slid a key into number twelve-thirty.

She hesitated, then figured out what to do. She slid her key into the companion keyhole. They turned both keys simultaneously, and he pulled a metal box the size of a dictionary out of the wall and handed it to her.

"Those are the viewing rooms," he said, pointing to two doors in a narrow hallway.

"Thank you."

She walked into the first room, shut the door behind her and sat at the small wooden table, trying to calm herself. She was sure her heart was going to burst. She looked down at the box. A gift from her father! She felt as though she was standing on the outskirts of a glorious, magical city. All she had to do was take one step forward to enter it.

She pulled up the metal lid and looked inside. It was empty.
No!

Stunned, she shook her head vigorously, as if to fix eyes which were malfunctioning. What was happening? She felt as though she had fallen into a pothole and was plummeting down into an abyss.

This can't be, she thought. The clerk had done something. Played a trick on me.

Her newfound hope deflated like a punctured balloon.

Then she saw something at the far end of the box, a gray envelope, its color exactly matching that of the gunmetal drawer, causing it to blend in. She snatched it up and tore it open.

Looking at its contents, her eyes lit up in delight. She smiled. Then her smile grew into a grin. In a lightning quick reaction of emotional alchemy, despair had transformed into elation. Just like that.

The envelope held five thousand dollars in neatly-folded hundreds fastened together with a rubber band. That was great, she'd never seen so much money, but the real gift was the paper it was wrapped in on which her father had written, "Dr. Edgar Porter, 3706 N. Hillside, Chicago. A colleague. Maya, see Dr. Porter first."

She read these words several times, just to be certain. One of them filled her with hope. *First.* "See Dr. Porter *first.*"

She raised her fists in triumph. He was sending her on a mission. It was exactly what she had hoped.

CHAPTER 3

At breakfast the next morning Maya ached to ask Muriel about David Orr. The urge was stronger than it had been in years. Intense dreams had awakened her several times during the night, and she found herself arguing with herself about whether or not to break the long-standing taboo of silence around this subject. Fear, as usual, had won out. Provoking Muriel could mean long days of suffering, and Maya didn't want to risk that, especially now, when she sensed a big opening in her life.

Dressed in a terry cloth robe, Muriel stood at the kitchen's sliding doors, sipping a fruit smoothie and staring outside in the direction of the oak tree that had held the journal and now held Livingston. Her hair was a mess, the dark roots easily visible beneath wild blonde tangles. There were faint circles under her eyes, which would probably disappear as they usually did, in the shower. Muriel was naturally attractive, with a model's high cheekbones and a sly, dimpled smile, though her face was gaunt from too much dieting and working out at the gym. When she did eat, it was usually just a salad, a tiny piece of chicken or a few strawberries.

"You know those big-screen TVs, those abominations that can ruin a perfectly good living room?" she said, still looking out at the yard. "I think I've got to get one. Henry is into sports. God, I hate sports."

"Our TV's pretty big," Maya said, sitting at the kitchen table, nibbling on a muffin.

"Not big enough."

"Does he have bad eyes?"

"No, he doesn't have bad eyes," Muriel shot back. "He's a man. Men need their sports, and they need them big, God knows why."

"Not the ones I know."

Muriel laughed. "You don't know any men, honey. Those friends of yours, they're just boys." She turned to look at Maya. "But, hell, there's time. You need to meet some new people, get out of your skin once in awhile. You've got your face buried so deep in those books of yours you couldn't see a decent man if he was pressing up against you. How's something real going to ever happen to you if you don't *do* something every once in awhile?"

Maya ripped off a piece of muffin, dropped it into her mouth. Muriel was right. She was one of life's great spectators. Until now.

"This might come as a shock, Mom, but I'm going to follow your advice. For once."

Muriel managed a gravelly laugh.

Maya said, "I'm going camping."

"Camping? What good is that?"

"It's a start."

Muriel shrugged. "I suppose. Who with?"

"Josh."

"Sheesh," Muriel said, shaking her head. "You can do better than that freaky kid. You're beautiful, kiddo, but you act like you don't even know it. Use it. That kid, he's got more earrings than me except I have the taste to wear one pair at a time."

"He can express himself any way he wants to," Maya said, bristling at defending a guy who had just dumped her. Still, strangely, she felt no real anger at him.

"There are better ways to express yourself," Muriel said. "Like showing up at a job, for one."

"He has a job, for your information."

Muriel looked away. Maya had been noticing a sadness in her mother's voice that she had never heard before. It was minor but telling, although Maya did not know what it meant.

Maya finished the muffin, then rinsed the dish and put it in the dishwasher. She said, "You must be serious about this guy Henry, buying a TV and all."

"I haven't bought anything yet. I'm just thinking about it," she said. "Henry is one fine looking man but he doesn't drink anything stronger than iced tea. I hope he isn't one of those AA types. I haven't figured him out yet but I will, don't you doubt that."

"But you like him, right?"

"Yeah, I like him. I like him just fine."

"Good," Maya said.

Muriel gave her a sidelong glance. "Yeah, good," she said, with that somber tone in her voice.

Maya headed back to her room to pack, but not for a camping trip. The next day she would be in Chicago.

*   *   *

She had been on airplanes before, on vacations with Muriel, but she had never arranged the details of a trip herself. As it turned out, everything fell right in place. Reserving the flight online was easy. Once she arrived at the airport, she left the car in long-term parking, hopped a shuttle to the terminal, paid at the ticket counter, waited through the security line, and finally made the gate.

Inside the plane, she stuffed her backpack up in the overhead bin, squeezed into the window seat beside a tall man whose knees touched the forward seat and jammed her *City Paper* into the netting in front of her.

She stole a glance at the man, a handsome guy with perfectly combed sandy-brown hair, a square jaw, and a calm, confident manner. He was going to Los Angeles. She *knew* it. She knew it because the thought had come to her with that peculiar feeling of certainty.

Outside, beyond the scuffed window, workmen probed a complex of gears protruding from an open section of the wing. Watching them, Maya found herself wondering what would happen if one of those parts broke while the plane was aloft. What if the wing cracked or the engines gave out? What if the plane crashed? What would it feel like? Would she resign herself, try to fight, or—who knew—embrace it?

She understood the genesis of these gloomy thoughts. She was afraid to fly. Her defenses were up. Her protection against anticipatory fears was to stage a preemptive strike on them: imagine the worst, play it out in the imagination—and thus avoid being taken by surprise. It boiled down to simple preparation. In some ways it was a costly way to prepare.

Sitting there, in total safety, she imagined it all: the stomach-wrenching descent, the crushing g-force pressure that would stretch out the skin of her face, the explosive impact and the shattering of her body parts . . . and then . . .

What?

No one knew what.

She had always tried to view death from a spiritual perspective, as a natural progression, a transition into something else, maybe a different state of consciousness. NBD—no big deal. Logically, to her, it made the most sense. Why did people make such a fuss about something as natural as a tulip closing for the night? It would open again in some way, in some form, somewhere.

It was easy to be cavalier about death when you'd never been around it. She understood this. She knew her theories were nothing more than mind stuff. She hadn't a clue as to what would happen when she felt the grim reaper's bony-fingered tap on her shoulder.

Down on the tarmac, thick-chested men tossed suitcases onto a conveyor belt that rode up into the plane's underbelly. All that baggage, all those people. One day, she thought, they would all receive the tap. And so would she.

"Don't like flying?" the man beside her said.

Startled, she jumped. "What?"

"It looks like you're trying to squeeze the air out of that book."

"Oh," she said, loosening her grip on the journal.

"Me, I figure if something's going to happen, at least it'll be quick."

"I guess."

"Do you live in Chicago?"

"No. I live in Maryland. How about you?"

"L.A."

Ha! she thought with satisfaction. Maybe her ability was

working again. But then, the guy did look more than a little bit Hollywood.

He said, "You look surprised."

Her cheeks flushed. "I guess I had a feeling you were going there."

"Oh?" he said. "Why's that?"

"I don't know. I shouldn't have said anything. I'm sorry."

"Not a problem," he replied good-naturedly. "Let's see if you can guess what I do for a living."

"No, thanks, I'd rather not."

"Come on, give it a try. You never know."

She shrugged. A thought came to her, a *knowing*. "You're in radio," she said. "But not *on* it. Something behind the scenes, helping, organizing, something like that."

"Wow," he said. "I'm a programmer for a radio station in L.A. What's my marital status?"

"Do you mind if we don't do this?"

"Sure. No problem," he said. "You know, psychics are the number one industry in L.A."

"I'm not a psychic."

"Maybe you are and you just don't know it," he said. He nodded at the journal. "What's that?"

"Just some of my writings," she said, tightening her hold on the book.

"Are you a writer?"

"Oh no. I just put my thoughts down. It's therapy."

He nodded. The cabin suddenly lurched forward as the plane began to back up. She watched the terminal slide out of view. The man began to read a magazine.

She gripped the armrest tightly as the plane lifted off. After it leveled off she began to relax. She put on her headphones and opened the journal, even though she had already read through it several times.

Consciousness, both individually and collectively, causes the physical world to come into existence. Nothing exists outside of consciousness. All else is illusion. The world comes into being in every moment through the interplay of consciousnesses. We don't see it because we experience reality through our senses, which limit our perception to what is physical.

Energy flows into the earth through energy vortexes and exits through them, too. You may not know the word. Some native peoples call them power points. In these places, thoughts manifest into events faster; the thoughts of groups of people more so, especially if they are emotionally charged. This is how social, cultural and religious movements take form.

Buildings that are constructed near vortexes endure longer while all else falls to time and the elements. The ancients often factored the in-flowing energy of vortexes into their designs. They understood how to use the angles and positionings, placing their structures carefully along these lines.

Unfortunately, no man-made instrument can perceive or measure this energy. At least not yet. But it can be done. The plants can function this way. It's why I want you to see Porter. We worked on this at the university. Ask him about the plants.

"The plants?" she wondered, as the plane touched down.

*   *   *

The taxi sped northward on the highway. She cracked open the back window and breathed midwestern air for the first time. Clean and warm. To the west, the late afternoon sun hovered over the splintered roofs of row upon row of houses built beyond a cement barrier that ran along the road.

She had searched for Edgar Porter's phone number but found nothing. She tried the Chicago phone directory, the libraries, the business directories, and all the online search engines she could find. There was no record of him at any of the area's universities, either.

She checked to see if North Hillside Drive existed at all, which, to her great relief, did. She thought about writing to him but decided she couldn't wait that long. She was hungry for a new experience; she had to get out of Plainfield, strike out in some way. She had the money, and so she figured she'd just show up—and in deciding this she had experienced an exhilaration such as she'd never known, the high of forging out into the complete unknown with no idea of what might happen.

Dusk was falling, the time of day she loved most. When the sun began to weaken and falter, her usual intensity would give way to a serenity she rarely felt at other times. She could sense her thoughts turning away from the world and its concerns toward the inner and the mysterious, like cars leaving a crowded highway onto a mysterious exit ramp that appeared only for a moment and then vanished.

The cab exited the freeway and made its way onto a residential road. Hillside Drive snaked up into the knolls of an old, established neighborhood where wealth oozed from the bricks and stones of every house they passed, each with a perfect lawn and well-tended garden. It had been a warm autumn and blooms were still visible. As the taxi climbed into the hills, she felt certain the trip would be fruitful, that she would gain critical insights into her father, as if the mere presence of wealth and beauty in the environs equalled success. Realizing this, she shook her head. Rubbish.

The car glided to a halt in the long driveway of 3706 North Hillside, an English Tudor estate set back from the road and surrounded by an isolating woods. The house was enormous. She paid the driver and watched the cab pull away. Walking to the front door, she suddenly felt foolish. What exactly was she supposed to say to the man?

Tell the truth.

She rang the bell. She waited. Two minutes passed.

She rang it again. A moment later the door opened but only a crack, just enough to reveal the pudgy face of a short man with furtive eyes.

"Uh, Mr. Porter?" she said, uneasily.

"That's right, missy," he said, opening the door an inch further. "What do you want?"

She drew back, surprised by his brusqueness, tried to force a smile. "My name is Maya Burke. I'm here about a friend of yours, David Orr. I was hoping I could talk to you about him."

The man pinched his chin. "Hmm, David Orr. David Orr. Can't say I recall him. Who is he?"

"My father. I'm looking for him. Actually, I've never met him. You knew him a long time ago, right? He taught at the university."

"He did, eh? Are you sure?"

"Yes."

"Absolutely?"

"Yes, I'm certain."

"Positively?"

She nodded, feeling increasingly uneasy. Was he testing her? Why? She said, "I don't know when exactly."

"Don't know when," he repeated, his eyes narrowing.

"You worked together," she said. "You don't remember?"

"Afraid not."

She tried another tact. "It was a long time ago. Twenty years. Maybe you've forgotten."

"Ah, well, yes, twenty years. That *is* a long time."

"He said—"

"Who?"

"My father."

"Not true, not true. You said you never met him."

She looked away, as her adrenal glands sprang to life, pumping chemical discomfort into her body, making her stomach tense up and her hands cold. "No, actually, he wrote me—"

"Wrote you? Sounds like you *have* met him. Now which is it? Either you met him or you didn't. Hmm?"

"I found something—"

"Found something? What's that?"

She opened her mouth to speak but it was too late. The descent had begun. It was all too familiar.

What would happen was this: her feelings would begin to paint. With the virtuosity of a Van Gogh they would paint an elaborate landscape, a dark and hopeless visage in which nothing worked, in which she was stuck at home and tired, brutally tired, and heavy, so heavy she could barely move. Her arms, heavy as granite, would be stuck at her sides. All she could do was summon her mother and ask—no, beg—for help. And maybe Muriel would help, maybe she wouldn't . . .

The door started to close. She watched it as though in slow motion, frame by excruciating frame.

"Wait!" she shouted. She ripped open her backpack, and frantically digging through it, pulled out a scrap of paper.

"Look! Here it is," she said, reading the paper. "Edgar Porter, Dr. Edgar Porter. It's right here, in his writing. I swear! Please, look!"

The door stopped, then creaked back open. The man's face came into view, this time smiling. To Maya, a frightening sight.

"You should have said so in the first place. That's my father. You want him, not me. I'm Jim. Jim Porter."

"Your father, yes," she said, breathlessly. "That's who I want."

"What's your name again?"

"Maya Burke. Tell him I'm David Orr's daughter."

"Wait here."

"I will," she said. "Don't worry."

*   *   *

"This way," Jim Porter said, motioning her into a wide hallway that bisected the house. She gazed around in wonderment. She had never seen a ceiling so high, a marble floor polished to such perfection. Walking behind him she stole glances at the rooms on either side, each a softly-lit chamber housing artifacts and artwork, treasures from all over the world.

She had known of the existence of private art collections but had always assumed they were small, a room or two of valuable pieces, certainly nothing compared to the bounties of the museums. But this, this was amazing. Here in the middle of a residential neighborhood stood walls displaying priceless oil paintings—two that she swore were Monets although she couldn't get close enough to be sure—marble and bronze sculptures including a Rodin she recognized, masters' drawings, walls hung with tribal masks, displays of stone disks, kachinas, spears, even some modern art pieces—hundreds of objects that had to be worth a fortune.

Walking as slowly as possible she felt a familiar serenity, a warm spreading sensation that melted away her anxiety. She had logged hundreds of hours at the Smithsonian Institute, just an hour's drive from home, in Washington, D.C., wandering through the various museums, gazing at paintings or sculptures or old cars or lengths of cable that held the Brooklyn Bridge aloft. She had stood before the Magna Carta and the Constitution, reading the texts. When her feet were tired she would park herself at a bench in the National Gallery of Art and pour out her feelings in a spiral-bound notebook.

The enduring works of humankind, the beautiful, the old, the timeless, especially the art, transcended the everyday world, took her all the way down, which was what made her feel so good—and also so alone, for none of her friends shared this appreciation.

"Come, come," Jim Porter said. "Yes, I know. Father's art is fabulous."

"Truly," she said, hurrying along.

They came to a greenhouse at the back of the house as the last rays of sun streaked the tall palms brushing up against the glass ceiling. A little stream trickled by her feet over moss-covered stones and into a collecting pool where ruby and orange flecked Koi swam lazily about. The water disappeared into an opening at the far wall.

They exited through a back door, arriving at a brick patio where an old man sat in a wheelchair.

"Maya Burke," Jim said to the old man. He then turned on his heels and left before his father could acknowledge him.

Edgar Porter was as ancient-looking as some of his art collection. He had an enormous head, a face so corrugated with wrinkles it looked like a topographical map, and a bald pate broken only by a few wisps of colorless hair. He was tall. Standing erect he would have been imposing, but folded up into the chair he was just a crumpled up heap in a baggy shirt and slacks. His blue eyes were laser-sharp, though, and they shone brightly.

"Sit down, Maya," he said, in a warm, welcoming voice. She took the chair beside him. He pushed a lever in the armrest of his wheelchair and it rotated to face her.

He opened his arms to indicate the property, with its stone paths, gardens and fountains. Though the sun had set, there was still light, the sky a deep blue.

"I come out here every day at this time," he said. "It doesn't matter what I'm doing, it can wait until the sun has set."

"That's interesting," she said. "I was just thinking how much I love this time of day, too."

"Understandable," he said, nodding his great head. "It's the time of the changeover. Maybe you love it because you are drawn to such things."

"The changeover?"

"A time of mystery, of possibility," he said. "When light becomes dark, invisible reveals itself, subtle becomes known. At dusk a window opens into other worlds. That is," he added with a wink, "if you believe the shamans."

She knew the term. "Medicine men?"

"And women, too."

He smiled. His lips were colorless, the pigment bleached out by the sun, or age.

"I'm sorry," he said. "I don't mean to lecture you, my dear. I suppose it's in the blood. I taught anthropology for years; not that it gives me a license to bore a lovely young lady."

"It's okay," she said. "I'm interested."

"Yes, you are," he said, studying her. "And you should be. Such matters drive the world."

He shifted the chair closer. "You resemble David, you know."

"I do?" she said. She paused, taking this in. She had always wondered. "I was hoping you might know where he is."

"I'm afraid I haven't seen David in many years." He paused,

watching her. "You're disappointed. I can see it in your face. I can tell you what I know. Maybe that will help. But tell me, how did you come by my name?"

"He mentioned you in a journal he wrote."

"A journal?"

Immediately she regretted saying it. The only thing of David Orr's she had ever known was the journal. She wanted to keep it to herself, and herself alone. But so far she had failed miserably. Josh knew, and now Dr. Porter, too. She knew this possessiveness was irrational but she couldn't help it.

"What kind of a journal is it?" he asked.

"Actually it was just a few pages," she said, backpedaling. "He wrote something about using plants to perceive energy. He mentioned your name. Do you know what it means?"

He fell silent, staring past her as if she weren't there. Then, with a twinkle in his eye, he said, "Long ago we both taught at the university, your father and I. You might say that David was my protégé, at least for a time. He was quite the idealist, your father. His predictions of what he called the post-scientific age—I suppose people call it the new age and other silly things now—brought him some degree of notoriety. He was a futurist, and quite daring in his ideas. Or reckless, depending on your point of view. He taught only briefly. He left academia for a position in Washington. That was a long time ago, you realize."

"Do you know what he did in Washington?"

The old man shrugged. "As I said, we fell out of touch long ago."

"Is there anyone you could ask? Friends? People he worked with?"

"Perhaps. I'll think on it."

She looked up at the sky. Now the dusk was over, giving way to night. A few stars were visible, faint twinkles of light. The temperature had dropped, and she buttoned up her sweater. The music of crickets filled the air, reminding her of home.

"David is correct about the plants," Dr. Porter said. "If you want, I can show them to you."

"Great," she said. "How does it work?"

He laughed. "Talking about it is wasted time. It's something you have to experience. But it's too late now. It'll have to be tomorrow. Are you staying in the area?"

"Yes," she said.

"Where?"

"A motel, I guess."

"My dear," the old man said. "Stay with us. My God, there's a wealth of guest rooms, more than we could ever use. That is, if you wish. You'd be safe, I assure you. Jim, for all his peculiarities, is quite harmless."

She pasted a smile on her face and considered the offer. No, of course she wouldn't be comfortable sleeping in a house a thousand miles from home with two men who were, well, unusual, to say the least. She thanked him and offered to take a cab to a motel, but he insisted she borrow a car. It turned out to be a Cadillac, which she drove down to a motel at the bottom of the hill, near the highway.

Dinner was a cheeseburger and fries wolfed down in a matter of minutes. She hadn't realized how famished she was.

The room was comfortable, and even though she tucked herself under the blankets prepared for a difficult night—sleeping in beds other than her own had always been a challenge—sleep came surprisingly fast. Maybe it was the soothing drone of the highway in the background.

She dreamed of her father that night. It was a dream she'd had many times, which she had described once to her mother's brother. Buddy was on the back porch swing that morning, as usual, when she came out. She was all smiles.

"What's with the happy face?" he asked. "Where's the usual morning grump?"

"I had a nice dream," she said.

"If it's that good, I want to know about it."

"It's personal."

He laughed. "Come on, kid, this is your uncle talking."

"All right," she said. "It was about my father."

He nodded solemnly. He had never met his sister's husband.

She said, "It starts out I'm sitting on a picnic table under a tree. There's a lake with reeds in the shallows and the smell of warm grass. It's summertime.

"There's a dirt path that winds up into the hills. I don't know where it goes. I don't know much of anything, except that I'm not supposed to turn around. I don't know why. It feels like I've been sitting on that table for all eternity, waiting. I don't care. I know I'm in the right place. I mean, I *can't* be anywhere else, I have to be there, and this thing that's going to happen is really important.

"There's a tap on my shoulder. It's him, I just know it. I turn around and look. He doesn't say anything but if he did it would be something like, 'That's a girl. Come with me,' in this father-speak kind of way. I know that sounds stupid.

"He takes my hand and I stand up, and we walk up the path toward the hills. The feeling is strange *and* good, like I'm bathing in light or something, and everything that's bad is gone. Whatever I was, I'm not anymore. This thing I'm feeling, it's more than just him. I've become part of something else, something bigger. I have no idea what it is, though.

"I ask, 'Where are we going?'

"'Home,' he says.

"That's when I wake up, feeling good, and it lasts."

She looked up at her uncle. "Weird, huh?"

Buddy smiled, then reached out and squeezed her arm. "You've got quite the imagination, Maya. That you do."

"I guess so," she said.

CHAPTER 4

"I did not choose the location of my home as some random act," Dr. Porter said the next morning as he wheeled down a hallway toward the back of the house. He stopped and turned to face Maya.

"When I bought this property thirty-three years ago I knew exactly where the real value was: in the land. But not the way most people think of it, not as real estate. As an energy source. This land possesses a property shared by only the rarest of places. It is home to a force indigenous to the area, a point from which energy flows. It is of incalculable value, but only to those who understand it. Do you know what an energy vortex is, Maya?"

Of course she did. David Orr had explained it to her.

"I've heard the term," she said. "But where is it?"

The edges of his bleached-out lips turned up in a smile. Though his face was pinched and wrinkled and even repugnant, it lit up at times, especially when he talked about energy. She imagined her father the same way.

He pointed down at the floor.

She said, "It's the house?"

"*Under* the house."

"Where are the plants?"

"Down there," he said. "Each and every one. Come."

He started down the hallway and she followed him. They came to a doorway in a small, unassuming foyer and he swung it open, revealing an elevator car. They got in.

"Going down," he said, smiling.

The descent was slow and Maya fought the urge to chew on her fingernails; anything to take her mind off the anticipation churning in her stomach.

When the door slid open, her mouth dropped open in

amazement. Before her was a cavernous room as big as a gymnasium, a nursery populated by hundreds, maybe thousands, of bushes, plants and trees extending out in every direction in long rows. An extensive irrigation system snaked along the floor, reaching into the soil of every container. Banks of lamps on the ceiling bathed the room in light. The air was warm and moist.

Dr. Porter extended his hands, palms out. "My instruments," he said proudly.

To Maya they looked like ordinary plants, exactly what she had labored over at the gardening section of Tomlinsen's Hardware, where she had worked weekends in high school.

"This way," Dr. Porter said, wheeling up a ramp to a podium containing banks of machines that glowed with colorful displays. He rolled the chair over to an instrument panel, and Maya took the empty chair beside him.

He turned a knob, and the overhead lights dimmed. Then the room fell to complete darkness, which was immediately broken by a faint reddish glow that emanated from a new, smaller set of ceiling lamps.

"Now watch closely," he said. "Keep your eyes out there."

She felt herself tighten up. Keep your eyes *out there*? What did that mean?

It must mean to look out, and so she peered into the shadowy jungle, hoping to see whatever it was she was supposed to see.

A few minutes passed.

"There!" he said. "Did you see it?"

She swept her gaze from one end of the room to the other but saw nothing, just a dimly lit expanse of plants.

"Keep looking," he said.

Another several minutes passed. Still, nothing.

She said, "Maybe I could do this better if I knew what I was looking for."

"Energy," he said. "You're looking for energy."

"Energy? What do you mean?"

"That which drives, that which animates, all things. The fuel, the material of which we are made."

"But you can't see that."

"You're wrong. You'll see."

She had always believed in energy—in theory. It explained a lot. She had never questioned the existence of an invisible force at work behind the animate and inanimate worlds, even though modern science had never acknowledged it or proved its existence. *Something* provided the power to run everything. Something energized the cells of the body, something propelled the movement of water. But where *was* it? Where was energy? You couldn't see it. You couldn't feel it, smell it, hear it, touch it. You had to take its existence on faith, and that usually led to problems.

She recalled her anthropology courses. Traditional cultures all believed in energy. Native American myths were rife with talk of energy and its manifestations. The Chinese had mapped its pathways through the human body millennia ago. The Hindus had a host of gods to represent the energy forces of nature. *Sanskrit* was a language that included a whole vocabulary about energy, down to the finest details.

Why have words for something that doesn't exist? Just because the eyes can't see it? Thoughts are invisible, too, but that doesn't make them any less real.

So where was all this energy?

Apparently here in this strange bio-lab right in front of her, and she was too dense to see it.

Concentrate.

She tried squinting and blurring and skewing her vision but still she came up empty.

"You're too tense," Dr. Porter said.

"Yep," she agreed.

"You have to relax," he said. He reached over and handed her a pair of lightweight headphones. "These will help you to get into an alpha state."

Alpha. She recognized the term. Her meditation teacher had used it all the time. Alpha was the technical term for the brainwave pattern of deep relaxation, an altered state just askance of normal waking, a kind of restful alertness.

At fifteen, Maya had convinced Muriel that meditation was the key to reducing her level of anxiety, which, even then, had been a problem. Maya had taken to it immediately, practicing twice every day. It worked.

To Maya, meditation was a welcome respite from pinball mind. And now that she thought about it, she determined to start it up again. The only problem was *doing* it.

The headphones played a simple tone, unwavering in pitch. Uninteresting.

"Close your eyes," Dr. Porter said.

She did, and a heartbeat later she felt as though she was moving. Suddenly, she felt the floor drop away from her. She was in free-fall. Frightened, she opened her eyes—

And the sense of movement stopped. She looked around. She hadn't gone anywhere. She was still in the chair, the quiet jungle all around her. She started to speak but stopped, startled by a sight a few feet in front of her.

A shimmer of light, just a few crackles, appeared over one of the plants. Quickly it disappeared.

"Did you see that?" she said, excitedly.

"Yes," he said nonchalantly. "When it comes back, lock your eyes onto it."

Again the sparkles appeared. When she focused on it, chills buzzed through her body. But that wasn't all. There was something else. She had the preposterous idea she had *awakened* the plant, and it was now aware of her.

And with this thought the whole room exploded in a blaze of light and electricity, like a thousand holiday sparklers shooting off all at once.

Then the colors came—rivers of ruby, scarlet and emerald that flowed and danced and melted and spurted out from the plants like little volcanic eruptions. They coursed in streams down to the floor and around the walls and up to the ceiling, spreading out everywhere.

"It's beautiful!"

And with these words, the show stopped. Again, she found

herself looking out at a giant room full of plants bathed in a ghostly crimson light. No movement, no color. Just stillness, and the sound of her quickened breathing.

"Am I not supposed to talk?" she said. "Where did the colors go?"

"They're still there."

"Where? Why can't I see them?"

"You can if you hold your questions for a moment. I want to try something. Take the headphones off."

She slipped them off and handed them back to him.

"We'll try it naturally, no props," he said.

Whatever that meant. "All right."

"Now try to return to the feeling you had at the moment you saw the colors. You'll have a memory of it. Try to bring it back."

She tried, and to her surprise it worked. Within seconds the great display of colors filled the room again. She turned to Dr. Porter. He, too, was glowing.

"Your body—"

"No. Out there," he said, pointing towards the storm of activity.

She turned her gaze back to the room and this time saw something different. Over by the back wall, a small tree of about five feet was emitting a strong blue light, far brighter than anything around it, blotting out her view of some of the plants.

Dr. Porter's voice came to her as if from miles away.

"That's the vortex," he said.

The blue light attracted her so strongly she couldn't pull her eyes from it. She didn't want to. It was incredible. It felt good. She wanted to move closer to it. She felt herself begin to rise, without even realizing it.

Suddenly, the ceiling lights came on, the colors disappeared, and she was shocked out of the hypnosis of the tree. Shading her eyes in the bright room, she said, "That was too weird. The *tree* is the vortex?"

"No," he said. "The spot it's sitting on."

She took a breath. "I'm tired."

"Don't fade on me yet," he said. "There's something else to try. Come."

He rolled down the incline into one of the long aisles, and she followed behind him, brushing her arms against leaves and branches as she passed.

She was bursting with excitement. She had gotten verification, finally: energy was real. There *was* something beyond the physical. A bristling, crackling realm of activity lived beneath what the senses perceived. Sure, you needed physical eyes to see it, but this "it" was only the outer shell of a deeper experience. How much was down there?

"It's a Fichus," Dr. Porter said, touching the tree that had glowed so brightly.

"Pardon?"

"This flora here. Fichus. That's the name. But it could be anything. Look at it. Just a normal tree."

She had hardly heard him. Her mind was still reeling, alighting on the implications of what she had witnessed. If she believed in energy—*really* believed in it—wouldn't that change her whole view of reality? There would be an invisible world to contend with. Immediately she saw the gap between herself and the people in her life widen. Again.

"Hello?" he said, snapping his fingers to get her attention.

"Sorry," she said. "I was drifting."

"It's easy to get lost in reverie here," he said. "You see, Maya, proximity to a vortex affects thought. People act differently around vortexes.

"There's quite the difference, say, between growing up in the Middle East versus here in Chicago. The great vortex of Jerusalem is one of the most powerful in the world. It's helped to birth religions that have shaped continents, wars that devastated whole peoples. Psychic activity runs unbelievably high in such places. Passions are stirred up. The energy gestalts there incite people to do things they never would have contemplated elsewhere. That's why it's so hard to keep the peace, or even, at times, maintain rationality. Here, thankfully, you don't have that kind of extreme intensity."

She said, "Are you saying that vortexes affect what people think and do?"

"Absolutely. Few people are aware of it, though. It can't be proven, at least not scientifically. That is, if anyone bothered to try. Too subjective, you see."

She looked at the simple potted tree before her, then at the floor around it.

"How did you know the vortex was here?"

"I searched for it."

"How?"

"You're very curious," he said, scrutinizing her. "David was like that, too. There are two ways to locate a vortex: directly or inferentially. Inferentially, you look for ruins. Many ancient civilizations built near vortexes. They understood how to use the energy in their building designs. The more direct method is through clairvoyants. Psychics. People who can sense energy. That's how I mapped this one."

He wheeled up close to her. "My dear," he said. "You were excellent."

She drew back. "What do you mean?"

"Most people—no, I dare say just about all—could not do what you did, see what you saw. Let me show you something."

He grabbed the edge of the pot that held the Fichus and rolled himself backwards, dragging the tree away to reveal an "X" that had been painted on the cement. Then he found a folding chair and pulled it over to the "X."

"Sit," he said, simply.

She stared at the chair. "Why? What do you want me to do?"

He paused, took a deep breath. "Why are you here, Maya?"

"I told you why."

"Tell me again."

"I'm looking for my father."

"Right," he said. "And this is an opportunity to find him. One, incidentally, that may not come along very often."

"I don't get it. How?"

"Simply by using your innate gifts, with the help of the natural energy here. We'll seek information about him. The information will come to you. Or it won't. Maybe you can't do it. There are no guarantees."

"Is it dangerous?"

"As dangerous as daydreaming. If you get uncomfortable, you simply stop."

Still she didn't budge.

"Please, sit down," he said, touching the back of the chair.

Sitting at the center of the vortex would mean interacting with it in some way, being subjected to a power which had the ability to change human thought, and do . . . what? She didn't know. She couldn't know. She could almost see the invisible doorway she was about to pass through, another step into the unknown.

She lowered herself into the chair.

"We'll start with some visualizing, or imagining," he said. "Close your eyes and sit for a few minutes, until I speak again."

She felt her chest tighten, her breaths shorten.

Relax.

She focused on her mantra, that simple, soothing sound her meditation teacher had taught her. It worked. Within seconds the muscles around her ribcage began to ease up, and her breaths became deeper and longer.

The pink of her eyelids fell to a deep scarlet, as the ceiling lights dimmed. Her mind began to drift.

"Place your father's image in your mind's eye."

She had no image of him to place anywhere, except for that forgotten old photo she had seen as a child.

"I don't know what he looks like."

"Just maintain a thought of him."

She imagined him. She couldn't see anything; she just thought of him.

"Now allow yourself to drift, but keep him in your mind's eye. If you have any thoughts, don't grasp onto them. Let them go."

She immediately felt light-headed.

She heard something.

"A guitar!" she said, excitedly. "I hear a guitar. I don't know where it's coming from—"

"Don't analyze. Just listen."

"There's singing, too. I can't believe this. I'm really hearing this. An old folk song, something about a country girl . . ."

"What do you see?"

"I don't exactly *see* it . . . but . . . huh, interesting. A baby. Wait. She . . . it's a girl, but don't know how I can tell. I usually can't visualize like this . . ."

"Don't analyze."

"A man with dark hair, holding her, her head on his shoulders . . . Oh, my God!"

"What?"

"It's me!" she said. "I think. I'm not sure."

"Keep going," he insisted. "Don't get caught up in it."

"All right." She paused. "Now it's a room, another place entirely. Lots of people. A building with thick walls. Underground. Uniforms. No. Suits. Men in suits. Someone giving a lecture. No windows, just walls. Concrete. Dread. I feel dread. Oh, God, there is something here I don't like . . .

"Wait! It's changing. It's a field now, a grassy field with sunlight. I smell something sweet. What is that? It's so familiar . . . yes, yes, I know . . . honeysuckle. There are mountains, huge ones. Close . . . no, far away. They just look close. People are running. I don't know what's happening. I think I'm looking through someone else's eyes. Who? I-I think it's him. Is it? Is it him?"

Dr. Porter said, "What does he look like?"

"I don't know. He's gone. There's a sign, a road sign."

"What does it say?"

"Wilton, Wy. What's that? What's Wilton, Wyoming?"

"A town. What else?"

"A settlement, like a camp. People cooking outside. Children. A blonde girl with freckles. Not the same as before. Different. She's looking at me. She's staring right at me! What should I do?"

"Nothing. Do nothing."

Suddenly she felt exhausted. "I'm tired. I'm so tired. I can't do this."

"Quickly," he said. "Imagine yourself with your father."

She was gasping for air. She felt as though the wind had been knocked out of her.

"Do it," he said. "Quickly."

"Okay, okay. Yes. I'm with him, I think. I can't breathe."

"What do you see?"

Struggling, she said, "Nothing."

"What do you see?" he said, louder.

"Nothing!"

"Let it happen."

"Wait," she said. "The planet. I see the planet."

"Which one?"

Which one? "A drawing of it. Earth."

"You don't see him?"

"No. Just the Earth, with some kind of a web around it."

"A web?"

"Yes . . . tired . . . stop . . . have to . . ."

"One more thing."

"No, no . . . can't . . ."

"Okay then. Come back."

"Yes . . . come back . . ."

*   *   *

She awakened lying on her back, her arms at her sides, in the most comfortable bed she'd ever been in. She felt as though she was floating on hundreds of pounds of feathers. She looked around but did not recognize the room. She leaned over and peered out the window to the backyard. Yes, she thought. I'm in one of the guest rooms.

Her head was fuzzy; she had trouble focusing. She shook it to clear it, then stretched her arms and legs. She made her way down a hall and lumbered out to the backyard. The old man was sitting in the exact spot she had found him in yesterday, staring at the trees.

"Are you okay?" he said.

"I don't know," she said. "How did I get inside?"

"You walked."

"I did?"

"I led you, under your own power."

"I don't remember," she said, rubbing her eyes.

"That's not unusual."

"How long was I in there?"

"A few minutes. Come, walking helps," he said.

He led her along the curved brick walkways of the backyard, as Maya breathed deeply of the sweet-scented air and did her best to try to remember what had happened.

She recalled the disjointed images that played out in her mind like a string of film clips. They seemed indistinguishable from memories. But she recalled nothing of how it had ended.

Anyway, the day was beautiful. Colors danced. Sounds popped. Sparrows darted between trees. Towering cumulus clouds floated high in the sky, opening up occasionally to let sunlight shoot through.

They stopped at a bench near a stone fountain where streams of water shot up in the air in big arcs, splashing down into a collecting pool. Maya dropped heavily onto the bench, transfixed by the splashing of the water, which sounded to her like the music of flutes. *So beautiful*, she thought, as though she'd never admired a fountain before.

"Congratulations," Dr. Porter said, wheeling up beside her. "You've borne witness to energy. If more people could do that, it would start quite the revolution."

"Revolution?" she said, still drifting.

"Oh, yes," he said. "Our culture is based on a mechanistic view of the universe, not on the interplay of subtle energies. If we began to see things differently, well, let's just say a paradigm shift in this area would create tremendous upset in society. When Copernicus proved that the Earth wasn't the center of the universe, the chain reaction it started brought down a centuries-old way of life. You see, Maya, people aren't comfortable with change. Especially radical change. Some of us prefer to move along slowly and predictably, at a rate that can be controlled."

He said something else but she missed it; she was drifting again. Her thoughts were hard to grasp, like fish that slid through her fingers every time she reached for them.

"Where is Wilton?" she asked.

"Wyoming."

"Is that where he is?"

"I don't know. You see, when you focused on being together you drew a blank."

"So we don't know anything?"

"Not at the moment."

"Then all that was meaningless?"

"No, not at all," he said. "You need time to digest it, to let it stir your memories."

She shook her head, frustrated. "Then I don't get it, any of it."

"You will. Maya, I want you to find David. This may not come as a surprise, but I would like to see him, too."

She didn't care what he wanted. She cared only about finding him herself.

Her brain felt like it was working right again, her thoughts becoming lucid. She said, "Why did he stop teaching?"

The old man took a moment to retrieve the old memory. "I'm afraid he was booted out."

"Really?"

"He ruffled feathers. Lots of them. He didn't always teach what he was supposed to. His classes inevitably came around to his pet theories. He had very specific interests: the mass psyche, Carl Jung, the collective unconscious, the *I Ching*—"

"The *I Ching*?"

She knew all about the Chinese Book of Change, had used it many times, tossing the coins, trying to divine the answers to her questions. But the cryptic remarks of the sixty-four hexagrams spoke a language she didn't understand. The book was inscrutable yet it was also compelling, even if it did respond to the simplest question with, "Hoarfrost underfoot betokens the coming of solid ice."

"The *Ching* summed up what David believed in," Dr. Porter went on. "That change is never-ending, circular, and therefore predictable. By using the book properly he believed you could map the changes of a culture, a life, a planet—any system, for that matter. David, you see, wanted to predict the future in a cultural or mass context. He wanted to know what the next global event, disaster, cultural change, or even religion would be."

"That's impossible," she said.

"You never know," he said, smiling inscrutably. "If he was able to do it he would be quite the popular fellow. It would be a damned useful skill.

"A damned useful skill," he repeated. Then he laughed, loudly, and it surprised her, for he had been soft-spoken until then. Maybe she was still off-kilter from the vortex, but when she examined him closely, his face seemed somehow different, in motion, as if something hidden beneath the surface was stirring, something wholly different than what she had seen up to then. Still he stared at her, unblinking.

A shiver ran down her spine and she felt the sudden urge to leave, as if his strange look augured something terrible about to happen. It was crazy, she knew, this paranoia. Maybe it was the vortex. Even so, she could not deny the power of these feelings. She stood up.

"I appreciate everything you've shown me," she said.

"I understand," he said, staring at her. "I know you'll find what you're looking for."

Yes, she thought, I will. And I know exactly where to look.

CHAPTER 5

The Rocky Mountains looked just as spectacular from Wilton's ramshackle Pine Tree Motel, Maya noticed, as they would have from the elegant Hanford Lodge down the street, which she could not possibly afford—or rather *would* not afford, since she did in fact now have the money, thanks to David Orr. Holding on to money was a habit that was hard to break.

Flying out of Chicago had been difficult. The flight delay began as a half-hour inconvenience. Then it stretched to an hour. Then it stretched again. And again. And again. Finally, after five uncomfortable hours of sitting on bench seats, grousing with the other passengers, watching planes take off through the terminal windows—when she no longer believed anything coming out of the airport intercom—she resigned herself to being stranded in Illinois forever. *Then* they boarded. It was as though she had had to give up what she wanted before it could happen. The flight to Wyoming's tiny Jackson Hole airport was uneventful.

The afternoon was long, and she was relieved to be finished with it. Now she was sitting on the edge of a springy motel room bed beside a wide open window, breathing the freshest air she'd ever known. And feeling terribly alone.

Maybe it was Muriel's voice on the answering machine. Maya had left a message saying that she'd be home a few days late, sounding calm and convincing as she fabricated the camping trip details, but as soon as she had hung up, uneasiness set in.

She decided to meditate for a few minutes, even though alone inside of her head was the last place she wanted to be. But it worked, and the discomfort passed.

The fact that Wilton existed at all, a place she'd conjured up in a vision—or an hallucination, she thought uncomfortably—

had begun to chip away at her, extending a hairline crack in the foundation of her beliefs, an already tenuous structure which recent events had caused to creak more than ever. The truth was, it was hard to be sure what was real and what wasn't anymore.

She had seen that highway sign, there was no doubt about it, and it was still there, stuck in her memory, waiting to be fathomed. She could snap it back into view as easily as she could the image of Van Gogh's *Sunflowers*, Josh's round-backed guitar or David Orr's erratic handwriting.

"Wilton, Wy.," in white lettering on a green sign.

She wondered: Could the image be nothing more than the forgotten scene of an old movie lodged in the backwaters of her mind, coughed up by a neuron in need of attention?

No. It was real. It had to be. Otherwise, being here made no sense. No sense at all.

Now what? She would sit awhile. She would sit, and eat, and then sleep, and in the morning go into town and, well, see. Be led, she hoped. Put her trust in the process.

Doubt, as usual, crept in. What if there *was* no process? What if all her efforts came to nothing? What if life was what it so often seemed, an unending stream of chaotic events, searching and tedium, spiced by a few highs here and there?

What if . . .

No. Stop.

Don't go down that road, she told herself. It's too easy. Don't put the pain out there when it's really in here, yours, yours alone, borne of a brain that is always working overtime. Prowling, stalking, devouring. Like a wolf. Yes, exactly: a wolf. *The* wolf.

The image fit perfectly. Her mind, that relentless predator, had to be watched. Managed. She couldn't let it roam. If she didn't point the wolf in a constructive direction, it would turn on its master, often with a vengeance. Or worse, on the nearest innocent soul.

College had been a godsend, for it distracted the wolf on a daily basis. The creature loved challenge. She counted her study time by the minutes, not the hours, at times hardly even caring yet making dean's list every semester and graduating *summa cum laude*. Her expertise lay in the storage and retrieval of facts. The wolf understood logic. The wolf loved logic. But the satisfaction of facts had peaked and faded. Logic and rationality, she had decided, had little to do with happiness.

During one emotionally tumultuous semester she kept regular appointments with the campus psychologist to learn if she could direct the wolf's incredible power, shift its obsessive nature toward more productive use. Why did it have such a tight hold on her? Why couldn't she control it? Who was responsible for the plummeting of her moods to unfathomable depths?

Therapy answered few of these questions. For Maya it was time spent mostly, surprisingly, and irritatingly, searching for memories of Muriel.

She could have talked about Muriel's long nights of drinking, of watching her sobbing alone or in the presence of a numb, uncaring man—or a series of men—who would slap her, call her obscene names, treat her viciously. Or her wild swings of emotion, and the way she would spew sentimental love for Maya one night and snarl what a worthless loser she was the next. But Maya didn't choose to explore these areas. She couldn't. It was just too painful.

Her early childhood was hard to locate. At times she had no recollections at all. Instead of blubbering away as the shrink had no doubt wanted her to do in that claustrophobic little room, she balked at the still festering wounds around those memories, and instead directed the wolf toward distracting ethical and moral questions. Did the fact that Muriel, lost in her own illness and alcoholism, *consciously* intend no harm absolve her of responsibility for the emotional damage she'd inflicted on Maya?

The wolf pounced all over these examinations. In the midst of her deconstructions, however, the shrink's face would turn vacant. He wanted feelings, not thoughts. He hated the wolf just as she did but for entirely different reasons.

Once she shocked him by asking about his personal life. Suddenly he became nervous and fidgety, and Maya had to chuckle to herself. The expression on his face was so forlorn, so bereft, so pathetic, that she dismissed him then and there. He seemed to be as lost as she.

As much as she had wanted to hold Muriel accountable for her own difficult psychology, for making life harder than it had to be, she just couldn't do it. People weren't responsible for bad deeds done in ignorance; they simply didn't know any better. That was her conclusion. One's life was one's own responsibility, even in childhood, when you were at the mercy of others. Maya hated this logic but she couldn't fight it. It made sense. Maybe therapy had worked after all.

The therapeutic process had also touched upon the missing parent, the man now known as David Orr. She deified him. He was a great man, a humane man, a loving man. He would be back. One day. It was a typical fantasy for those in her predicament, she had learned, so deeply ingrained it seemed impossible to alter. Changing the internal David Orr would be about as easy as redirecting the Colorado River. The canyon was cut. The river's course was set. There was little to do about it.

For years she had poured her fantasies of him into the heroes of movies and novels, and he would come alive for a time. But no more. Now she wearied of the strain of pumping life into those sagging fantasies. It felt foolish, tiresome. The focus and concentration necessary was not even possible anymore except when she was at the apex of her energy, and this had not happened in awhile. When had she last read a novel? A year ago? Two? In her teens she had gobbled up Casteneda, Vonnegut, Wells, Borges. Now such flights of fancy felt leaden. They were lies. Television and movies, the same. Perversions, shams.

She looked down at her hands, balled tightly into fists.

She thought, Why am I so angry?

Stop it. Stop it now.

She took a long, cleansing breath, turned her attention to the window, where cool air was wafting in. So fresh, so clean, so pure.

So sweet.

Sweet? Yes. She recognized the scent—recognized it but couldn't place it.

What was it?

Suddenly she knew the answer, and in knowing jumped up from the bed and dashed over to the window. Again she inhaled deeply, just to be sure.

Honeysuckle!

She looked out at the line of mountains which stood imperiously along the horizon, as if holding the darkening sky aloft.

It's them, she thought. The very ones.

She examined them closer now, as her excitement grew. The shape of the peaks matched exactly those she had seen in her vision. She wasn't crazy, after all. She hadn't dreamed it. It was real. In some way.

Tracing her finger along the outline of the ridges, she laughed. Tall peak in the center, mesa-like plateau, skull-shaped rock on the right . . . exactly. Exactly as she had seen. With a difference.

This was real.

The snapshot that had developed in the darkroom of her mind in Dr. Porter's forested basement was merely an abstraction, a paper-thin image that fell far short of the imposing, all-too-solid landscape that stood before her. But there was more. The mountains seemed to be transmitting a message—not only to her, she felt, but to all who would listen. The message was this: Stretch. Stretch yourselves. Enlarge yourselves.

She did not know what this meant, nor did she linger on it. Shivering with excitement she stared out, gripping the window pane tightly, as though to keep herself from being sucked out through the glass, into something larger and more vital than anything she had ever known, into a plan set in motion in ancient times that dwarfed her little life the way the sun dwarfs a light bulb. In that moment she began to undergo an internal shift. The feeling was one of separation, of falling away, of moving from the familiar toward the mysterious, of reversing, of entering into the unknown.

Anything seemed possible. All she had to do was let it happen. She recalled one of her father's scrawls.

Only by accepting that the impossible is possible will the path open to you. Then the meaning of your life will come into view. Don't wait. Do it now.

*   *   *

She awoke the next morning shivering, clutching herself beneath a blanket that was too thin for comfort. The wool comforter she had snuggled beneath hours earlier had fallen to the floor. She leaned over and peeked outside. The sun wasn't up yet. The western half of the sky was dark, the eastern a pale blue.

She defrosted under the groaning shower, threw on her clothes and walked outside. The sky was gigantic, frilled at the edges by wispy clouds. Dew glistened on the grass like thousands of pearls.

A hundred yards down the empty road a traffic light hung limply from a high cable, its glowing green dot the only color in sight. Farther down the road she saw the lights of a roadside store, bustling with cars and shoppers. The other buildings scattered along the road were dark and still.

She walked to the store. Pickup trucks and sport utility vehicles clustered like cattle in the parking lot. Men and women in jeans and cowboy boots nodded hellos to each other, walking up the wide wooden steps of the porch.

She went inside, sliding on the sawdust-covered floor, almost doing a split, catching herself just in time. Dust was everywhere— on the shelves of groceries, on the cans, the boxes, in the air, on all the surfaces.

A bushy-bearded man with an enormous belly that strained at the fabric of his shirt stood behind a lunch counter, his hands resting on the ivory-handled levers of a soda fountain. He nodded hello, his smile gap-toothed.

"Haven't seen you around here, miss," he said.

It was too early to smile but she did her best. "I just got here," she said.

"Vacation?"

"Kind of."

"Uh-huh," he nodded.

"Can I have a large coffee? And this, too," she said, holding out a shrink-wrapped blueberry muffin.

The man reached for a paper cup. "One size fits all. Refills are free. You're a cream and sugar gal, right?"

"Yep."

"Bingo!" he said so loudly that she jumped.

She looked at the coffee pouring out of the carafe, then at the muffin in her hand. Caffeine and white flour—two habits she wanted to break. She was already awake, she didn't need a chemical lift. Being on the road provided that. But here she was, doing it anyway.

She hated being dependent on things. Or people. It was weakness. When they were gone, what then? Yet she seemed powerless over certain urges. She *had* to have the coffee, or she'd feel miserable.

Maybe Uncle Buddy was right. Buddy asserted that habit was the strongest force in the universe, bar none.

He believed that every process in existence was stuck in grooves of varying depths, which explained why real change was so rare.

He even went so far as to claim that habit literally held the universe together, keeping natural laws such as gravity and magnetism in place, which had been set in motion at the dawn of time and performed consistently merely by dint of habit, just as a top spinning in outer space would never stop since there was no friction to slow it down. Theoretically, it would spin forever. Or until something altered its motion. Then it would do that forever.

Habit.

According to Buddy, stars, buildings, tadpoles and people all followed the same tendency: to keep doing what they'd always done. The only force that could change habit, he said, was persistent, willful effort. Then, after a suitable period of time, change might occur.

"Nothing like a good hot cup of coffee in the morning," the big-bellied man said as he handed her the coffee.

"I know but it's a tough fight," she said, and the man looked at her strangely.

She sat at a table on the porch and waited. She drank and she breathed, and she wondered how to begin. She worried. She checked the store's bulletin board. She warmed her hands on the coffee and nibbled at the muffin. An hour passed. The sun drifted up over the ridge, warming the air.

Cars pulled in and out of the parking lot. She waited for a sign. Something. Anything.

Then she changed her mind. No, she thought. I won't begin like this.

Waiting was the old way, the old Maya, a habit that would change right now, and to hell with Buddy's suitable period of time. Maybe Josh was right. Maybe you did make it up as you go.

The situation required a display of intention, an act of will. A statement of commitment. She would oblige. She would move. She would search, probe, inquire, and hopefully find out where Wilton, Wyoming fit into the puzzle of her life.

And so she walked.

And walked.

By dusk, a dull throbbing in her feet had spread up into her calves and thighs. She had strolled the streets of Wilton, meandered through its parks, visited its gift shops and real estate offices and cafes. She had peeked around every corner of the little downtown, searching people's faces for a sign, a spark, a recognition. Anything that might begin the conversation that would change everything.

It didn't happen. Her hellos were met with innocuous responses. "Yes, it *is* a beautiful day." "How are *you*?" "No, never heard of the man."

She'd never given it much thought but the fact was, she didn't know how to meet people. She'd never tried it. Socially, she just flowed with whatever was happening at a given time.

The following day, more of the same. More beautiful walks she didn't enjoy, more searching the faces of strangers. Only now the townspeople were noticing her, walking alone, looking upset.

No one had heard of David Orr.

The next morning she scheduled a taxi to the airport. She was disappointed yet also relieved—she had tried, hadn't she? She couldn't be faulted that. The universe obviously had its own timetable. She had a feeling something would happen, but in its own time.

It sounded good, anyway.

She made her way to the store for a last caffeine and sugar fix. Dolefully sitting on the porch under a dark, unfriendly sky, she sipped at her coffee.

A young girl, tow-headed, ear-to-ear in freckles, bounced up the stairs and shot into the store like a guided missile. Maya smiled to herself. The girl's alert eyes and quick manner reminded her of herself of a decade ago.

Maya wanted to get back to the motel and pack, but she hesitated. Something about the girl nagged at her and she didn't want to leave until she had figured it out.

Her mind searched, drifting back . . . She could feel the wolf grasping, reaching, seeking a memory, an image . . .

Then she had it. The blonde girl had appeared in her vision! Just like the mountains, Maya had *seen* her.

Maya looked up just as the girl bounded out of the store. She stopped, turned and grinned, and as their eyes met, Maya felt so unnerved she froze. Oblivious to Maya's internal churnings, the girl hopped down the stairs and jumped on a bicycle that was leaning against the side of the building.

Slowly, Maya's voice returned. "Wait," she stuttered.

The girl looked straight at her—and did exactly the opposite. In a single swift movement she kicked up the kickstand, pushed off and began peddling furiously down the road.

"Hey!" Maya yelled out, now starting after the girl. Frantically she waved her arms and called out but the rider was too fast. The distance between them opened up; the bike grew smaller and smaller until it had sunk below a rise in the road. Maya's long strides petered out, and she came to a stop on the black tar road, breathing hard, feeling confused.

She retreated to the porch to try to fathom what had happened. There could be no doubt that the girl was the reason Maya had come to Wilton, the connection to David Orr. But why did she run? Did she recognize Maya? That would be impossible—but then so were visions and energy vortexes and plants that gave off fireworks that nobody else could see.

"Hi."

Maya spun around.

The freckled girl, grinning mischievously, a glint in her eyes, dropped into a chair opposite Maya.

"Nobody can catch me," she said proudly. "I'm the fastest rider in town." It was a declaration, uttered with a perfect balance of certainty and challenge.

Maya just stared at her, still feeling shaky. It was one thing to see a mountain in one's mind and then in the real world, but here was a flesh-and-blood human . . .

The girl sat quietly, smirking. Maya could barely even think because looking at the freckled child was like gazing upon a younger version of her own self. Was the resemblance important?

"You're pretty fast," Maya said.

"*Pretty* fast?" the girl said, frowning.

"Extremely fast," Maya said.

On hearing this, the girl grinned, revealing two large front teeth with yawning gaps on either side.

Maya said, "Where did you go?"

"Oh, I circled around back. You didn't see me, right?"

Maya shook her head. "You totally fooled me."

"Why are you here?" the girl said.

"*Do you know me?*"

The girl rolled her eyes and laughed.

Maya said, "I just thought . . . yeah, pretty stupid, I guess."

"It's just the tourists are gone and you don't look like one."

"What do tourists look like?"

"Dumb. Busy. They smile too much. You don't smile and you don't look busy."

"Thanks," Maya said. "I think."

"I hate tourists," the girl said. "I'm Gathering, by the way."

"What are you gathering?"

"Ha, ha. Very funny."

"I don't understand."

"My *name* is Gathering."

"Oh," Maya said. "Sorry."

"My parents were hippies. That's the answer to the next question, right?"

"No."

"Good," Gathering said.

"Gathering, my name is Maya, and I only have one question."

"Well, okay."

"I'm looking for someone who used to live here, an older man. Maybe your parents can help me."

"I doubt it. They live in Idaho."

"Who do you live with?"

"People," she said. "Some are old, if that's what you mean."

"Who takes care of you?"

Gathering's lips curled mischievously. "I take care of myself."

"I bet you do a real good job, too. Now these older people, can I speak to them?"

"Maybe," Gathering said slyly. "If you can catch me." She jumped up out of the chair.

Not again, thought Maya, as Gathering dashed over to her bike and started down the road again. This time, mercifully, she slowed down and waited for Maya to catch up.

"I live over that hill," Gathering said, pointing.

Ten minutes later they arrived at a two-story brick house. Two cars were parked on the front lawn, a sleek black Audi and a crusty old pickup truck. Gathering yanked open the screen door, banging it so hard off the wall that Maya just barely got her hand out to stop it from slamming into her nose.

"Whoops," Gathering said.

They walked through a narrow hallway girded on both sides by floor-to-ceiling pegboard sheets on which dozens of pots, pans, skillets and other kitchen tools hung. The floor was old and scuffed, the air rich with the scents of cooking food.

They came to a brightly lit kitchen where a man and a woman sat at a kitchen table examining blueprints and architectural drawings. Several pots were boiling away on the stove, steam rising from the rattling lids.

The woman was much older than the man. She was large-boned and muscular, with a tanned, leathery face and long silver hair that flowed down her back, braided and tied in a style that Maya somehow knew was as constant as the sunrise. She peered at Maya through wire-rimmed glasses that rode low on her nose, and smiled a curious Mona Lisa smile which made the years seem to vanish from her face.

"Here they are," Gathering told Maya, her defiant attitude now gone, her voice deferential, eager to please. To the man and woman Gathering said, "She's not a tourist."

"That's good," the old woman said, humoring her. She then turned to Maya. "I'm Georgia Roussey and this here is Brandon McGowan." The man, who looked to be in his thirties, had dark wavy hair and a slender, intelligent face.

Maya took a chair beside them, and immediately something disturbing began to happen. Georgia was speaking, but Maya, distracted by the phenomenon, couldn't hear her. A week earlier such an occurrence would have resulted in an all-out panic, but now, after the vortex, she wasn't as shocked by her eyes showing her impossible things. Nevertheless, the sight was unsettling.

At first she thought it was an optical illusion caused by a play of sunlight, only the sun was behind a solid wall of clouds. Then she thought it might be an aftereffect of the vortex, which may have been true. She had no way of knowing.

A thin luminous fog encircled Georgia's Roussey's head, almost a halo, blocking out a portion of the wall behind her. The lower corner of a painting hanging on it had become an unfocused blur.

Suddenly Georgia's voice flowed back into her awareness. "Are you all right, dear?"

As these words registered, the luminous fog vanished, her eyesight returned to normal, and the face of the sturdy old woman resumed clarity again, as did the corner of the painting. The whole episode had lasted just a couple of seconds.

"What?" Maya said.

"Are you all right?"

"Yes. Why wouldn't I be?"

Georgia and Brandon exchanged a glance. Then Georgia pushed her glasses up her nose and in a warm voice said, "What can we do for you, Maya?"

"I'm looking for someone, a man who once lived in Wilton. His name is David Orr. Have you heard of him?"

Georgia shook her head. "Sorry. It doesn't ring a bell."

"Me neither," Brandon said.

"If he's still here, though," Georgia added, "finding him should be a snap. This isn't exactly New York City."

Maya, disappointed, slumped down. Another blind alley. She looked out the window and saw many buildings outside, structures that hadn't been visible from the road. The house seemed to be part of a large complex.

"What is this place?"

"An intentional community," Brandon said.

Georgia said, "A kind of village, only one that didn't evolve naturally. It was designed, intentionally."

"I've never heard of that."

"Harvest Road is a collective farming settlement," Brandon said, and now Maya identified his Southern drawl. "We live simply, focus on cooperation, hold service to one another in high regard. We're like an Israeli kibbutz in many ways. Everyone who lives here also works here. A lot of our people have outside jobs, too. We're democratic. Everyone participates in decision-making and governance."

Maya's mind, the wolf, perked up, thinking: cult. The expression on her face must have given her away because Brandon immediately responded.

"We're not extremists," he said, "if that's what you're thinking. This is a peaceful place."

"In a way we are," Georgia said. "But so were the founders of democracy, modern science, and every other dominant belief system that's found a foothold in the world. Our goal, Maya, is to help people blossom by creating a microcosm of trust in this one little corner of the world. Now, that's not such a bad idea, is it? Most of our people . . . How many are we now, Brandon?"

"Two-hundred-twenty-one."

"Many of whom have lived here for years."

Gathering, who had been leaning against the sink, stepped forward. "But we're moving, right?"

"Some, yes," Georgia said. "We've acquired some additional land. That's what these plans are about."

"It sounds impressive," Maya said, uncertainly.

"I'll make some inquiries about your David Orr," Georgia said. "In the meantime, why don't you take a look around. You may find us interesting."

CHAPTER 6

Strolling through the settlement with Gathering, Maya couldn't believe how much more there was than she had seen from the road: a long dormitory with at least a dozen bedrooms, several cottages, paved roads, a few industrial buildings, an orchard, and a two-story communal dining hall.

They stopped at a playground near an old cobblestone plaza where a group of toddlers scampered around a jungle gym beneath the matronly gaze of two caretakers sitting on a blanket. People of all ages passed by, some in cars, others on bicycles, many on foot, engaged in a variety of tasks, hauling gardening supplies, working in the greenhouse, accepting deliveries, picking up trash.

"That's the factory over there," Gathering said, pointing to a loading dock behind a barn-like building that hummed with activity. "They make parts for tractors or something like that."

"I see it," Maya said.

She had never been anywhere like Harvest Road, and to her surprise she found herself attracted to the busy purposefulness of it. It was alluring, this sense of community, and this seemed to be a real one, not a phony collection of people like the sororities or sports teams she'd flirted with in school. She thought: wouldn't it feel great if one's life was intertwined with so many others in a way that really mattered?

Everyone seemed to be . . . integral. So needed. She had never felt that way. She'd always considered herself optional in the world. It wouldn't miss a beat if she was gone. Who relied on her, even in the smallest way?

She thought back to her youth, how much of it was spent trying to escape the discomfort of this feeling of extraneousness, especially at home, where Muriel often saw her as an annoyance.

She had expended so much energy in pursuit of a sense of belonging. When she was Gathering's age she used Rachel Stein's home for this purpose, without even knowing it, losing herself in her friend's sprawling family, watching cable television, playing video games and mingling with their eccentric guests, many of whom stayed on for weeks at a time. For a few hours she escaped the brooding silence that awaited her at home.

In those days Muriel would pull into the driveway at seven every night, slide a frozen dinner into the toaster oven and collapse in front of the TV while Maya would seal herself inside her room and disappear into the plots of novels or television shows, often in search of home.

Once, Maya had found a *National Geographic* in Rachel Stein's basement with photos of a South American tribe engaged in elaborate ritual dances, clad in ornate costumes, their faces painted in bright colors. What had captured her imagination was how absorbed they looked, how present in the moment—how unlike Americans rushing to their next appointment. She'd seen the same thing on the streets downtown, even amid the poverty, a joyfulness that sprang naturally from a sense of community, a phenomenon she had rarely witnessed in Plainfield's subdivisions.

Like the Steins, the residents of this community seemed to lead close-knit lives. Walking around, Maya hadn't heard a television or even a radio yet. From what she could tell, these people *interacted*.

A crack of thunder struck, far off, just at the edge of hearing. The scent of a storm was in the air; heavy clouds cast a pall over the countryside. A sudden gust of wind shook the trees, springing many leaves free, that spun and fluttered to the ground. The toddlers, oblivious to the plummeting barometer, continued their antics. The women began to herd them in, calling out their names, which ricocheted through the monkey bars and swings and slides.

"Spencer! Tyler! Justine!"

Maya turned as the Audi approached, bumping across the grass. Brandon leaned out of the window.

"I'm heading up to the new site," he said. "Why don't you come along? I can drop you in town afterward."

Maya turned to Gathering.

"Rats," the girl said, frowning. "I have to work. Kitchen, as usual. I'm already late. You were my excuse."

She spun around and dashed off, calling out good-byes.

Maya turned to Brandon. "I guess so."

They drove out of the compound, past a couple of teenagers lying on the grass wrapped in each other's arms, alongside an abandoned car with weeds growing out of the dashboard, and by a car driving past them to which Brandon waved. Once he was out on the main road he stomped on the accelerator and the car sped off, creating a wake of wind that left a road sign vibrating as they passed.

"Wilton, Wy," it read, in green and white.

Maya gasped as the sign quickly shot behind them.

Brandon turned to her but she just shook her head. "Don't ask."

Brandon was open and friendly. His voice slowed at times as if his brain was processing lots of information as he spoke, or maybe he was just being careful of what he said. It was hard to know. Maya pegged him as the sort who could devise plans and follow them through to completion with total confidence of a successful outcome. It was a quality she envied.

He lived in California. He had moved there from Atlanta to run an export business, shipping clothing and electronics to Eastern Europe. He visited Wilton monthly and was active in building its community.

"I'm in it for the long run," he said.

"What exactly *is* it?"

"An alternative."

"To what?"

"To the way that you live." He smiled. "You'll see."

He took a sharp turn, then pulled the car onto a grassy hill. They got out and walked to the top of a ridge overlooking an expansive valley. Tall grass flowed in the wind as far as the eye could see, and the landscape was dotted occasionally with trees. Just down the hill stood a cabin with a small mountain of logs stacked beside it. Gazing down into the green velvet expanse, Maya spotted the tops of some rocks.

"What's that?"

"I'll show you," he said.

They made their way down the hill to a round cement pit filled with burned wood and cinders.

"Some of our people practice tribal rituals," he said.

"Why?"

"They're useful," he said. "Rituals reconnect you to the deeper aspects of life. They remind you that there's more than what you see, and that you're a part of that, too."

"Burning wood does that?"

"That's only the metaphor." He looked up at the sky as if sizing up the coming storm, then turned back to her. "Modern culture has lost its connection not only to nature but to the self," he said. "Just look around and you can see what that's wrought. We derive our meaning from externals. Things. That's not where the heart is. And that's not all. The way we live is not just crazy, it's dangerous. At the rate we're going we'll exhaust the earth's supply of raw materials in a few decades. That's a documented fact."

"You sell things for a living," she protested. "You support consumption. You support that way of life."

Her objection did not faze him. "One must work within the system to change it."

"Can anyone *really* change anything?" she asked, echoing the greater lesson of her education. "I mean, haven't things been this way since the first caveman clubbed his pal on the head and took over the clan?"

"You're pretty young for that point of view," he said.

But she did think that way. She looked down. The grass appeared so soft and welcoming that she sat down on it, and he sat beside her.

"Do you know how this country was founded?" he asked.

"I know what I learned."

"And what was that?"

"Well—"

"In simple terms."

"Okay." She knew the story well. She began, "Back in the seventeen-hundreds, a bunch of guys, the legendary Founding Fathers, seized an opportunity that was rare in the history of the world: the chance to invent a society that valued individual freedom instead of spending all of its energy on satisfying the indulgences of a few aristocrats or a despotic ruler. It's a long story but the idea was to guarantee freedom for everyone. Well, the white ones, anyway, but that's another story.

"They wrote up their ideas in some enlightened documents. The Declaration of Independence, etcetera. England—mom and dad—tried to stop them. That was the Revolutionary War. The parental units lost, which meant that our guys—women didn't exist then—could run the country however they pleased. They decided democracy was the best thing going. Simple enough?"

"Yes," he agreed.

"I studied history."

"So I see," Brandon said. "Now, this 'bunch of guys,' your legendary Founding Fathers, what do you think of them?"

"They had chutzpah, man."

"Why?"

"They made the ultimate sacrifice. If they'd lost, they would have been hung from the rafters."

"And if that had happened, where do you think you'd be today?"

"At a pub, hoisting a pint," she said, laughing.

Brandon didn't smile. He just sat there, waiting for her to quiet down.

"Consider for a moment," he said, "how dangerous it is to try to do what they did, to attempt to create a new society, to rebel against the powers that be, powers that are backed by fighting men and the weapons of an empire."

"I have," she said, soberly. "I've always wondered if great and humane leaders are born all the time and are routinely killed off as they come into their power, like Martin Luther King and Kennedy.

Maybe guys like that are constantly being eliminated and we never know about it. Maybe that's why the political dramas never change."

Brandon's look was so intense it chilled her.

"What?" she asked.

"Things *are* changing."

"What do you mean?"

"A revolutionary change every bit as big as the one you've just described is happening, right now."

"Right now?"

"Through the land."

"The land?"

"The earth's natural energy centers," he said, watching her closely. "Its vortexes."

Her jaw dropped. She stared at him in disbelief. "What did you just say?"

"I said that the earth's energy centers are being used to create change."

"That's what I thought you said." She turned away, trembling, and tried to collect herself.

This was no mere coincidence. No way. Far beyond it. From the writings of David Orr to her inner travels in Dr. Porter's basement—and now off the lips of Brandon McGowan. Vortexes. Clearly she was on a path of some kind.

"That's why I'm here," she said, feeling shivers crawling up and down her back. "I was just at a vortex. I had a vision. I *saw* this place. Wilton, I mean. And Gathering. It's crazy, I know, maybe it was just an hallucination. I mean, *I just came from a vortex.* He was trying to get me to see where my father was."

"Who? Who was trying to get you to see where your father was?"

"An old colleague of his in Chicago."

"Edgar Porter?"

"Yes!" she said. "You know him?"

"I know *of* him."

"Who is he?"

"A vortex researcher," Brandon said. "Did you tell him you were coming here?"

"No. Why? Is that important?"

"No. Not really."

"What do you know about vortexes?"

"It's an area of interest," he said. "Many people are studying them now. But tell me, what happened with regard to your father? Were you able to get information on him?

"I'm not sure. I just saw Wilton. That's why I came here. I figured maybe he was here. Are you sure you don't know David Orr?"

"Yes, I'm sure."

"He was into all this stuff, too."

"I suppose he may have been here," he said. "The community has been here a long time."

"This stuff is tripping me out. I can't believe you know about it."

He waited for her to look at him, then said, "You saw something back there in the kitchen, didn't you?"

"What do you mean?"

"An energy pattern around Georgia."

Shocked, she said, "How do you know that?"

"I *saw* you seeing it."

Her eyes widened. Panic churned in her stomach. Again she felt the strain of her beliefs stretching to a breaking point.

Brandon, seeing her reaction, said, "Easy. There's nothing to be afraid of."

"I'm not afraid," she said quickly.

He locked his eyes onto hers. "Good," he said. "You should know something then. There are George Washingtons and Thomas Jeffersons alive today. Do you understand what I'm saying?"

"No."

"Change is afoot. Great change."

Change. Great change. Monstrous change. Unpredictable change. Uncontrollable change. Yes, yes. I get it, she thought. As much as I can. But what does it mean?

Even through her fear and confusion she realized that Brandon was speaking of exactly the phenomenon David Orr had written about. Maybe his change was really happening, even after all the years his journal lay untouched in the ground.

"You're having trouble with this," he said. "I can see it."

"I want to understand," she protested. To understand meant to get closer to the truth of David Orr, the bull's eye at which she was aiming. "Tell me about this change. I want to know."

Suddenly lightning flashed overhead, illuminating Brandon's face. Then thunder cracked over the distant fields. The afternoon sky had grown dark and ominous; rain was only moments away.

"Cultural change begins as an intention on a mass psychic level," he said. "Whether it is realized in the world or not is a matter of momentum. Let me give you an example: The Vietnam anti-war movement of the nineteen-sixties. The protests started out with the intention of a small, inconsequential group but grew large enough to affect a country of over two-hundred million. At a certain point, a critical mass of intention was reached psychically, and change effected.

"Or take the abolition of slavery in the Civil War. An astute politician like Lincoln can read the group mind before even it knows what it's thinking. Though the war wasn't about slavery, strategically he wanted the slaves to be freed. At the time the move was politically unpopular, and critical mass was weak, change harder to manifest. As it turned out it was enough and he eked by. Critical mass was reached and the slaves were liberated."

"But what about now?" she asked. "What kind of change is going on now?"

"Unknown at present, I'm afraid."

"Then how do you know it's happening?"

"The research shows it. Manifestation has sped up. The velocity of cultural change in the world has increased. Look how fast technology is advancing, how rapidly trade is crossing borders, how quickly political systems are shifting. Human society has never been so fluid. That's only the beginning.

"Manifestation does not occur in a vacuum. It's willed. Mostly unconsciously, but it comes from *us*. The velocity of the medium—the earth environment—has increased. It's become like a greased bowling alley; there's no traction. Nothing sticks. We've seen more cultural change in the last century than in all the others combined. Why?"

Lightning flashed and thunder cracked so loudly they both jumped. The storm seemed to be just down the hill. Still the rain held back.

She wasn't going to be distracted. She said, "Okay, why?"

"Because large-scale cultural, social, and political change is being manipulated."

"Manipulated? How?"

"In much the same way that you did it. By *consciously* manifesting." He nodded at the land around them. "How did you get here?"

"You brought me."

"Yes, but why here of all places? Why Wilton?"

"I told you. I saw it in my vision."

"Exactly. And who are you talking to? Someone who knows about vortexes, who understands what's happening, of all the people you could have bumped into. *That's* manifestation. You created this very interaction back at that vortex. Coincidence? No. You are part of it now. Your experiences will propel you toward a specific destination. At this moment your unconscious is hard at work trying to manifest the intentions you set in motion in your vision. The moment you veer from them you will know it. You will feel sapped of energy, unfulfilled, lost."

As if to bring the point home, lightning lit up the great field in a burst of electricity, and another thunderclap struck. The swollen mass of clouds finally opened, and raindrops began to tap at her face.

"We'd better go," he said, but she did not move.

She seemed to be stuck there on the ground, overwhelmed by this new, weighty information. Brandon pulled up his collar.

"Who are you?" she asked.

"A concerned citizen, someone who wants to see this world survive the coming years."

Survive the coming years. Another David Orr-ism.

Perhaps a deluge really was coming. Maybe that gnawing feeling of some ineffable *something* looming just over the horizon wasn't mere paranoia. Full-moon craziness was on the rise in the world, anyone could see it. The newspapers screamed it on a daily basis. The center *wasn't* holding. Maybe the ubiquitous stress that permeated the lives of just about everyone she knew was not only real but warranted, the chilling prescience of an uncertain future.

If there were an explanation it lay in the journal. She was certain of it. Armed with Brandon's information, she would plumb its depths and bring to the surface its secrets. What was a book but a topographical map of a psyche, a guided tour of a mind? David Orr's mind held the answers, and so she would travel beyond his words, derive the meaning she had missed, and proceed from there. But not here. Not in Wyoming.

The rain came down now in a deluge. Sheets of water fell from the heavens. Brandon and Maya sprinted up the hill and jumped into the car. He started it up and pulled onto the road.

Sitting in the Audi as they approached town, her hair drying in the hot air of the dashboard vent, the rain pounding against the roof like machine gun fire, she wished she could stay longer at this unusual community, get to know its people.

He drove her to the motel and waited as she packed her things, then he drove her all the way to the airport, talking more about the change, until her mind was so loaded with information all she could do was nod when he looked over at her and stare out of the window as much as possible.

"We'll see each other again," he said at the curb of the airport's departure area. "I have a feeling."

"I hope so," she said. "Goodbye."

"Goodbye, Maya."

That evening, sitting on a long cushioned bench in the airport, waiting for her flight, she watched a TV that hung from the ceiling. In front of her, travelers strode down a long hallway, disappearing in both directions.

Wilton had opened her eyes. There were other ways to live,

lifestyles far removed from the urban-suburban scene she knew so
well. There was so much she didn't know. Of alternative ways of
living she had only known what television had shown her, the
most extreme communities, the cults and gangs and militias that
the media milked for entertainment value. Like everyone, she had
soaked up the carnival-like coverage of these disturbed
countercultures. But there were other ways, too, benign alternatives,
like the one she had just left. Perhaps these would form the
fountainhead of the future.

What she watched on the airport television that evening
confirmed to her that a transformation was indeed occurring.
Disputes among nations were erupting like brush fires in a parched
backwoods, as usual, yes—but with a difference. Now it was
everyone's business. The Earth had shrunk, its neighborhoods had
blended together. People were stepping, however tentatively, across
the boundaries of their prejudices. Information that had been
hidden was now available. The identities of those who poisoned
the air and the water had changed. It was no longer *them*. It was
us. This shift in perception was as real as the sound of a beating
heart.

What was *the change*? Was this it?

She had learned that throughout history catastrophic events—
earthquakes, geological upheavals, cosmic disasters—had been
predicted to accompany great change in the world of human affairs.
David Orr saw these phenomena another way.

> *Such predictions are metaphors. The physical shaking of
> the earth symbolizes change. But not physical change—internal
> change. Change in people. The world as we know it will be
> "shaken up," life as we know it will "cease to be." There is no
> external cataclysm. Physical reality as a whole is a metaphor for
> that which is internal. The definition of apocalypse is revelation.*

She sipped from a carton of orange juice she'd bought at the
airport store. The tanginess felt good, burning away the stale taste
in her mouth.

Her life had become dream-like. Dream—reality. Which was which? The events of the past days, the people, the places, the dramatic changes to her belief system, resembled nothing she'd ever experienced. She had never felt so engaged, so vital. So alive. If this was a dream, then she didn't want to wake up.

She had studied the great civilizations of the past, knew how the corrupt and indulgent ones had collapsed from the weight of their own excesses. She wondered if America was sliding down that same slippery slope, with its disintegrating communities and broken families, its corporate greed and culture of guns and violence, its ever-growing gap between rich and poor. Sometimes she became upset just thinking about it. Was her fear justified? She didn't know. Maybe she was projecting her own frustration onto the world and then complaining at how bad it all looked.

She often envied the optimism of her mother's generation that came of age in the nineteen-sixties, when it seemed an individual's voice could still be heard over the drumbeat of corporate expansionism, when old America still existed and people weren't stressed out all the time. What did it feel like to be hopeful about the future? She didn't know. She had only known that stressful sliding feeling and its shifting fears.

Maybe, just maybe, this change of her father's, of Brandon's, would bring back an easier world. Maybe things could be different.

She was about to find out.

CHAPTER 7

She arrived home at two in the morning. Muriel was out. She dropped her clothes in a pile by the bed, drew a bath and soaked in the warm water until her skin was soft, and sleep within easy reach. Then she lifted her pruned body up out of the tub, toweled off, and slipped into bed with a satisfied smile on her face.

She awakened to the sun blasting at her window shade. She got up and shuffled down toward the kitchen and stopped suddenly in the hallway, startled to glimpse a lone figure sitting on the living room sofa. The shades were tightly drawn, the room nearly dark.

Muriel, in jeans and a denim shirt, was swirling a glass in her hand. Maya could hear the familiar sound of ice cubes going around and around. Muriel looked as though she hadn't moved in hours, and Maya wondered if her mother had been in that same spot, ghost-like, the whole time she'd been home.

Muriel smiled, but it wasn't really a smile. It was a thin line turned up at the edges. "You could have said something," she said.

Maya felt her body go cold. Her first thought: Muriel had seen Josh somewhere and knew that the camping trip was a lie. Or worse: she had somehow found out about *him*.

"How long were you gone?" Muriel asked, her tone accusatory. "Three days?"

"Three days," Muriel repeated. "And did you call?"

Why was she asking? Calling hadn't been a problem for some time. "No."

"Why not?"

Maya remained quiet.

"Maya, I don't care what you do or where you go, but as long as you're living in my house, I want to know if you'll be gone for the better part of a week. Is that clear?"

"Yes," Maya said. "It's clear." Relieved, she exhaled a sigh of relief. Muriel didn't know, after all.

"You're a selfish girl."

Whatever.

"Oh, never mind about that," Muriel said. "How was the trip? Did you at least have fun, even if it was with that oddball?"

"Sure," Maya said. "It was like last time. Hiking. Rivers. Flies. Fish. Tent. Hard ground."

"Try selling real estate," Muriel said, continuing to swirl the glass. "That's hard ground, too."

Maya went into the kitchen and came out with a bowl of cereal. She sat on the easy chair opposite Muriel.

"What about work?" Muriel said. "Are you even looking?"

Maya's eyes were glued to her mother's hand, which was shaking so badly the glass was vibrating. Muriel had had the shakes before, but never like this. The liquid was practically jumping out of the glass.

Maya ignored the question. "How's Henry?" she said.

"He's fine," Muriel said. "But you're changing the subject. Why didn't you major in business? Do you know how much opportunity there is in business today? Don't you want some options?"

"Me? Business? You've got to be kidding."

"Money comes in pretty handy, kiddo. So does learning how to make it. When you leave this house you're going to find that out, I can assure you of that."

Muriel ran her hand through her hair, then looked over and caught Maya staring at her. "What?" she said, suspiciously.

"Nothing."

"You're looking at me."

Maya said nothing, took a spoonful of cereal.

Muriel said, "What's going on here?"

"Maybe you look a little different."

"Different? Different how?"

"I don't know. From how you looked a few days ago."

"What's that supposed to mean? I'm still me. See," she said, patting her cheeks in an exaggerated way. "Same old me. Sitting here enjoying the morning."

"In the dark?"

"So what? The light's going to be out all day."

"Okay, okay," Maya said. "You're right. I'm tired. I'm going back to sleep."

"You've been asleep all night. It's ten o'clock."

"What about you? Have you been up all night?"

Muriel didn't answer. Maya had some more cereal and kept silent, which was the best course at such times. Her mother's emotions moved in unpredictable ways, like a river that wound through vastly different terrain, disappeared into caves, dove underground, dropped down unseen waterfalls. Maya had expended much energy adjusting to Muriel's currents, and although she had tried to give up the practice, she suspected it was still going on in the back alleys of her mind and always would, siphoning off valuable energy.

Muriel stared down at the glass in her hand. "This sucks."

"What?"

"Iced freaking tea, that's what."

"You're drinking iced tea?" Maya said, surprised.

Muriel gave her the dead-eyed stare that had always made Maya's blood go cold. "What of it?"

"Nothing."

"Okay, then." She had another sip and grimaced.

Maya rinsed off the bowl in the kitchen sink, and put it in the dishwasher. "See you later," she called out.

"Do whatever you want, I don't care," came the reply.

Back in her room, she leafed through the journal to a passage he'd written about relationships.

You needn't decipher all the tangles, nor even understand them, to do what's right. Try to act from the noblest possible place in your dealings with others and you will "create" the best possible outcome. Use that exquisitely powerful tool, your imagination. Imagine you are loving and serene, act from that perspective, and you will be.

Anger is a reaction to an event that does not conform to your expectations. It can also be a plea from your repressed self. When you become enraged, someone may be displaying a character trait you possess but are afraid to act upon. It remains in hiding as trapped energy, a caged animal that hungers for freedom. Free it. The bars on your cage are of your own making . . .

The phone rang at noon the next day.

"Maya Burke?"

"Yes?"

"This is Albert Fiske. I'm an associate of Edgar Porter's. He told me you were looking for your father. I knew him. I worked with him."

"You did?" Maya said excitedly.

"I should say that I don't know where he is, Maya," he said. "But I might be able to help you find him. There's a lot I can tell you, but I'd rather do it in person."

"Yes, of course. Where are you?"

"I'm in D.C., just off the Mall. Do you know the area?"

"Absolutely," she said.

Of course she did. She knew the National Mall intimately. How could she not? Without it she might never have emerged from the great abyss, that bottomless pit of despair that had swallowed her up like a sinkhole in search of a soul. Those days were the darkest of her young life, ones she did not long to revisit. Strangely, her salvation took place at the Mall.

*   *   *

The peacefulness of the garden at the National Museum of Oriental Art emanated from its design. Curving brick walkways wove through flower beds and fountains like paths through Eden. All this, just a few feet from bustling Independence Avenue, a major Washington artery on which morning traffic hummed and honked as commuters converged on the city.

She had arrived early, spied a bench in the garden and waited, watching people walk through the monolithic entrance of the museum, the only part of it above ground. A gardener walked by, singing to himself as he watered the flower beds. On the other side of the gate, along Independence Avenue, thousands of government workers strode the busy sidewalks, many of them disappearing into a large office building across the street.

A stone's throw away, the well-worn grass-and-dirt path of the National Mall ran all the way from the Capitol building to the east to the Washington Monument and Lincoln Memorial to the west. In between stood the museums of the Smithsonian Institution complex, a city within a city, with its vast and priceless collections of historical art and artifacts.

But the district belonged to the country's politicians, not its historians and curators, and year after year, decade after decade, they descended on Washington to wrestle for power and try to mold America along the lines of their own beliefs. If they succeeded, they might achieve a bit of immortality, securing their name on a piece of legislation, a program, or a process.

Maya's fascination with history began as a seed that Uncle Buddy had planted and carefully watered. Buddy Burke, Muriel's only sibling, was two years her senior, a retired air force pilot who had flown a B-52 bomber in combat. He came to Plainfield for a visit when Maya was sixteen and stayed for six months, a period that had affected her profoundly.

Many a summer evening had seen uncle and niece sitting on the porch swing, with Buddy regaling her with his stories, translating the political dramas of distant nations into terms she could understand, occasionally punctuating his discourses with the swack of a mosquito. His voice was hypnotic. Transfixed, she would hang onto his every word, eager to escape the dullness of Plainfield for the great cities of Europe and Asia.

To Buddy, countries possessed personalities just as people did, inborn programming that never changed. America was an adventurous, brazen young explorer. India was a nurturer, feminine, a keeper of secrets. Mother Russia and Germany's Fatherland had their personas and gender leanings, too.

Every land mass, he told her, infused its innate personality traits into the collective psyche of the people who lived on it, creating a foundation for their behaviors and actions. America, he said, was unique in that it was a young country. Whereas other nations' behaviors had become calcified over long years, the ink on America's story was still damp. It was far more changeable than the others.

Buddy and his theories. Oh, how she missed him! She loved him as she would have loved her father, if only she'd known David Orr. Even as a teen she felt she understood her complex and conflicted uncle. His cheerful front couldn't hide an existential pain that simmered beneath the surface, and his effort to veil it made her love him even more. What had happened to Buddy?

He disappeared into New York or Philadelphia, she'd last heard. He was a salesman of some type, a hustler who had always led a difficult existence. He hadn't written or called in years. The last letters she sent him were returned undelivered.

She checked her watch. It was time. She got up and wound her way through the garden to the Mall, then headed in the direction of the Capitol. At one point she had to step aside to duck out of the way of a German man snapping a photo of his family. People from all over the world filled the area.

Maya, like the German tourists, marveled at the dome of the Capitol building. High up, at the apex, standing proudly in the cool autumn wind, was a bronze statue of a woman wearing a Native American headdress. Maya knew the piece well; she had written a paper on it. Even now she felt the piercing irony she had experienced then: the very men who had treated the Native Americans so brutally had chosen to crown their primary legislative building this way. The statue's name was Freedom.

Maya's beliefs told her that history was not static. It was fluid, ever-changing. Though the deeds of the past could never be undone, they were continually being rewritten. As a girl, Maya had learned about a heroic visionary named Christopher Columbus who had discovered a new continent. Then, in young adulthood, amid a changing political landscape, the man had become nothing more than another European plunderer, anything but a hero. Though he had not drawn a single breath in half a millennium, suddenly he had begun to act differently.

She had learned that Europeans brought civilization to a continent of savages in a place known as the New World—another fact that had metamorphosed over time. In reality, the indigenous peoples were treated like weeds in a field that needed to be cleared, their cultures deemed worthless.

Buddy taught her that recorded history was nothing more than a series of lessons in perspective, point of view. "One guy's colony is another guy's graveyard," he had said.

Perspective.

*　　*　　*

She arrived at the Museum of Natural History. Long lines of people crept slowly through the entrance doors, delayed by a security check inside. School buses pulled up and dropped off crowds of children. Pigeons bobbed along the pavement. The aroma of popcorn from sidewalk vendors filled the air.

She hesitated at the top step, as the role of this building in her personal history hit her with full impact. She now regretted her choice of meeting place.

The big crash, as she would later call it, struck when she was seventeen, squeezing the energy out of her with ferocious swiftness. Dr. Yanikowski, the psychiatrist whom Muriel had recruited to help Maya, had called it a clinical depression. Maya didn't care about labels. All she knew was that she was in constant agony.

A foreign consciousness seemed to have taken possession of

her, filling her body with molasses-like heaviness and her mind with hatred for itself. Maya took up residence in bed, weeping spontaneously at all hours, praying for relief, feeling so physically weak that she could barely summon the energy to lift her hand and wipe the tears from her cheeks.

It began with Buddy's departure. He had given no explanation for leaving; he just said a quick goodbye and disappeared one day. A week later she awoke distraught and tired. She thought nothing of it. She was no stranger to sadness.

But her mood worsened, until after five days she had become despondent. Whenever she tried to pull herself up she would immediately drop back into bed, feeling as though she was burdened with a hundred additional pounds.

Her thinking processes began to change. The things and people she cared about no longer mattered. Her thoughts turned increasingly morbid. She began to detest the world, largely for the energy it required of her. She had none to give. All thoughts were the cause for suffering. She felt victimized, but by whom? No one had harmed her. Who, then, was to blame? Herself? If that was the answer, then the situation was even more terrifying.

The organ of thought, the brain, the wolf, that indefatigable miracle of evolution that could treat the world with such cool dispatch . . . that was the very part of her that was ill. Compulsively it looped over and over with the same bleak thoughts, the same unanswerable questions, the same boorish complaints. There was no escape. The beast had dominion over her. She could stop it no more than she could stem the flow of clouds across the sky.

The episode lasted two weeks—an agonizing fortnight that battered her psyche like the screams of torture victims, scarring her deeply. She knew she would never be the same.

But she outlasted it, her will won out, and gradually her energy began to return. At first, the best she could manage was to shuffle around the house like a weary foot soldier who had survived a terrible war at great cost. Strenuous tasks were out of the question. If her mental to-do list filled up, anxiety chased away her newfound energy, bringing her thumping back into bed. Dr. Yanikowski had prescribed antidepressant medication but she tossed it unopened in a drawer. Mind-altering medicines frightened her more than the illness itself.

His advice, though, did interest her. He told her to find easy, enjoyable things to do until she returned to normal. He taught her a self-therapy technique she would continue to practice, a kind of mental jujitsu that dispersed the obsessive negative thoughts before they could gather together and initiate another descent. She took to it immediately. It consisted of writing down her negative thoughts along with their opposites. Beside, "I am weird and no one will like me," she would write, "Everyone is unusual in their own way so I am really normal." Next to, "I will get depressed and kill myself," she would respond, "I will live in the moment and the future will take care of itself." And so on. Amazingly, it worked, and usually in a matter of minutes.

Her healing process was also tied to the Museum of Natural History. After the worst was over, she found herself thinking often of this museum, which she, like so many other youngsters, had visited on a grade school field trip. So she drove there, purely out of curiosity. Only later would she understand why. The reason was this: her bruised soul sought convalescence in a location unrelated and unfamiliar to anything in her life or even, as it turned out, her world. She wanted a completely neutral place where she could heal and expand and let the scabs of her wounds fall away.

She spent whole days at the dinosaur exhibits, traveling back tens of millions of years to a time when the life she knew remained undreamed of, for people had not yet arrived to dream it. Her voracious mind, her hungry wolf, happily swam in a waterfall of facts and theories.

She—it—devoured the information. Every plaque, every exhibit. She took the audio tours. Her vocabulary grew with words she would never use. Mesozoic. Brachiosaurus. Iguanodon. Such names became the lyrics to her new anthem. The names and places and dates washed over her in a cleansing ablution, and she grew stronger. Contemplating the nuts and bolts of the life of the dinosaurs satisfied the wolf—although she often had to suppress a cynicism at the certainty implied in the declarations of knowledge that adorned the exhibits.

When it came down to knowing when the Triceratops stomped through the countryside, how it spent its afternoons, why it had disappeared, the only information she had were the latest theories. As new theories were posited and old ones discarded, whatever one took as reality at a given time would undoubtedly become incorrect one day. What then constituted truth? she wondered.

When Muriel was in grade school, dinosaurs were thought to have been slow-moving reptilian clods. When Maya reached the same age, they had become quick, bird-like creatures. Which was it? There were plenty of theories to go around. How about this: human beings are actually the cloned offspring of space aliens on shore leave at a blue-green planet.

Wasn't all knowledge really just theory? How could you know anything for certain? Every so-called fact, every agreement upon which you based your understanding of the world, was really shifting, changeable, not at all rock solid, not something you could bank upon.

The wolf's eyes glowed with a red, hellish fire.

Stop.

At the top of the steps she took a long breath. She maneuvered into the entrance line and soon was through the door, in the museum's crowded atrium. Corridors radiated out from this central hub to all the exhibit halls—sea life, rocks and minerals, mammals, reptiles, native cultures, the dinosaurs. A pungent, stale odor filled the air, the smell of dusty exhibits and sweaty people, one that Maya had come to attach to natural history. Actually, she liked it.

The atrium's centerpiece was an African bull elephant, its trunk reaching permanently for the sky, sealed in place by the taxidermists of nineteen-fifty-five. "The modern world's largest land animal," read the plaque. A throng of chatty children gazed up at it, making jokes and laughing.

She walked slowly around the elephant until she spotted a man holding a newspaper under his arm, just what Albert Fiske had said he would be doing. She waved to him.

He walked over, shook her hand, his grip firm. He said hello in a husky voice.

"Can we walk?" he said, pointing toward the door.

"Sure."

Albert Fiske was in his mid-fifties, youthful-looking, with bushy black eyebrows, a black crewcut, and a thick, muscular chest. His gray trousers were neatly pressed. His starched white shirt, tie, and loafers were conservative. He was only slightly taller than Maya. She had never found clean-cut guys attractive, but he had a masculinity that would have been pleasing on one of her boyfriends.

They walked toward the Washington Monument. "I've lived in D.C. for twenty-five years and I've never been up in it," he said. "Downright unpatriotic, wouldn't you say?"

She was impatient. She wanted to get right down to business. "Was my father patriotic?"

He said, "I can let you decide that for yourself."

"How do you mean?"

"You'll see," he said. "My office is right across the street."

He started toward Independence Avenue, where she had been earlier. He stopped, turned toward her.

She hesitated. Here it was, she knew, another doorway leading to David Orr. There was no question about what she would do.

"I'm coming," she said.

CHAPTER 8

"Your father was a talented man," Albert Fiske began, as he settled into the squeaky chair behind his desk and leaned so far back that Maya braced herself, certain he was going to topple over backwards. He didn't. He just hovered there, suspended at a one-hundred-and-sixty degree angle, gazing down his cheeks at her. She straightened her back, sat up tall in the low chair opposite the messy desk, trying unsuccessfully to hike herself up to eye level with him.

He had led her into an office building just behind the government building she had watched earlier from the bench in the garden. There was no sign on the front of the drab cement building, just its street address.

He had strode into the lobby with authority, flashed his ID badge at the three guard stations they passed—each one leading to windowless lower levels—and was waved through every one with a deferential nod.

Maya sniffed the air in the office; it was moldy, stagnant.

"You've received the quickest background check I've ever authorized," Albert Fiske said. "The equivalent of a secret clearance. Of course at your age there isn't a whole lot to check."

"Why do I need a clearance, Mr. Fiske?"

"Just 'Fiske,'" he said. "Everyone calls me Fiske."

"Okay. Fiske."

He said, "The reason you need a clearance is so that I can tell you what I'm about to tell you. It's what you came for. Can I offer you a drink first?"

"Do you have a Coke?"

"Sure."

He got up and walked out of the office, and Maya surveyed it.

Dank gray concrete walls, dirty floor, stale smell. Almost like the museum. Two posters on the walls, one a street scene of the Champs-Elysées, the other a whale leaping high out of the ocean. Both ripped and stained with age. Fiske's desk was a trash heap of papers.

He returned, handed her the Coke, and took his chair. This time he didn't lean back in it. He sat forward, facing her, his elbows on the desk. She took a long swallow of the soft drink, put the can on a small table at her elbow.

"Is this the government?" she asked.

"Yes," he said.

"Which branch?"

"I'll get to that," he said. "First things first."

"Not much for décor."

"We don't splurge in that area."

He reached into a desk drawer, pulled out an 8-by-10 photo and handed it over the desk to her.

"Guess who?" he said, clearly enjoying the moment.

She didn't have to. It was obvious. The black-and-white image showed a young man standing beside a blackboard, staring intently at mathematical equations written on it. He seemed composed yet excited.

The shape of David Orr's mouth matched hers exactly, wide and full. He was tall and slender, like her, with dark angular features, intense eyes, and disheveled hair, a dash of irreverence in an otherwise neat appearance. He was wearing dark slacks and a light cardigan sweater.

She asked, "When was this?"

"Long time ago. Twenty years."

The photo was so clear and crisp she could almost read him. She stared hard at the eyes, trying to bring them to life; maybe, she mused, if she focused hard enough, they would be able to see her, too. She had initially thought his expression was a smile, but now she wasn't so sure. It was hard to tell.

Fiske, smiling broadly, said, "You probably want a copy of that."

She nodded.

"I'll take care of it."

She handed the photo back across the desk to him.

Fiske said, "You want to find him pretty bad, I bet."

Again, she nodded.

"Maybe we can help each other. I'm looking for David, too."

"Why are you looking for him?"

He stretched his arms out and tilted his neck to one side, and she heard a sharp but barely audible *crack*. Then, ignoring her question, he said, "Have you ever heard of remote viewing?"

She shook her head no.

"You'll need to know about it because that's what your father was doing when he disappeared."

"Disappeared?"

"Make yourself comfortable, Maya. I'm going to tell you a story that's like nothing you've ever heard before."

He reached for a Styrofoam cup balanced atop a stack of papers on his desk, brought it to his lips and swallowed whatever was in it—she assumed coffee—while his eyes never left hers.

"Do you know much about the Cold War?" he said.

"Sure," she said.

"What do you know about it? Tell me," he asked, a hint of condescension in his voice.

His tone made her feel defensive. "A period of intense economic and political problems following World War II. A conflict between the capitalist West and the Communist bloc characterized by military buildups, economic competition and bad diplomatic relations. Is that close enough?"

"That's good, very good," he said, impressed. "Then maybe you'll know some of the background."

He put the cup back on the stack of papers. He said, "That's where the story starts, in the sixties and seventies, when Soviet Russia began to study extrasensory perception, or ESP. You know what ESP is, right?"

Maya looked away. God, the man was patronizing. And he probably didn't even know it. But never mind, she'd have to cut him a break because of what he was telling her. It was difficult to admit but he was also appealing in an obnoxious ultra-masculine way. He probably owned guns.

"It's being able to see things without being there," she said. "Knowing things in advance."

"Right," he said. "But it goes further than that. Some people can observe things without using *any* of the five senses, so it comes down to perception that's completely nonphysical. That, believe it or not, is the capability the Russians were developing. And do you know what? It worked. Guess what happened next?"

"We got into the act."

He paused, sized her up again. "You really know your stuff."

"Who exactly is this 'we'?"

He extended his arms. "The good old U.S. of A. Now, the Soviet intentions weren't exactly friendly. Their aim was single-minded: to spy on us. Period. And since they'd had a head start, when our budget came through we had some catch-up to do."

"I'm surprised we got funding at all."

He paused, challenge in his eyes. "Why do you say that?"

"When have Americans taken metaphysics seriously?"

"Care to elaborate?"

"We deny the existence of anything science can't explain. Just read some of the literature of the past millennia. There's loads of first-hand accounts of ESP and unexplainable phenomena, but just because of the occasional hoax, it's all discredited. That's backwards. The phenomenon that *breaks* the rule should be the thing to study, not the predictable stuff."

Fiske's eyebrows had been slowly creeping up as she spoke, toward the wavy lines that zigzagged across his forehead.

She stopped, drew back, ashamed of herself, knowing that her opinion would only serve to alienate her, as it always had. But her words had the opposite reaction on Fiske. He was interested.

"Tell me," he said. "Are these the sorts of things you think about?"

She shrugged. "I guess."

"Tell me more."

She felt too self-conscious. She shook her head. "I don't know. Now what were you saying about ESP?"

"Okay," he nodded. "Now the Russians had their technique for observing phenomena at a distance, which they called remote viewing. How can I explain it . . ." He paused, searching. "I guess it's like 'throwing' your consciousness, the way a ventriloquist throws his voice. A remote viewer receives mental impressions. He doesn't go anywhere per se; he's just sitting in a room, eyes closed, following a mental regimen that by the way, is quite complex."

He leaned back in his chair, which now squeaked and groaned louder than ever.

"So we began our program. Our early remote viewers were psychics just like the Russians, hand-picked for their abilities. It seemed a logical place to start. We began with modest goals like identifying the contents of sealed boxes, and believe it or not, it worked. It's the damnedest thing." He shook his head as if he still didn't believe it.

She asked, "How does it work?"

"After a prep routine the viewer is given coordinates, pairs of numbers that correspond to a location. He focuses on them and receives images, which he notes and diagrams. With no idea of what the numbers represent, he 'travels' there.

"Now, as I said, we started small. In one trial the viewer reported a small, moving gray mound. The target? A mouse in a box we had placed in a room across the hall. *Boom.* Direct hit. That's how it works—not perfect, but correct. Shapes and colors come in the strongest. Sometimes you get details, other times you don't. It depends on the viewer, the situation, and who the hell knows what else, the phases of the moon, for all I know.

"We moved in stages from the sealed-box trials to actual locations, starting with rooms in the building, then going farther out to other places, other states, even foreign cities—statistically successful all the way. It was amazing. Our access seemed to be unbounded. The images float in and the viewer notes them. The information literally comes through the viewer, but it's a subtle process. *Really* subtle. A bad dinner can skew things. Or a bad date. But that's not all. Even subtler factors come into play, like the *thoughts of the person* guiding the viewer."

Maya laughed. "That's pretty subtle, all right."

Fiske shook his head. "It gets worse. The guy who chose the coordinates two days earlier can affect things."

"Honestly," she said, shaking her head. She liked far-out theories, but this . . . this was going way out on the limb.

"It's true, all of it," he said firmly. "Now, one day—I remember this like it was yesterday—someone says, 'How about an extraterrestrial target?' When we stopped laughing we thought, why the hell not?"

"We chose Jupiter. A NASA satellite was due there on a fly-by so we knew we could check its data against ours. I didn't expect anything, of course. Nobody did. The viewer did his thing and reported a ring around Jupiter. Which is ridiculous. Jupiter has no ring. Maybe, we laughed, he overshot and bumped into Saturn's rings by mistake. As it turned out, the joke was on us. The satellite data came back showing a ring around Jupiter that was previously unknown. Boy, did we have a few drinks that night. After that, funding flowed into our little project. We were in business. We trained a team of viewers and discovered things every bit as incredible as the ring around Jupiter."

"Like what?"

"Like that our viewers could see into the future. Now hold on a minute. The future doesn't exist, of course, but the *potential* future does. Think about it. The future is a work in progress. You can't see the finished product because it hasn't happened, but you can see the construction site, the partially completed structures. What might happen."

Maya perked up, interested. "I should have figured the government was into all this."

"Initially the CIA and the Defense Intelligence Agency," he said. "Nowawdays, a few independent groups do remote viewing."

"Which one are you? What's this building?"

"CIA, Maya. It's not about who, though," he said. "It's about what. Everything I've told you has been declassified. You can read about it at any bookstore. Just look up 'psychic spies.'"

"Then why the security check?"

"For this."

He reached into a drawer and pulled out two large sheets of paper which unfolded into maps, one of the United States, the other a Mercator projection of the world. He laid the U.S. map on top.

Blue and red dots peppered the map. A series of blue dots, about a dozen, appeared in several states, mostly in New England, Montana, the Southwest and around the West coast. Hundreds of smaller red dots were sprinkled throughout the rest of the country.

"Energy vortexes," he said. "Yes. Just like the one at Porter's house. The blues are majors, the reds minors."

The familiar chills now started to move wavelike through her body. She leaned forward, peering at the map. She pointed to a red dot near Chicago.

"Yep. That's him," he said.

"A minor?"

"Correct."

He then put the U.S. map aside, revealing the Mercator projection, also covered in red and blue dots. He slid his finger to a blue dot east of the Mediterranean Sea.

"Jerusalem," he said.

He ran his finger south to Egypt.

"Giza."

And further east to the Himalayas, stopping again on a blue dot.

"Tibet."

Then to Central America.

"Guatemala."

Maya's brow wrinkled as she watched.

Fiske asked, "What do these places have in common?"

Maya considered it. After a minute of thinking hard, she looked up.

"Influential cultures," she said. "The pyramids are in Giza, the Mayan culture was in Guatemala, and Jerusalem is home to the three great Western religions. Religions began in all those places. So you're saying the vortexes are related to religion?"

Fiske was smiling and nodding. "Exactly. Exactly right."

She recalled what Dr. Porter had said about the mental and psychic intensity that exists around vortexes, stirring people up. She asked, "Why isn't this known? It seems so obvious, and so important."

"The mystics of indigenous cultures know. But why share the knowledge? Would you? There's an old saying: 'He who doesn't know, says. He who knows, doesn't say.' These people don't say."

"Then how do *you* know?"

Fiske smiled. He folded up the maps and returned them to the drawer. Then he leaned back in the creaky chair and Maya again grimaced, waiting for him to splatter onto the floor. Now, though, she realized what was happening. He knew what she was thinking, and was enjoying it. She'd been looking at his powerful chest most of the time, never at his face, so she had missed it. She felt like a fool, and just shook her head.

He said, "The vortexes have always been there. The difference is that now we have the remote viewers to see them."

Suddenly, a thought struck her, a *knowing*, and she sat up straight. "My father was a remote viewer."

"Yes."

"He was a psychic?"

"Was," he said. "And still is."

Her first reaction was relief. It explained a lot. Her abilities. Her sensitivities. The way she often knew people's moods the moment she laid eyes on them, their thoughts before even they did. At times this so overwhelmed her that she would have to run home and hide out in her room, sometimes for hours, lying in the dark, just to recover from absorbing all that information. Now she knew why.

"David was the best of my viewers," Fiske said. "You're talented, too, Maya. Don't look so surprised."

Maybe so, she thought, but she wasn't about to sit on another vortex and take that strange trip again.

"Let me finish," he said. "The vortexes form a communications network, each one a node connected to all the others. If you want to know what happened at Porter's, why you received those images, here's your answer: you received a communication."

"A communication? From whom?"

"A group called the Mandala."

"The who?"

"A group of people who live in a kind of commune in Wyoming. That's why you picked up the reference to Wilton."

She looked away, toward the whale poster, feeling that familiar spinning sensation. She held her hands low, so he couldn't see them shaking. Fiske knew of the people in Wilton.

"Why are they called the Mandala?" she said. "What does it mean?"

"The word comes up in a few cultures, actually. The origin is Sanskrit. A Mandala is a circular design or picture, a kind of symbol showing aspects of a person's life, or a tribe's history. The Mandala I'm talking about are a group of people who have learned how to use the vortexes."

"To do what?"

"It may be possible to incrementally influence cultural evolution. We think they have discovered a way to do this, possibly of ancient origin. You see, several probable futures exist at this moment. Our remote viewers have observed them. The Mandala have seen the same thing."

Fiske picked up the empty coffee cup and flung it into the waste can. A few brown drops flew out onto the wall and crept downwards. He ignored it, and turned back to her.

"Three probable futures show up in our research. We call them continuation, low-tech, and post-disaster. Continuation is essentially no change from today's world. Low-tech represents a breakdown of bedrock institutions and a return to a kind of tribalism, with all of its ills. No communications infrastructure, governance, transportation, medicine, and so on. A giant step backwards. Post-disaster is just as it sounds, the worst case scenario, annihilation of our way of life with the surviving population retreating into ruins, the urban areas savaged."

Maya, listening intently, recalled her father's predictions of change, how tumultuous it might be. Had David Orr worked out the details as Fiske seemed to have? If so, he hadn't included them in the journal.

Maya felt the soda swishing around her stomach, irritating it.

"What we're trying to do here," Fiske said, "is to ensure the continuation future. That way our critical systems don't break down, there's no collapse, the government doesn't fold, there's no rioting and social strife. The other futures don't paint such a pretty picture. We can't deal with a collapse, Maya. That, I'm afraid, is what the Mandala want. Not directly, but as a result of their real intention."

"Which is?"

"What they call a spiritual renaissance. A peaceful world, free of hunger, war, disease. Sounds good, eh? We understand their desires. We want that, too. But they are going about it all wrong. It can't be done without incurring irreversible damage; it requires too big a revolution in thinking. Without such a revolution, anarchy will reign. Then we'll have lost the ball game, centuries of achievement."

"But wouldn't a spiritual revolution be peaceful?"

He shook his head no.

She said, "How can you be so sure?"

"Listen to me," he said. "The Mandala possess a deep knowledge of the vortexes, possibly even the ability to affect people's minds. It doesn't matter where they are physically; they can be in Timbuktu. It's not a matter of place. It's a matter of ability, of intention. Their goal is to affect the collective mind. What do you think will happen when they reach into the fabric of human thought and begin to force changes?

"You have to understand: they *want* a meltdown. They see it as necessary. In a way, they are no different from terrorists. They are psychic terrorists." He paused, looked at her. "I'm asking for your help, Maya."

"Me?" she said. "What can I do?"

"The Mandala have attempted to contact you."

"But I didn't know that," she said quickly.

She thought about Brandon and Georgia and Gathering and their . . . commune, as Fiske called it. She liked the place. She liked the people. She found it impossible to imagine them harming anyone. They seemed so benign. He didn't know she had visited them, nor would she tell him. Not yet, at least.

He said, "I want you to help us learn about them."

"How?"

"They'll contact you again," he said. "When they do, I want you to let me know."

She nodded uncertainly.

CHAPTER 9

Her attention was continually drawn to the dull pulsing coming from somewhere behind her eyes. A headache was brewing. The air was warm and stuffy. The ceiling fan was spinning but not doing much to cool the room, its blades turning so slowly she could almost make out the details on them.

She had given in, and now she wondered if she had made a mistake. She glanced at Josh lying there beside her, his breathing rhythmic, his consciousness adrift in dreamland. Why had she let him back in?

She was weak. That was what she told herself. That was how she had decided to see it. He had called so many times, apologized so profusely, groveled so convincingly—that she had had no choice but to give in. Or maybe she was just lonely and frightened. She hoped she wasn't that pathetic.

He said he had changed his mind, he didn't need time alone, after all. That's all it took. With those words she had caved. He told her he missed her. So he said. He wanted to be with her. Did she forgive him? No. Yet here she was.

The wound, though still fresh, was not festering. It was not even accessible at the moment. His cold words of the other night seemed to be part of a dream already half-forgotten. Was her uncharacteristically quick forgiveness of him another aftereffect of the vortex? Maybe, because it was something she'd never have done before.

She had opened up to him, but only to a point. Physically she had given in, yes, and mentally, too. But emotionally, no, not really. This night? It didn't mean much, she told herself. She needed it. She needed a friend. Maybe it was a mistake because three a.m.

had arrived and she was wide awake, staring up at a dirty ceiling through eyes that hurt.

The frustration of their conversation of the last night still lingered. Most of all she wondered: *Why didn't he understand?*

Quietly she slipped out of bed and went over to the window, wearily looking down to the amber glow of street lamps that fell on the empty sidewalks of Plainfield. The only movement she could see was the stirring of the trees in a gentle breeze.

Plainfield at night. So familiar. She recalled the many early mornings in which she would emerge from the back of her house onto streets just like this, her body surging with nighttime energy, animated by the rush of the late night movie. She would walk the ambrosia-scented streets bathed in a clarity she rarely felt in the light of day. While the neighborhood slumbered, her worries would loosen and slide away. Finally: no one to please.

Sometimes she would sit on the steps and strum simple chords on her guitar—she had never advanced from the beginning stages of playing—sending music softer than the wind down the dark sidewalks. That same sense of blissful unconcern, borne in those teenage years, wrapped itself around her now, as she stood quietly at Josh's window.

She turned her gaze to the composition of the room, to the concert posters tacked up on the wood-paneled wall, the guitars propped up in a corner, a crusty dish of who-knew-what left on the table, clothes strewn about the floor. At this bewitching hour all seemed animate in some strange way, as though the music waiting within the curved wood of the guitars could be sensed, the months of willing service in the jeans apparent. It was crazy, but she felt these things to be alive.

Her eyes closed for a moment, and she imagined the neighbors in their beds sleeping, the two other renters in the old Victorian house. The three-story structure was divided into apartments, each small yet possessing an essence of the whole house, like holograms. Josh's five rooms, at the top, were marked by a V-shaped ceiling and a woodsy aroma. The creaky outside stairway that led up to it emerged from the tangles of an abandoned garden that surrounded the house like a weed-filled moat.

Josh's eyelashes flickered. He shifted under the blanket, then stretched and rubbed his eyes. Maya tiptoed around the bed and slid under the covers before he fully awakened, and smoothed her hand across the skin of his shoulder.

She had not been able to hold her tongue, had told him everything, every detail. The story of Chicago and Wyoming shot out of her with the force of pressurized steam. And to her surprise, he didn't understand. He tried but in the end he couldn't, or wouldn't, embrace her fantastic story. He listened, at first perplexed and then doubtful, shaking his head the whole time without even realizing it.

To Maya the conversation was unfinished, hanging in the air like a half-deflated party balloon. Impossible to avoid. When he opened his eyes, Josh realized this. He was starting to understand her.

"What time is it?" he said, stretching.

"Four. I think."

"That early?" Instinctively he reached for her, then brought his hand back.

"You're still thinking about it," he said.

"Uh-huh."

"I'm sorry. I just don't think it's possible to alter the future."

"I know," she said.

He yawned, sat up on his elbow, facing her.

She said, "I think I can explain it."

"I'm happy to listen," he said. "I don't know if it'll make a difference, though."

"It might," she said. Then she announced: "The hundredth monkey theory."

"The hundredth what?" he said, pulling mindlessly at the elastic of his boxer shorts, snapping it against his skin.

"Just listen."

She pulled herself up to a sitting position. "There's this group of islands populated by monkeys that live on bananas, only they don't peel them before they eat them. They just pop them in their mouths and spit out the peels afterwards. Then one day, a brilliant, creative monkey comes along and out of the blue decides to peel a banana before eating it. Then others follow her lead—"

"*Her* lead?"

"This is *my* story, okay?"

"Yep," he said, obediently.

She paused, looked at him. He did seem to be listening.

"Now, when the number of peelers reaches a hundred, something amazing happens."

"They make smoothies?"

"No, stupid," she said, punching his arm. "The monkeys on the neighboring islands start peeling, too."

Now he stopped fidgeting with his underwear. He nodded, thinking.

"That's right," she said, watching him.

"So, they're in communication somehow," he said.

"Exactly. When a certain number of monkeys exhibits the new behavior—say a hundred—a shift occurs. They advance, culturally. Or technologically. Or whatever. Likewise when Brandon, or Fiske, talk about creating change they mean being able to somehow prompt the first one hundred people to do something new and different, starting a chain reaction that will alter things."

Josh nodded, taking it in.

She said, "Like the way the same inventions happen in different parts of the world or identical myths pop up in cultures that are separated by oceans. How do you account for that?"

"Me?" he said. "Actually I don't."

"Well I do," she said. "And so does he."

"Who?"

She switched on the lamp, and the mystery of talking in whispers beneath the gossamer cloak of night, with its conspiratorial feel, disappeared like a puff of smoke in the wind. She reached down for her backpack and pulled out the journal.

Josh was interested. He said, "Can I see it?"

She hesitated, then gave it to him, carefully, as one would a handful of eggs. He opened it, turned the faded pages, inspected the handwriting. Maya was not surprised when anxiety stabbed at her chest.

"That's enough," she said, taking it from him.

"Possessive, are we?"

"Maybe a little."

She flipped through the pages until she located the passage she wanted. Then she turned to Josh. "Do you want to hear this?"

"Are you kidding? This thing rules you. Read, please."

"Okay," she said. "He says that people communicate with each other constantly, telepathically, though we're not aware of it. Through something he calls the inner medium."

"Go ahead, read it."

She began.

> The inner medium is an environment, a landscape, a state of consciousness—all are true. It is one of many levels of reality which underlie the world as we know it.
>
> The inner medium is where the unconscious desires of humankind coalesce, forming psychic structures that grow into matter and events. It is where the seer glimpses the future as it forms, much as a meteorologist forecasts the weather.
>
> Imagine we are at a seashore, curling our toes in the sand (a wonderful thought). A wave laps in. Then another. And another. Though we can't see it from our vantage point, these waves originated hundreds of miles away, shaped by the tides, the moon, the weather, the ocean floor, the currents . . . dozens of factors. If you fully understood these factors you could predict the movements of waves.
>
> Cultural waves are similar. One who can perceive them might see the political, social, technological, even the spiritual, direction of the future. The world's enduring cultural movements all started out as such waves. Ancient Greece, Rome, the Renaissance, American Democracy, the world's religions—all originated as collective desires.
>
> The ones that endure do so because they are propelled by

great emotional intensity. Does the human race want an artistic resurgence, a cleansing war, technological progress, a new religion, or perhaps, unconsciously, a population-reducing epidemic? These questions are answered constantly and collectively by the species.

Every human being who walks the earth contributes to this endeavor. We are all connected to each other through the inner medium, and constantly infuse it with our desires. And so all of humanity contributes to the vast undertaking of creating the world in every moment . . .

She stopped there.

"Interesting," he said.

"But what do you think?"

"I think it's interesting."

She could hear it in his voice: he was just agreeing with her. Did the text come alive for him, stir his imagination, thrill him as it did her? No. God, it was frustrating. Everyone was the same. They all preferred the tangible, the concrete, the predictable, the rock-solid *fact* over the flowing, elusive possibility. She wasn't even remotely like that. Yet she could sense him trying to meet her at her beliefs, wanting to get closer to her. But his reaching out only made her feel sad.

"What do *you* think?" he asked.

"I think that people in different places and times and cultures have the same ideas because they're fishing in the same psychic ocean."

"But where? Where is this ocean?"

"In here," she said, tapping her temple. "Where your thoughts are, only deeper."

Suddenly he sat up, his face brightening. "Wait a minute," he said. "Wait just a minute. I think I get this. Tell me if this is right. The first monkey to peel came up with the idea all on its own, correct?"

She nodded vigorously, urging him on.

"But not until the hundredth started peeling did the wave gain enough momentum in the inner medium to become real in the outer world, and when it did, the technique was absorbed into the culture as a whole. Right?"

"Yes!" she said, and kissed him. "And nobody asked why or how. They just noticed, wow, we're peeling bananas."

He said: "We're driving cars."

"We're watching television."

"We're believing the news."

"We're doing what everyone else is doing."

"What *they* say."

She jumped up out of bed and began to pace around the room. Suddenly she stopped, turned to face him. "I know what's happening. The Mandala are using the vortexes to manipulate the inner medium. Like Fiske said, they're encouraging certain probable futures, trying to tweak what happens. Which means . . ."

"Yes?"

"That the world is being controlled. Things don't just happen."

"Whoa," he said.

She knew this was an insane idea, and a stupid thing to say. The world was not being run by a few people. She, for one, could do whatever she pleased. So could he. So could anyone. The whole world? It was too big, too messy. Too chaotic. There were *billions* of people out there . . .

Right?

Suddenly she felt exhausted.

She shuffled back into bed, fell back and let her head pound into the pillow with a thud.

"Are you okay?"

"Just overwhelmed. I think I better leave this stuff alone, try to get some sleep. Is that all right?"

"Sure," he said, with a note of relief in his voice.

She nuzzled up close to him, pressed her cheek against his shoulder, felt the warmth of his skin, which meant that she was cold. Thinking made her cold. Thinking *was* cold. He reached over and stroked her hair. It was the last thing she remembered.

She fell asleep. In his arms.

In the morning she realized what she had done. She had not had to burrow into her own blanket, had not had to break free from a cozy union in order to feel comfortable enough to drop off to sleep. She had relaxed completely with another human being. It was a rare event. Maybe things were getting better, after all.

She leaned her head up and hovered over Josh's face, near enough to see his eyelashes shiver in the dim light sneaking past the edges of the shades, close enough to feel his breath tap against her lips. She pressed her mouth gently down on his.

"Too early," he mumbled, his eyes still closed. Then he reached out and tugged the window shade all the way down and turned his back to her. Within seconds he was snoring.

She looked up. The blades of the ceiling fan were still turning too slowly, but it did not bother her now.

The headache never came.

She was getting what she had asked for and she knew it. The winds of her life were picking up speed. Though she could not know it yet, a gale force was gathering that would build into a hurricane. To fulfill her destiny, she would have to leap up and be carried off in its winds.

CHAPTER 10

Maya was not prepared for what she saw when she returned home the next morning. She couldn't have been. The gale force winds seemed to have already touched down—in the Burke's living room.

She stood at the front door, mouth agape, staring in disbelief at a room in shambles. Muriel's beloved sofa had been gutted, its stuffing strewn about the floor like the disemboweled entrails of a brownish yellow beast. The chairs had been slashed open. The coffee table and end tables were broken into pieces, photos and paintings pulled from the walls. The TV was a jagged mound of broken glass, wood, and wires. The carpet had been pulled up, and the drawers from the wall unit removed and crushed.

She stepped cautiously inside. She wasn't scared. More shocked than frightened. What danger could exist now, with sunlight streaming in the open windows, cars passing by, neighbors out and about? The whole world was calm and normal.

She tiptoed into the living room, weaving through shards of plastic and glass and splintered wood, past broken picture frames and fractured shelves, and made her way into the kitchen, where a junkyard of broken dishes, smashed appliances and scattered cooking utensils greeted her.

What had happened? Her first thought: Muriel had gone stark raving mad. She *had* been acting strange of late.

But this . . . this was too much, even for Muriel. Muriel's eruptions, though volcanic, usually petered out quickly, resulting at most in a plate or two launched against a wall, or some knife-edged words hurled at Maya. The worst Maya had ever witnessed happened five years ago, when Muriel had smashed several pieces of her best china over the retreating body of a boyfriend. The next morning she hadn't even recalled him being over, blaming everything on Maya instead. It so unnerved Maya that she spent the next two nights at a friend's house until she was certain that Muriel had calmed down.

Where *was* Muriel? Was she all right? Now Maya began to worry. She dashed down the hall to her mother's bedroom.

Muriel was lying in bed, sobbing quietly, the blanket pulled up to her chin, balled-up tissues all over the floor. She turned her tear-soaked eyes toward Maya. At that moment Maya actually felt sorry for her. She seemed so helpless. Maya ran over and sat on the bed. "Are you all right?" she said.

Muriel, sniffing hard, stared blankly at her.

"What happened?"

Muriel's voice was so weak Maya could barely hear it. "We got robbed. My life is ruined."

"When did it happen?"

"I was out with Henry last night. When I got home . . . ." Her words melted into sobs.

"Did you call the police?"

Muriel closed her eyes. Her head moved slightly up and down. A nod.

"What did they say? Was anything taken?"

"Jewelry, a VCR . . . I don't know . . . can't look. Did you see that mess? My living room, my wonderful living room. Sweet Jesus, what am I going to do?"

Maya didn't know what to say. She had no idea how to comfort Muriel. "Don't think about it right now, Mom," was the best she could do.

Muriel's room seemed to have gone untouched. Why? Then, suddenly, Maya realized she hadn't seen her own room. Terrified of what she might find, she ran out into the hallway.

At her doorway, she froze. Her room was a mirror image of the living room. Only these were the essentials of *her* life in shreds.

"Oh, no."

Her most intimate space, completely violated. The drawers to her bureau had been yanked and dumped, the shelves pulled off the wall. The closet floor was a mountain of clothes, many of them torn. Everything that defined her had been trampled upon. The pain of invasion was almost unbearable.

Stunned, instinctively she reached down and began to gather up her things—books, drawers, clothes, photos, the remains of her computer. Then she stopped, too stricken with grief to go on. What was the point? Everything was finished. Useless. She slid down to the floor and just sat there, dazed.

The wolf suddenly sprang to life, seeking answers: Why? Why did this happen?

Then it seized on something.

The journal.

Of course! Whoever had done this was looking for David Orr's writings. What else could it be? Thank God she'd taken it with her to Josh's, the one bright spot amid all the wreckage. She had come to consider the journal as valuable as any of her possessions anyway.

She had to hold it in her hands, right now. Just to be sure.

She went into the living room in search of her backpack. Hadn't she tossed it inside the door as she often did? Frantically she searched among the ruins but it was nowhere to be found. She began to panic, started ripping up the already shredded chairs, throwing bits of table around, kicking through the magazines all over the floor. She had dropped the backpack inside the door. She was certain. So it had to be here, somewhere.

No.

Idiot!

She ran for the phone but then stopped. Josh wasn't home. He was at work.

"Damn, damn, damn," she said, sprinting down the hallway, yelling a quick goodbye to Muriel, then leaping from the front doorstep toward her car.

She got in, started it up, and sped away, muttering to herself, "It's there, it's got to be there . . ." How could she have forgotten her backpack?

Five minutes later the Corolla bounded up over the curb onto Josh's lawn before she turned it back onto the street with a jarring bump that stalled it out. Never mind. She grabbed the keys and ran for the door.

She took the stairs two at a time. Josh never locked his door; there wasn't any point. Breathing hard, she threw it open.

The room was exactly as they'd left it. Her backpack was on the floor, propped up against the bed. She grabbed it, dug inside and pulled out the journal, wrapped safely in her sweater.

"Thank you, God," she said, hugging the book in her arms.

She fell back on the bed. She had worked up a good anxiety sweat. Her forehead and neck were covered in perspiration.

Breathe.

She counted off some long, slow breaths and gradually her sense of panic subsided, replaced by an awareness of the outside world. The sounds of the neighborhood drifted in: children playing next door, a plane droning overhead, the distant roar of a lawnmower.

She sat up. She didn't want to go home. Muriel was a mess. Maya would somehow have to deal with that. She had no idea how. What if she got worse?

She would deal with it, that's all there was to it. The break-in was more on her mind right now. Could someone really have unleashed so much destruction due to the journal? No, she told herself. She was just being paranoid. Nevertheless, she thought back to everybody she had told about it. Fiske, Dr. Porter, Georgia, Brandon, Josh. Was that all? What about the man on the plane? Had she told him, too? She hoped not but she couldn't recall.

She heard a sound downstairs. Immediately her body stiffened. Her breaths, which had become long and easy, now became staccato gasps. Her palms went cold.

Calm down.

Josh? Unlikely. A neighbor? Yes. It had to be a neighbor.

Footsteps coming upstairs.

They paused at the second floor, at the other renters' doors. Only Josh's unit was on the top floor.

The footsteps continued up.

Shut the door!

She took a step forward but it was too late.

A man stepped into the doorway. No . . . it was a woman. Small and narrow-faced with spiked blonde hair and severe, thin lips, wearing a black miniskirt revealing short, muscular legs.

She stepped inside—Maya drew back instinctively—and walked right up to Maya. The woman's hand reached out. Maya saw that there was an envelope in it.

"This is for you," the woman said.

Maya, petrified, said, "Wha-what is it?"

"Go ahead, read it."

"Who are you?"

"It's all in there," the woman said, pointing at the envelope. "Why don't you open it?"

Maya slipped her finger under the flap and tugged it open. She reached in and pulled out a single sheet of paper, a computer-generated printout. She turned to the woman to ask what it was but all she saw was an empty doorway. The woman was gone, heading down the stairs.

"Hey! Wait!" Maya called down the stairwell.

She dashed over to the window just in time to see the blonde woman disappear into a car parked in front. Immediately it sped off.

Shaking her head, Maya sat on the bed examining the printout, a simple two-column table. A list of icons ran from the top of the page to the bottom: a windmill, a car, a house, a face, a gun, a book, the sun. Beside each one were the names of cities. Amsterdam, Berlin, Buenos Aires, London, New York, Paris, Sydney, Tokyo . . . .

One of the icons gave her a start. The webbed earth. Exactly the shape she had seen in the vision: an outline of the planet covered by a web of lines. She could not believe her eyes. Here again was another internal experience made manifest in the outside world. Or was it the other way around? She wondered, Who knew about the webbed earth? To this there was no answer.

Yet.

The city name beside the symbol: Los Angeles.

She looked back to where the woman had stood just moments before, as if the physical space she had occupied could somehow help Maya decipher what was happening. No such luck.

Carefully she folded up the sheet and returned it to its envelope, then tucked it inside the pages of the journal.

She wondered, had others "seen" symbols, too, in visions of their own? Maybe she wasn't alone in this. The idea was comforting, anyway.

*   *   *

Maya had offered many times to help in the reconstruction of the house but Muriel would have none of it. In the weeks following the break-in, Muriel's attitude had changed dramatically. The initial shock and sadness and anger had lasted only a few days. The real losses were few—some furniture, carpets, old jewelry and electronics, many of them items that Muriel had wanted to replace anyway. Once she had settled down emotionally, she realized this. All she had needed was a push to begin the process of reinventing the house, and she had gotten it.

Henry Rossmore, whom Maya had learned was a veteran insurance claims adjuster, had made a few calls on Muriel's behalf, and a sizable reimbursement check was delivered to the Burke household in record time. The robbery, then, to Muriel at least, had become a stroke of luck, a sort of divine intervention lifting her out of the doldrums. For the first time in years she felt passionate about something.

The most shocking observation, from what Maya could see, was that Muriel had touched no liquor through the whirlwind of activity taking place in the remaking of the Burke house.

From the crack of dawn Muriel could be heard barking orders to the workmen, overseeing the painting, guiding the repairs, directing the placement of furniture, handling every detail with patience and fortitude. Her tireless, compulsive busyness seemed to be the perfect filler for the vacuum left by the drinking, if indeed that was what was happening.

Muriel was as optimistic as Maya had ever seen her. She had seized upon an opportunity and was milking it for all she could get. And Henry was spending more and more time at the house, which also seemed to make her happy.

Once again Maya had allowed her mother to pick out her bedroom furniture, only this time not out of passivity but out of conscious acquiescence. She knew that her room would soon become a guest room, that her remaining days at the house would be few. She didn't know how she knew it, nor where she was headed. Maybe Muriel suspected it, too, because the elegant rosewood furniture she chose for the bedroom wasn't even remotely Maya.

There were times that Maya half-wondered if her mother had arranged the robbery herself, because it sure benefited her.

Sometimes, she decided, it was best to leave things alone.

*   *   *

A warm breeze stirred the leaves of Canyon Park's oldest cedar, as Maya lay on her back beneath the gnarled branches, staring up at the bits of blue sky that twinkled through the leaves. Her hair flowed into the grass. She had propped her knees up, her feet resting on a flat rock wedged in the ground.

A difficult month had passed since the still unsolved break-in. Muriel had finished the redecoration of the house. The search for David Orr was stalled out. Life had become mundane again. Summer was definitely over; the nights were cooling off. All had been quiet. Maya had mailed out some resumes, had even taken a couple of job interviews, but nothing had come of it. Probably, she thought, her mood had scared them off. She could understand this. She wouldn't have hired herself either, the way she answered their questions so listlessly, met the interviewer's eyes so rarely, and sighed so much.

Should she keep looking for work in this state? Move out? She had no idea, no clue. No direction. Maybe it was time for both, though she felt little enthusiasm for either. She knew what was happening. The dreaded black clouds were creeping in. The signs were all there: the despair, the fatigue, the feeling of standing outside of life, of drifting away from people. The world seemed to be spinning a little too fast, and her efforts to keep up were increasingly met with weariness.

She feared another depression more than anything in the world. She would not go through that torture, would not go gently into that dark night, not again, no matter what. She would intervene. She knew what to do. She had defenses now, thanks to Dr. Yanikowski.

She began by focusing on the leaves as they flickered in the wind. Her mind immediately fought it. It wanted to fill her imagination with fearful thoughts. Every time it started to do this she would bring it back, back to the leaves. To the leaves and the branches, and the sky and the wind. She would lead it away from its circuitous obsessions, toward the body and the land, to the world of flesh and bone and wood and stone.

I am in control.

Then it would wander—again. And she would bring it back. Again. And on and on it went.

She slid her headphones over her head, blasted the music so loudly that no thought, no anxiety, no despair could find a foothold in her vibrating consciousness. Her intention: to blot out the mind, the tyrant, the wolf; focus only on the senses. The cure. The catharsis would come. In time. It would come and she would feel the rush, the release. Afterward, she'd be lighter. For today, anyway.

Let go.

It began with the chattering of voices. Faceless, disembodied, imploring. From the inside, but not of her—of them. Her mother. Her friends. Boyfriends. Teachers. Authors. Filmmakers. Advertisers. They were all there, pushing, urging, manipulating. It was essential to ignore them, to deny them energy, to let them shout themselves out, out of her mind, out of existence. *Don't heed them.* Let them wail and scream and beckon. Then, only then, would they lose energy, weaken, falter, become hoarse, and finally go mute.

At these times she felt a kinship with the tortured souls of the past—Van Gogh, Plath, and Cobain were her favorites—the hyper-sensitives who had scaled the dizzying artistic heights and then fallen to their dooms, as if mortally pierced by the world. At times Maya had circled the foothills beneath those high peaks herself, but had always pulled back, afraid to venture farther.

She breathed deeply, as the music worked its magic. Music and nature. Music opened the channels upon which the emotions could drain away; nature absorbed and recycled them. If she found just the right song she would listen to it over and over, sometimes for weeks at a time.

It was happening now.

And . . . done. So fast!

Like the pop of a balloon or the blast of steam from an opened valve, the fetid air whooshed out, leaving her fresh, calm, equalized. It was over. She would do no more. She didn't have to. She pulled off the headphones.

Traffic sounds floated over from the far side of the field. Her mind was at peace, contracted, like a billowing skirt suddenly smoothed down. Her senses were crisp, unfettered.

A bird fluttered by. The scent of freshly cut grass wafted over. A breeze brushed at her cheek. It was all good.

She gave herself permission to mentally drift, to tiptoe across the wavering leaves, to leave the human, the drama, behind. Maybe life really was a bottomless, unsolvable tragedy as it so often seemed. But not at this moment. Not now. Now she detached from all that. She felt fresh, liberated.

She sat up, rubbed her eyes. A maintenance man at the other end of the park, spiking trash on a pole, waved to her. She smiled and waved back.

She didn't turn on the radio the whole drive home, just rolled down the windows and let the wind wash over her. If her father was to remain a mystery, so be it.

The next day Georgia Roussey called.

CHAPTER 11

The third floor student lounge was a colossal area of couches and tables and panoramic windows that looked down at the soccer fields, baseball diamonds, and the university's main gymnasium building. On arriving, Maya had marched directly over to her favorite couch, dug herself into a corner of it and grabbed a campus newspaper that was lying on a table in front of her. The lounge was almost empty but for a sprinkling of students.

She had spent hundreds of hours in this room, often in this very spot, highlighting passages in textbooks, memorizing the dates and locations of battles and treaties and discoveries and inventions. She had analyzed theories, pored over maps, wrote papers—whatever her professors had asked her to do. And she had jumped through the hoops as well as anybody.

Reflecting on all of the energy she had expended at school, she had to wonder: How much of it would prove to be of real value if everything was about to change?

She felt a tap on her shoulder. She turned around, and there was Georgia Roussey, grinning at her. Maya stood up, and the old woman practically lifted her off the ground in arms that were surprisingly strong. Maya, startled, realized that Georgia was only hugging her.

"Interesting place," Georgia said, looking around.

"You said public and crowded."

"I did. And so it is."

They sat on the couch. Gazing at the amiable old woman, Maya found Fiske's warning more unbelievable than ever. This great big bear of a woman seemed about as dangerous as Santa Claus.

"There's something I've been wanting to ask you," Maya said.

"Go ahead then."

"Well, when I met you there was a halo around your head."

"That's because I'm an angel," Georgia said and then erupted in laughter. When she had settled down, she said, "No. What you saw was energy."

"Can anyone see it?"

"Oh, no, dear," Georgia said. "Only the gifted."

The gifted. Maya liked the sound of that. She liked Georgia. Just being around her felt good. Even so, Fiske's face kept flashing in her mind, warning her.

Georgia said, "Maya, actually, that's just the sort of thing I came here to talk to you about. You see, there are certain special abilities that when witnessed for the first time might seem like magic. But they aren't. They're just latent human abilities. Precognition, telepathy, out-of-body travel—these are some. Then there's what happens at a vortex, which can be viewed as a kind of magic, too." She paused, and stared at Maya.

Maya said, "Brandon told you what happened to me."

"Yes, and I'm glad he did. You have to understand, Maya, that at this time in history such 'magic' is finding its way into the lives of people and our culture as a whole more and more. People are learning how to use it." Then she added: "And not always with the best of intentions."

She glanced around the room, and satisfied with the innocence of the surroundings, turned back to Maya. "You've heard from Albert Fiske, correct?"

"Yes. How did you know?"

"Simple, dear. You visited Edgar Porter. Naturally he would have contacted Mr. Fiske. Ours is a small community. And did Fiske tell you about the Mandala?"

Maya nodded.

"Good," Georgia said, "First I need to straighten something out. I do know your father. I couldn't tell you this in Wilton because we couldn't risk your passing this information on to Fiske. I'm sorry but it was necessary."

"Do you know where he is?"

"I'll get to that in a moment. What you need to know right now is this: Albert Fiske is not his friend."

"He said the same thing about you."

"Of course he did."

"What is the Mandala?"

"An alternative way of life, just as Brandon told you."

"But that's not all."

"No."

"Fiske says you're using the vortexes to try to disrupt society."

Georgia laughed. "Let me educate you, Maya. First, your Dr. Porter is not what he seems. Edgar Porter is an extraordinarily wealthy man with ties to more secret organizations than I could even name. He speaks five languages, has homes all over the world. He is a very powerful man. The only reason for his relationship with Fiske is a common interest: vortex research. What he wants to do with it is anybody's guess."

"Why is Fiske looking for my father?"

"Long ago, dear," Georgia said, "your father worked for him. David was a remote viewer, as Fiske has probably told you. The two of them discovered something new, a process called active remote viewing. In active remote viewing you don't just observe. You influence. You try to change things: people, events.

"They used many methods, including performance-enhancing psychotropic drugs. Under Fiske, your father did work that some would consider highly unethical. The targets of the active remote viewing were influential people. Business executives, politicians. Fiske wanted to build a capability that would allow him to influence laws, business deals, alliances, financial decisions. He had interests in all these areas.

"Your father wrestled with the ethics all along. I believe he continued on purely out of blind scientific ambition. Eventually, when he couldn't justify it any longer, he left. He walked off the project."

Maya recalled a passage in the journal.

. . . *recently I left a project of great importance.*

Georgia continued: "He was the best of Fiske's group, the only one who had succeeded at active viewing. He was popular among the other viewers. When he left, several of Fiske's team went with him, ruining a key demonstration Fiske had planned for a group of high-ranking officials. It flopped, and soon Fiske's funding dried up. Humiliated and discredited, his career took a turn for the worse. Only recently, after all these years, he's bounced back. He's making a comeback. What is troublesome is that he's managed to build up a following and restart the work."

"What does he want from my father?"

"Our guess is information."

"Why can't you tell me where he is?"

The old woman took Maya's hand. Georgia's hand was large and warm. "You'll need to be patient, dear."

"Is he alive, at least?"

Georgia nodded. "Yes, he's alive."

"Well, that's something," Maya said.

"There's more at stake here than your personal needs. You must trust me."

I have to, Maya thought as she slumped down in the couch.

Despite Georgia's refusal to reveal much about David Orr, Maya was thrilled with what she'd heard. He was alive. And this woman sitting next to her knew where he was. Fiske did not.

In her excitement, Maya accidentally kicked the table, toppling over a paper cup which spilled water all over the tabletop. She dug into her backpack for a tissue or a napkin but she had neither.

Georgia, ignoring the spill, said, "Listen carefully to me. I too can *see,* like a remote viewer, like your father. Like you are beginning to. I can project my mind and receive images. You didn't stumble onto us, dear. We called you. That's what happened at the vortex. You received a summons. Porter didn't know this would happen, but when it did, he used it."

"Used it? For what?"

"To try to locate your father."

"*He's* looking for him, too?"

Georgia nodded. "What did you tell Edgar Porter about your vision?"

"Everything," Maya said. "Everything I saw."

"Tell me."

Maya recounted it all: the man she had encountered whom she assumed was her father, the blonde girl, the scent of honeysuckle, the mountains, Wilton, the webbed earth—everything she could remember. Georgia listened attentively, remaining quiet for some time after Maya had finished.

"Did you see anything familiar in the printout you were brought?"

The printout—of course! She had all but forgotten it. "That was from you?"

"Yes."

"I recognized the webbed earth, like I said. What does it mean?"

"Different symbols become visible at different levels of awareness. That one appears at a very deep level."

"Meaning what?"

"That you're enabled."

"Enabled?" Maya said. "To do what?"

"To use the vortex communications network."

"I am?" Maya looked away. There was so much to absorb.

Georgia reached out, touched her shoulder. "I want to be honest with you, dear. We're running out of time. I may need your help."

Maya's eyebrows shot up.

Georgia said, "David is a very important man in the Mandala, and Fiske is getting closer to finding him. If that happens you may not get the chance to see your father. I'm sorry to have to put it that way but it's true."

Maya was reeling. "What do you want me to do?"

"Come to California."

Instinctively she said, "I can't just leave," then quickly realized how crazy of a response this was. Nothing was keeping her from going anywhere. She could do anything she pleased.

Ever patient, Georgia said, "In this life you get what you think. That's the only rule. Think about what you've set up here. Consider the journey you're on. Don't you see what's happening? The events of the past months were designed to bring you exactly to this point."

Maya's thoughts were jumping around wildly. She didn't know what to do, think, or say. What Georgia was implying—and Brandon had told her the same thing—contradicted her core beliefs about life. Was one's life choreographed in advance? What about free will?

Then she thought back to all the synchronicities that had been occurring since she found the journal. They did seem to form a path that was plain to see: Stumbling onto the journal. Experiencing the vortex. Having the vision. Discovering the Mandala. Meeting Fiske.

"Others have taken longer to arrive where you are today, here with me," Georgia said. "You're talented. You know it. You can materialize your desires with great acuity."

Maya laughed glumly. "And my problems."

"As the world grows more troubled," Georgia said, "your keen awareness of it causes you no end of unhappiness. You choose, due to your youth and immaturity, to manifest your life burdened by this handicap. This kind of thinking creates a circular loop that reinforces itself. One day, Maya, you will create positive events, even on a canvas that appears to be dark.

"We don't have the luxury of time. A global change of real magnitude is on the way. We're at a point in history that is ripe with potential. If you had a hand in deciding what might happen, what would you do?"

Maya raised Fiske's warning. "Wouldn't big change create big chaos?"

"Growth and pain are bedfellows, Maya. It's always been that way and always will be. The Mandala is attempting to raise humanity's collective mind to a higher level. Think about it. There are enough natural resources on this planet to take care of all of us. Imagine a world without war, where cooperation is the rule rather than the exception, where aggressive energy is channeled into exploration, building, creating, healthy competition. What I'm talking about is the experiment that has never been tried. Now we can do it. The opportunity has arrived."

Maya wondered how the Mandala might actually do such a thing. But before she could ask about this, someone approached, a tall, dark-haired man with muscles bulging under a loose, untucked shirt. Georgia nodded to him.

Maya said, "I have so many questions."

Georgia took the younger woman's hands. "I will answer them. In time. For now, I want you to follow some precautions. Do not talk of any of this to anyone. I trust you because I believe I know you. I know your father. You *will* be reunited.

"Act as though you are being watched, for this may well be true. This will all play out soon. Try to live as normally as you can. The next time we see each other will be in Los Angeles."

Georgia kissed her on the cheek, then turned and walked away with the muscular man at her side, leaving Maya to slump back onto the couch, surrounded by students studying textbooks and writing papers in preparation for their future in a world that seemed to be on the verge of a mind-bending change.

"'Live normally?'" she thought. As if.

*   *   *

She took the back roads home instead of the highway, ablaze with excitement. Abington Road snaked through a beautiful, densely wooded area that led to Glendale, a tiny town situated halfway between the university and Plainfield. Maya whistled as she drove, occasionally stealing glances at a crystalline stream that swirled alongside the road, crossing underneath in places and then popping up on the other side, back and forth, all the way to Glendale.

Glendale's lone gas station was built in the nineteen-fifties, its red and white pumps small and rounded in the style of the period. Passing by, Maya saw a sign in the station window which had probably been unmoved for decades: *Friendly Service*. Friendly, she thought, just like the town itself. She had always liked quaint little Glendale, and especially the Town Restaurant, where she had spent countless afternoons loading up on coffee and studying for exams. The whole of Glendale was just a few blocks long, a stretch of maybe thirty sturdy old houses of stone and wood set far back from the road. There was even a log cabin at the north side of town.

She approached the traffic light at an easy thirty miles per hour when an overwhelming urge to stop the car took hold of her. She had no idea why she felt this way. The street was quiet, not a car in sight. The traffic light was green. Yet the impulse to stop was so strong she couldn't deny it. Strangely, she felt as though she was being forced to stop.

Panicked, yet unable to resist, she found herself stomping hard on the brake pedal. Only later would she realize that this feeling had the same quality as the one in the backyard that had led her to dig in the spot that held David Orr's journal.

The tires screeched, leaving long black marks on the road, and her body shot forward, sending her head toward the steering wheel. Then the seat belt went taut, catching her in mid-flight, ricocheting her backwards. She slammed back into the seat, shouting out as the car skidded to a stop just short of the traffic light, which was still green.

Her body was trembling. She couldn't move her foot. It seemed to be glued to the brake. The rubber of the pedal and the sole of her shoe had somehow become inseparable.

She heard a loud drone coming from her left. Then something blazed across the intersection just inches from her bumper, a long metallic flash that sucked the air from around the Corolla, leaving it rocking back and forth. Immediately a violent metallic *crunch* pierced the air, like the arrival of a rocket from the peaceful Glendale skies. She'd never heard such a loud sound.

Grimacing, she turned to look. A truck had smashed head-on into a light pole, was accordioned to half its size and now stood eerily still, the pole sticking out its crumpled engine like a stake in the heart. The only movement was a wobbling back fender that slowly came to rest.

The people of Glendale streamed out into the street, some running to the truck and its driver, others standing back with fearful looks on their faces. It seemed that no one had noticed the little Corolla sitting alone in the road, just fifty feet away.

Go! she thought. *Get out of here! Go!*

Her right foot was vibrating, but at least it came up off the brake. With intense focus she brought it over to the accelerator.

Down.

Careful!

She touched her foot to the pedal. The car edged forward.

Carefully she pressed a little harder, and the car picked up speed. She didn't turn to look at the wreck or to see if the people of the town had noticed her. She just stared straight ahead, concentrating on the road.

Glendale flowed by, and a few seconds later was gone.

Breathe. Her lungs filled with fresh air, and she exhaled with an audible *ahhh.* Her driving seemed all right. Now it was just her, the winding road, the woods, and yes, that strange rubbery feeling—not just in her legs but all through her—making her have to concentrate a little harder than usual to keep the car safely moving down the road.

Drive, she told herself. You'll normalize. She checked her rearview mirror every few seconds, each time seeing nothing more than the empty road disappearing behind her. She had no idea where she was, though she could not be far from home. She pulled over by some woods and lay her head on the steering wheel for a few minutes. She knew she hadn't done anything wrong in Glendale yet she felt she had to leave. She just couldn't remain near that wreck.

She rested, and then found her way home. She'd only been a couple of miles away. At home she took a shower, rocking back and forth under the hot water, allowing it to massage her neck, sore now after the hard stop.

Afterward, she took the journal and sat on a lounge chair on the back patio, watching Muriel cooking dinner through the kitchen window. Henry was on the living room sofa, watching the big-

screen television she had bought for him. Everything felt normal—
except for her.

She couldn't stop thinking about what had happened, the way
she had jammed on the brakes before she saw the truck, as if she
had known of its arrival in advance. That was impossible, of
course—unless she believed David Orr. Once again his journal
seemed to be explaining things in advance. It had a funny way of
doing that. She had read the passage before but it had meant little
until now.

> *Many layers of consciousness reside simultaneously inside of*
> *us, from the higher abstract thinking processes of the mind on*
> *down to the lower, mundane maintenance functions of the*
> *body. This latter type, "body consciousness," is not just program-*
> *ming, as some would think, but intelligence. While it controls*
> *the essential activities of circulation, respiration, and diges-*
> *tion, it is not without will. Every cell possesses consciousness.*
> *Body consciousness can act of its own accord, circumventing the*
> *higher functions . . .*

Years ago Uncle Buddy had almost been run down by a car as
he crossed Bellington Road. He leapt to safety only at the last
instant. Maya, terrified, had witnessed the whole thing.

Sitting on the curb afterwards, she asked him how he had
managed to jump out of the way so quickly. His answer didn't
make sense. At least not then.

"I didn't jump out of the way," he said.

"Then who did?" she asked, half-jokingly.

He had no answer. He just insisted that he didn't do it. One
second he was in the road, the next he was leaping lightning-fast
out of it. But *he* didn't do it?

"Some things just happen," he said, shrugging it off.

Maybe now she understood. The initiator of his life-saving
move wasn't a who, but a what, an intelligence internal to the
body, one that perhaps had taken over control of it from the mind,

engaging his muscles to throw him out of harm's way. He—his mind—hadn't even realized he was in danger until it was over.

Buddy had said the force was not him. But it *was* him. It just wasn't his brain. It was his body.

The same way, Maya surmised, her body had sensed the oncoming car and had acted of its own accord, pushing her mind out of the picture. Body consciousness, then, had saved her, too.

She realized this was just a theory. Maybe it was all wrong. She certainly couldn't prove it. She liked it, nevertheless. It resonated. What were the odds of it being accurate? Buddy would have asked for a numerical estimate. And she would have told him: ninety-percent probability. One-hundred percent was impossible, of course, for it implied absolute certainty.

> *The truth seeker must release, revise and enlarge his beliefs mercilessly over the course of his life, incorporating new truths as they emerge, letting go of old ones when they no longer serve. Grasping a truth too tightly makes you a slave to it. You will constantly alter reality to conform to it in order to prove yourself right. Instead, release old truths as you outgrow them, just as you have let go of the belief in Peter Pan and the Land of Oz.*

Satisfied, she closed the journal, went inside, and ate dinner in the dining room with Muriel and Henry. The lovebirds.

She went to bed early. She needed a good night's sleep. The next day she would try to discover the truth about Albert Fiske.

CHAPTER 12

Fiske exited the lobby of his building and flowed easily into the rush-hour crowd moving down the sidewalk. He buttoned up his jacket in the cool evening air and checked his watch. A newspaper was folded up and tucked neatly under his arm.

Maya, standing behind a pillar at the side of the building, watched him closely, waiting for him to advance a little further. She was eager to get moving.

Now.

She fell into the pedestrian traffic a safe distance back. The long train of people marched toward the Metro station as efficiently and purposefully as ants across a kitchen floor. Fiske wasn't very tall; Maya had to keep jerking her head from side to side to keep an eye on him.

Spy on the spy. The notion had been exciting the evening before—until she had considered just how stupid it might be. But she wasn't about to back down, not now, not with such a buzz of excitement coursing through her. What was the worst that could happen? If he caught her, she would offer up the innocent young girl defense. She was just a harmless kid, fresh out of school, acting outrageous. Right? Or maybe say she'd lost his business card on the way to see him. But then she could have gone up to him right now and tapped his arm. She didn't.

Firmly encased in the crowd, Fiske rode the escalator down into the Metro station. Maya remained twenty feet back, still struggling to keep him in view. The crowd had a mind of its own, pushing him forward faster than her. As the distance between them grew, she feared she would lose him.

At the bottom of the escalator she dug her Metro card out of her pocket, as Fiske passed through the turnstile and walked toward

the Virginia-bound platform. The line ratcheted slowly through
the turnstile, then stopped suddenly as a man fumbled to figure
out how to slide his card in. Anxiously Maya leaned on the woman
in front of her. Finally the man succeeded with the card, pushing
his way uncertainly through.

Maya finally made it through and approached the platform,
where she huddled behind two tall men and glanced Fiske's way
far too often. He was leaning against the railing a good distance
from her, reading his paper. The approach lights on the Virginia
side had not yet begun to flash; the train was still a few minutes
away. The crowd was huge but calm; the station could have been
noisier given the large numbers of people in it. Everyone seemed
so well behaved.

At last the train pulled in. The people on the platform edged
toward the doors, waiting for the train's riders to exit, but few of
them got off. Everyone was leaving the city, not entering it. The
throng poured in through the open doors, carrying Fiske in with
them. Maya ducked into the car behind his, relieved that she could
watch him through the forward windows.

Soundlessly the train sped across Washington. As each stop
approached, Maya's gaze shot to the forward car, but Fiske never
moved from his seat. Watching people exit the train, she tried to
devise ways to use them for cover. The stops came and went. Federal
Triangle, Metro Center, McPherson Square, Farragut West, Foggy
Bottom. Still Fiske didn't move.

As they neared Arlington, the first stop in Virginia, he folded
up his paper and stood up, holding the overhead rail for support,
his face lit by the strobe-like tunnel lights that flashed through
the windows.

Maya readied herself. The train hissed to a stop, the doors slid
open, and Fiske stepped out. She remained in her car until the last
possible moment and just as the doors were about to shut, she
leapt out.

Twenty or thirty people separated them. Enough. If he had
turned she would have been caught. But he just followed the flowing
caterpillar of people up the long escalator and out of the station.

The train ride had brought the night with it. Arlington was a city of tall office buildings, cut evenly by a grid of streets, the Potomac River just a few feet away. The lights of Georgetown glowed brightly across the river. Despite its many buildings, Arlington seemed deserted, like a ghost town. Pedestrian traffic was only a trickle. Following Fiske down the dark street, she felt vulnerable.

He came to a corner and stopped. Maya quickly turned to face a newsstand she was passing, just as its proprietor, a burly man with a long beard, reached up to pull the awning down for the evening. He smiled and began to say something to her but she turned back toward Fiske. Seeing that he was no longer at the corner, she began to hustle down the street. The man at the newsstand yelled out to her, but to no avail. Within seconds she was around the corner.

She saw Fiske open the door of a church across the street and disappear inside.

She took a long breath. Her adrenaline was up. She was on edge, hyper-alert. She took quick note of the contrast of this feeling to the malaise that often permeated her days. This could be addicting, she thought.

She started to step off the curb but then stopped. Fiske had reached his destination, a place she surely could not have happened upon by accident. If he saw her now, the game was up. There was no way out.

She didn't care. She leaped off the curb and jogged across the empty street, then climbed the steps to the church. The inside foyer was dimly lit, the only illumination a flickering bulb. The door closed behind her with a whoosh and a click. She stepped into the hallway and saw the entrance to a large auditorium, its doors wide open. A sign in front read: Parents Without Partners. She could hear voices inside.

Idiot! What a fool I am, she thought, intruding on the man's personal life like this. Fiske was just a dad in search of a date. All she had wanted was to talk to him, which would have been easy enough in Washington, but instead she had screwed it all up and now could do nothing but retreat back home, accomplishing nothing.

Suddenly, across the hall, a door swung open—the men's room—and a man came out, smoothing his hair back.

Fiske.

She winced.

Standing in the shadows, a few feet away, she held her breath, praying he would walk by without seeing her. As if that was possible. As soon as he started for the auditorium he would be close enough to reach out and pat her on the cheek. Or smack her. She imagined the look on his face. Jesus! She was going to have to explain herself. How?

But Fiske didn't walk toward the auditorium. Instead he went in the opposite direction, down a hallway that was so long it disappeared into darkness. Relieved, Maya exhaled, straining her eyes to see where he'd gone. But it was too dark. Forgetting her near humiliation, she tiptoed after him.

She came to a doorway at the end of the hall and peered into a pre-school classroom, lit by shafts of light that slid past the blinds from a parking lot in the back of the church.

A door at the far end of the classroom was slightly ajar. Where else could he have gone? She stepped carefully into the room, maneuvering through the clutter, past blocks, toys, games, crayons, books, and papers, and pushed open the door.

Stairs. Leading down to a narrow passageway, so constricted she had to shuffle sideways to advance through it. The air was dank and moldy, and she almost sneezed but she clamped her fingers down over her nose just in time, and the urge passed. Inching forward, unable to see, she prayed that the floor wasn't as cluttered as the classroom. Luckily it wasn't.

She came to a set of double doors bisected by a vertical slot of light. She heard voices on the other side. She recognized them.

Startled, she shook her head. This can't be, she thought.

It was impossible.

Her heart began to race. She tried to look through the crack in the doors but it was too narrow. She pressed her ear against it, listened closer.

Georgia: "They're intercepting our communications."

Brandon: "Have you been able to raise David?"

Georgia: "No. Not yet."

Brandon: "What do you want to do?"

Georgia: "What else can we do?"

Maya gasped. How could this be? She pressed her ear closer to the crack in the door. If she heard more, maybe she could make sense of it.

The door moved. The catch hadn't been clicked into place. Slowly both doors began to swing open.

Bright light hit her in the face. She raised her hand to shade her eyes; squinting, she could make out some of the room.

A table. Chairs. Dirty cement floor. A window. And Fiske, standing in front of her, staring into her eyes. A tape recorder sat on the table beside him from which the recorded voices of Brandon and Georgia played. He reached over and clicked it off.

Fiske said, "Sound familiar?"

"No," she said. "Who are they?"

"The Mandala."

Shaking his head in an exaggerated way, he said, "Maya, Maya, what am I going to do with you?"

"Boy, is this ever embarrassing."

"Yes, it is."

"Why didn't you—"

"Say something earlier? On the Metro perhaps? Or how about the street? Or maybe outside my building?"

"You knew the whole time?"

Fiske laughed. He didn't seem particularly angry. She felt relieved.

"Am I in trouble?"

"That depends."

"On what?"

"On whether you'll let me buy you a drink before I send you home. It's been a long day. I could use the company."

He seemed safe, in his suit and tie, and penny loafers. Like a typical Washington bureaucrat or businessman. And maybe he was—but then, he wasn't, not really. What had Georgia said? That her father might disappear if Fiske found him first? Why?

"There's a place near here," he said.

"Sure."

They walked through the deserted streets to a tavern, a large dark room where several men sat hunched over a long bar. Gloomy, wood-paneled walls formed the interior, there were no windows Maya could see, and country music played on a jukebox. Fiske led her to a table by a dart board and ordered beer from a waitress who had come around. Maya asked for wine. The drinks came quickly. Feeling edgy, all she could think was: thank goodness the Metro station was on the next block.

"Did you know we were robbed?" she said, watching his reaction closely.

"No," he said, evenly. "I'm sorry."

"They shredded our house."

"Did you call the police?"

"Of course. I just thought you might know something."

"Me?" he said. "Why?"

"Maybe it was the Mandala."

"You don't know about them, remember?"

"Obviously they know about me."

Fiske picked up his beer and downed half of it in a single swallow.

Maya said, "Do they know where he is?"

"You heard the tape."

"How did you get that?"

"Routine surveillance," he said. "Homeland security at work."

"I thought that was for terrorists."

He shrugged. "You just have to get the paperwork right."

She had a sip of wine. "Can I ask you something?"

"Go ahead."

"You said my father disappeared. How?"

"I meant he left my project. He wanted to move on to other things."

"Oh. You mean he didn't disappear?"

"He did leave suddenly, but it was his choice."

"Where did he go?"

Fiske picked up his beer, had another swallow. "He didn't say. David was a private kind of guy."

"Were you close?"

"Sure, I'd say so."

"Then why don't you know where he is?"

"Like I said, he did things his own way. I don't know where my college buddies are, either."

He finished the beer and ordered another. He stared at her a long time, until she grew uncomfortable. "You know what?" he said, finally.

"What?"

He turned away. "Ah, nothing."

She was curious. "What?"

He took awhile, then said, "You remind me of someone."

"Who's that?"

"Don't take this the wrong way," he said, "but my brother. I'm only talking about personality here."

His next beer arrived. Maya wanted to know more. "Why do I remind you of your brother?"

"He was a pain in the ass, too, but engaging, like you."

She didn't know how to react to this. She said nothing, just sipped her wine.

"Passion misdirected, the both of you," he said. He shook his head, apparently angry at himself. "I'm sorry. I didn't mean that."

"It's all right. Where is he?"

"Arnie? Gone," he said. "He fell off an oil rig. Maybe he jumped. Who the hell knows."

"I'm sorry."

"Sure," he said. "Ancient history."

"Is it?"

He looked up at her. "What do you mean?"

"The love of a brother."

"I don't follow."

"Never mind," she said. "I'm just being intrusive."

"No," he said. "Go on."

"I was thinking that maybe you express your love for him by trying to protect others."

He laughed. "Yeah. Sure, right." He finished half of the second beer.

"No—you protect people from harm. The work you're doing." She couldn't believe what she was saying. It just came out.

His voice suddenly became grave, his look intense. His expression frightened her. "Have you ever been in a city that's been bombed out?"

"No."

"Well, I have. Here's what happens. Riots, looting, rape, murder, criminal behavior on a scale that would scare your boots off. The thugs come out of the woodwork. Nice, innocent girls like you get . . . well, it's not pretty. Not pretty at all. That's exactly what's going to happen if the people—those people you say I care so much about—aren't protected from your friends.

"Like most dangerous people, the Mandala aren't inherently evil, only misdirected. They give the common man too much credit. People don't act civilized of their own accord; it's not in their nature. The law—some kind of law—must be imposed. You're a student of history, you know this. It's the glue of civilization. The Mandala are anarchists, plain and simple, with no idea of what they're doing."

His eyes bored into her. He said, "I'm asking you to consider your role in this."

"*My* role?"

"What did Georgia Roussey tell you?"

Maya froze. "What?"

"You spoke to her."

She had been absent-mindedly twirling the stem of the wine glass in her fingers. Suddenly Fiske reached over and grabbed her wrist. She released the glass, as he squeezed until she grimaced in pain.

"What are you doing?"

"You're lying."

"I'm not."

He squeezed tighter. "Tell me what happened."

She was near panic. She could have called out but she didn't. "Nothing. Nothing happened. What are you talking about? Let me go!"

He stared long and hard into her eyes. "What happened in Wilton?"

She had to tell him something. "Yes, yes, I was there." He loosened his grip but only slightly. "They talked about their wonderful egalitarian society. It was interesting, but that was it. I don't know anything about what you're talking about. I swear."

"And Brandon McGowan?" The grip tightened.

"I met him, yes . . . stop it!"

"And?"

"He told me about rituals. Stuff about the commune, if that's what it's called. Please stop hurting me. No one told me anything."

He released her. She immediately grabbed her wrist, rubbing it to soothe the pain.

He said, "What did you think of them?"

"Think?" She desperately wanted to leave, to get away from him. She said, "They were strange. I've never seen a place like that."

"How so?"

"It was like a cult."

He nodded, satisfied. "What did they say about your father?"

"They didn't know who he was."

He laughed. Then he leaned back, stared at her.

Now she had a long sip of wine—one for the road. She put the glass down and started to rise. "It's getting late."

"Wait."

She looked at him, impatiently, fearfully.

"You're not the enemy," he said. "But know this: they will come for you. Once they do, they won't let up. I'm sorry I was abrupt with you. You understand my urgency. Think about what I've said. If you want to talk, you know where to find me. You can still do the right thing, Maya."

"Okay."

His face softened. "But next time use a phone. You almost lost me coming out of the Arlington Metro. I had to slow up a few times."

"Goodbye," she said.

"Yep. See you around," he said, reaching for the mug.

Once outside, she dashed for the Metro, unwilling to linger in Arlington any longer than necessary. Her car was where she had left it, at the Rockville Metro stop. On the drive home, she felt a familiar tightness in her rib cage, hopefully just stress working its way out.

She wondered: How much did Fiske know?

Did he know about the trip she was about to take, the one she had so carefully tried to hide?

CHAPTER 13

Rain pounded down on the sloped awning above her and ran down into the rain gutter, sluicing in torrents onto the front lawn. Some of it flowed over the edge of the gutter, falling like a waterfall onto the concrete patio below. Puddles grew and spread on the front lawn, which was starting to resemble a marsh. The rain had fallen steadily since dawn.

Huddled on a bench under the canvas awning, Maya recalled the last downpour she had been in: her short time with Brandon. Now, she was preparing for another trip. Maybe the rain had become an auger of transition for her. "A good rain means Maya is about to change. Again."

She laughed. As if she were the center of the universe.

She stared out into the storm, considering it. On this day the rain seemed a unifier, bringing together the disparate parts of the world, illuminating their common ground: that water is the blood of all life on planet Earth, the glue of every ecosystem. Within the rain hides the promise of a new day for every organism, from the tiniest microbe to the most mammoth African bull elephant.

A cold mist swirled up onto the porch. She zipped her raincoat all the way up to her neck. Stormy weather often relaxed her, even made her feel dreamy. Dealing with practicalities seemed unnecessary on these days. All she wanted to do was ponder, think, consider.

She stared absently at the puddles on the lawn, imagining the vast networks of roots beneath them, the snaking tendrils suddenly roused to life, sucking water up the thick tree trunks to leaves that jumped around in the wind and rain.

Beloved old souls, the trees. If they were people they would surely be sane. Tempered, dependable. The trees watch the world speed past, while they themselves remain still and unchanging. She wondered, Why do we go so fast? Why don't we slow down like the trees?

Perhaps, she considered, it is to blur the evidence of our eyes, the suspicion that we are actors in a drama with neither plot nor theme, that may ultimately hold no meaning. We don't know where it will go from one moment to the next.

Do the trees know this of us? Maybe. Their knowledge, after all, is older than ours, by many millions of years. Perhaps it is clearer, truer. Maybe they are wiser than us, she mused, and that is why they remain silent, like parents who smile knowingly at the antics of small children, withholding explanations that are too complicated for them.

But they watch, the trees. She was certain of it.

Someone had told her once that during the rain we can glimpse this, if we are quiet, if we allow ourselves to slow down to the speed of the trees.

How?

By sitting, by waiting. By allowing ourselves to enter into the rain.

The rain's hypnosis, like the dance of a fire, or the song of the surf, seeps into the psyche, a warm salve. During these times we can come forward. If we choose.

A car passed by, its tires spinning up water, its shimmering headlights distorted by the thick mist and rain. I am reaching out to that car, she thought.

She let her mind relax, and yes, it seemed to go out.

If nature was making a statement for this day it was one of union, a fusing of separates, a reminder of the interdependence of all things. Everything joins together in a water-melted landscape. She felt this to be true, not just another fantasy, and wanted very much to remember it.

A storm drain in the gutter had clogged, the runoff swelling back into the street, creating a fast-growing pond. Soon it would be a lake, edging up the tires of parked cars. So what?

She unfolded the Sunday paper in her lap—and the spell of

the rain and the trees was broken, the wall restored. The message: *We* are the rulers, *you* are the vanquished. Or so it seemed.

She decided: no. I won't go there. Not now. She closed the newspaper, dropped it under the bench on the soaking-wet cement, where it became waterlogged within seconds.

The front door opened and Muriel came out, arms crossed, grimacing. She was wearing a long coat. "Nice day, huh?"

Maya shrugged. "I kind of like it."

"You always were a little different."

Maya looked over to appraise Muriel's mood. It was an unconscious act. Muriel seemed steady.

Feeling adventurous, Maya baited her. "Whatever do you mean?"

"About what?"

"Me being different."

"You mean you haven't noticed?"

"I was just wondering where I get it from."

"Oh," Muriel said. "Not from me."

"Hmm," Maya said, hoping for more. Wishing for more. She got it.

Muriel's next statement flew in the face of twenty years of silence on the subject of Maya's paternal heritage, and made Maya's heart skip a beat.

"You get it from your father," Muriel said, simply, as though making the most ordinary comment in the world.

Maya, stunned, turned around. Muriel was staring wistfully out at the rain. "We weren't married when you came along, kiddo. We got married afterwards."

Years seemed to pass before Muriel spoke again.

"This is what you want to know, right?"

Maya nodded.

"He worked in Washington," she said. "He came to the university to meet with some of the professors there. Sometimes he taught. I was a secretary in the department." She paused, walked to the edge of the porch, stood in front of a sheet of rain pouring down from the awning.

"He wasn't interested in a life with me, Maya. I knew that. We tried anyway. Maybe it was stupid. He was unhappy. I was unhappy. I guess I've held it against him all these years. Maybe you can change that kind of long-running feeling. I don't know, it's like trying to change the course of an ocean liner. Pretty slow."

Maya watched as Muriel reached her palm out into the waterfall, then brought it back, soaking wet, and examined it. This wasn't Muriel-style behavior. None of it.

"I know what you think about Henry," she said, changing the subject too quickly. Maya said nothing. She had learned long ago not to try to manipulate Muriel.

"For your information, yes, Henry is in Alcoholics Anonymous." Now Muriel turned to face Maya, startling her. Maya, instinctively tightened.

Muriel said, "Not everything's my fault, you know. Some of it is this, this, illness. I guess I never saw it that way but that's how I'm trying to look at it now. Do you understand what I'm saying?"

It sounded like Muriel was saying she had a drinking problem. Maya just nodded.

"As for your father," Muriel said, "after you were born, we split. He left. That's about it, Maya. I know you're looking for fireworks, but there aren't any. It was fast and then it was over."

Maya wondered: Did he tell you about his work? About Fiske? About remote viewing? Anything?

"Did he say anything about his work?" she asked.

Muriel shrugged. "He worked in Washington."

"But doing what?"

Muriel didn't answer. She didn't know. She just kept reaching her hand out in the rain and pulling it back.

"Did you love him?" Maya asked, holding her breath.

Muriel turned and gave her the death stare. Then, to Maya's surprise, her face softened. Things *were* changing.

"Yes," she said. She hesitated, and then added: "And no. It changed, somewhere in there."

"Did he love you?"

Muriel gave a guttural laugh. "I'm not sure he *could* love. Not people, anyway. He loved ideas. Me, I was just a person. Do you see? I admit I liked the idea of having him, though I suppose, looking back, it wasn't the right way to go about it."

Muriel turned and walked toward the door, but before she got there, Maya said, "Do you ever want to see him again?"

Muriel thought about it. "A lot of water's flowed under that bridge. I don't know, to be honest."

Hearing all this brought up not just relief in Maya, but anger, too. She thought: All this time you've been taking it out on *me*.

The urge to lash out was strong, but Maya would never do it. Muriel would flatten her if she tried. No, Muriel was opening to new ways of seeing things, new behaviors, and it could only benefit Maya. Maya had only to wait and see how it played out, whether any of it would stick.

"This AA thing has got me thinking a lot more than I want to," Muriel admitted. "Makes me want to drink more than ever."

Maya, wanting to be helpful, said, "If there's anything I can do—"

"There is," said Muriel. "Don't bring it up, any of it."

Maya nodded. "I won't."

"This humidity is sure as hell messing up my hair," Muriel said, as she reached for the door.

Suddenly a loud groaning sound erupted from above them, then a sharp *snap* sounded, as a support pole for the awning broke loose. The released tension shot the pole high into the air, toward the front lawn. It made a sweeping arc before bouncing down in the grass. The awning began to sag all the way down to the patio on one side, pouring rain all over the concrete. Maya and Muriel both stepped closer to the house.

Muriel just shook her head and went inside.

Maya stood up under the drooping awning. She had an idea. Maybe what she did then was symbolic; maybe it was just silly. It didn't really matter. All that mattered was that things were changing.

She walked to the front of the porch and stood facing the lawn, her nose just inches from a clear plane of water that poured down from the remaining section of awning, and poked her finger through it. She turned her palm up and extended all of her fingers out, tilted them up, and then watched as water ran onto her sleeve. She pulled her hand back quickly. That was her reflex, to pull out at the first sign of danger. She had done that all her life. But that was the past. Now things were different.

She wanted to shout out her new resolve to the world: I will risk. I will embrace the unknown. I will accept what is.

It was a course change that had been building in her for some time.

Instead of thinking—for reason could be an enemy of action—she kicked her shoes high into the air. They landed far out on the lawn, near the sidewalk. Then off came her socks. Next she rolled up the bottoms of her jeans and stepped on the lawn, off the safety of the porch. Into the rain. Her naked feet sank into the cold, soggy turf. She could see Muriel watching her through the window. Muriel probably thought she was crazy. Not the first time, either. She didn't care.

Digging her toes into the mud, feeling the cool rain soak through her hair and her clothes, she twirled around in circles on the lawn as if in a primal dance, whipping her water-logged hair about and grinning like a mad woman. Maybe it was a rebellion against the ordinary, against the expected. Perhaps it was a preparation for letting go.

Euphoria charged through her and lit up her face, and for a moment, for a tiny sliver of time, she stepped authoritatively out of the rut she'd been in, out of the pre-programmed existence she had adopted too quickly and uncritically, and struck out against . . . what? She didn't know. Nor did it matter. The past was dead. All that mattered was now. Right now. She wanted to weep with joy—just for the moment. Just for the moment. Wrapped inside the rain, she felt so free.

CHAPTER 14

As the Los Angeles-bound plane rose up off the runway and began its climb, Maya recalled her mother's one and only story about her father. Maya was five. Muriel had told her that late one night, long, long ago, a magical airplane had landed in the backyard while Maya was sleeping and carried her father off to a mystical land of kings, knights and princesses.

"When is he coming back?" the little girl asked.

Muriel laughed and lit a cigarette. "Sorry, kiddo. He's not," she said.

"Why not?" Maya asked, puzzled, too young to understand.

"He doesn't love us enough, sweetheart."

For weeks the girl wrenched her little head skyward at passing jets, squinting, waving, hoping, but the magical airplane never returned. Gradually her hope faded, and the first seeds of futility took root within her.

In grade school shame had hounded her, for single-parent families were uncommon in the conservative, former farming community of Plainfield in those days. At sixteen she finally, consciously, decided not to give a damn about what people thought of her. This was a near impossible task for a teenager, but trying it out was far better than facing the pain of shame and rejection, which cropped up often for an unusual person like Maya.

She became a contrary, a rebel, doing exactly the opposite of what people expected of her. She tried many strategies. For a time she acted like a boy, dressing in baggy sweats, buzz-cutting her hair, shunning all things feminine, reading science fiction and comic books; even attempting, unsuccessfully, to join a boys' baseball team. To her amazement this strategy actually resulted in a brief period of high school popularity, exactly the opposite of what she had intended.

Sinking back into obscurity was not so easy. The nihilism she had embraced, or appeared to have embraced, actually *furthered* her standing as a person to know. All she could do was shake her head at the ridiculousness of it all.

Finally, she took a different approach. She wore the geekiest clothes she could find, stopped combing her hair, didn't look anyone in the eye, shunned all friendships, and hid out in her room as much as possible. Eventually the kids gave up on her, and she was able to melt back into being simply the weird girl who read too much and looked unhappy a lot of the time.

Suddenly the cabin pitched in some turbulence, shaking her back into the present moment. She pulled the seat belt tighter and glanced out the window, through thousands of feet of air, down to the forests, farms and rivers of Maryland edging slowly out of sight. Home.

"Goodbye," she whispered, the word falling soundlessly into the roar of the engines.

Georgia had taken no chances. The ticket had been delivered directly into her hands by a Mandala courier, a small nervous man who had sped off as soon as his mission was completed.

Maya had fed Muriel another lie about a trip with Josh—a longer journey this time, down to the Ozarks—and told Josh about it too, with instructions to avoid Muriel at all costs. But it was unlikely he would run into her. Henry Rossmore was taking her to his Ocean City condo for a week's vacation. The timing couldn't be better.

*   *   *

Through the tall, tinted windows of the airport terminal hallway she could see that Southern California was bright. No surprise there. It didn't take brains to know this. Backpack in hand, she strode toward the baggage claim area, as instructed. And as promised, someone approached her.

Maya recognized the woman immediately: the mysterious messenger with the spiked blond hair who had delivered the letter to her in Josh's apartment. Only she looked far different now. Her hair was auburn, combed down in a conservative style, and she was wearing a business suit.

"Hello, Maya," she said. "I'm Kira." She extended her hand, and Maya took it. Smiling, Kira looked far more approachable than she had in Plainfield.

"I'm sorry about that moment of drama at your friend's apartment, but Georgia likes us to keep a low profile. I didn't want to risk having to answer any questions. I hope I didn't put you off too badly."

"I survived it," Maya said, genially.

Kira led her outside to a car idling at the curb and got in front, beside another person Maya recognized, the muscular man who had whisked Georgia out of the student lounge. "I'm Serge," he said.

"Where are we going?" she said, settling into the backseat.

"To Brandon's house," he said as he started the car.

Within minutes they merged onto a highway, as Maya watched the late afternoon sun flash through a line of tall palms. The car was silent, too silent, the windows rolled up tight to keep out the hazy warmth, the air conditioning blowing loudly. She focused on the land outside, mostly flat with some small hills densely covered in houses and apartment buildings.

They came around a bend and immediately slowed in heavy traffic as a beach scene materialized with the abruptness of a movie cut. Maya immediately recognized the sunny Southern California of television and movies. Excited, she brought her face up to the window, wanting to stop and experience it firsthand. But she knew this would be impossible.

"Where are we?"

"Santa Monica," Kira said.

A curving pathway ran for miles along the beach, a fast-moving capillary of bicyclists, roller skaters and joggers. Maya looked on in wonder as a six-foot tall woman skated past everyone in sight—

backwards. She saw more blond hair and sculpted bodies than she had seen in her whole life. It seemed to her an alien world, strange and fascinating.

They passed several more beaches, and driving faster, soon came upon hundreds of beach-front homes, tightly packed together for long stretches, cutting off the view of the ocean. A few more miles, and the traffic thinned out. Now, to her right, canyons and hills came alive with wildflowers, and the density of buildings on the ocean side diminished, opening up great swaths of blue ocean.

The further north they traveled, the less commerce she saw. Older, more established stores and offices now lined the road, proudly displaying the word Malibu on their signs.

Serge turned off the Pacific Coast Highway onto a smaller road, and the whoosh of speeding cars faded behind them. Here was the first dense woods Maya had seen in the area, and it was beautiful. After a few turns, they ascended a long driveway and pulled into the garage of Brandon's house, a Spanish-style estate, complete with a red-tiled roof, courtyard and arching walkways.

Maya followed Kira to the house, passing through a gate and alongside a swimming pool.

The living room was sun-lit and filled with antiques, which struck Maya as being somehow out of place amid all the bright sunlight. One wall was completely made of glass, with glass doors in the center that opened out onto a redwood deck. Kira led Maya to the deck and told her to wait. Flowers and vines flowed like waterfalls over the railings.

Standing there she saw that the house was built high atop a ridge, with a dramatic ocean view. She hadn't even realized they had climbed. The driveway actually was a steep grade. From here, the ocean appeared not as a thin blue line but as an aquamarine oval that complemented the vastness of the sky.

Brandon came out and greeted her warmly, looking more casual than he had in Wyoming, where he had been in jeans and boots. Now he wore neat pleated shorts, a pullover and deck sneakers.

"We're glad you came," he said.

"It's beautiful here," she said. "I've never been anywhere like this."

"Are you hungry?"

"Famished. Thanks."

"We can take care of that."

They ate outside, sandwiches and fruit, and Brandon asked her many questions, following each of her responses with the next logical query. He never drifted in his listening, as she always did when people rambled on about themselves. He was always right there with her.

"Actually," she said, finishing a turkey and avocado sandwich, "I'm kind of in the dark about why I'm here. Georgia didn't say—"

"I know," Brandon said. "Hold those questions just a little longer. She'll answer them when she gets here."

"Okay." Maya got up and walked over to the railing, looked out over the ocean. The sun was nearing the horizon line. "The view is amazing."

"It can be even better."

"How?"

"From the beach," he said. "Come on, I'll show you."

Brandon led her—and Serge and Kira, who had joined them in the driveway—to a hiking trail across the street. The group filed down a dirt path into a lush canyon.

Walking under the near-solid canopy of trees, Maya noticed houses perched up on the steep ridges, held aloft by long, metal stilts, looking as though they would topple over in the slightest disturbance. She asked about this, and Brandon told her that even earthquakes had failed to budge them.

They stopped at a clearing where the sky opened up through the trees. A chain link fence barred their way, coils of barbed-wire enmeshed throughout it, its gate locked.

"This is a private beach," Kira explained, "only accessible to residents."

Maya frowned. It seemed a grave injustice to hoard so much natural beauty for a chosen few. But then she recalled the chaotic beach scene she'd witnessed earlier, with its skaters and bicyclists and overwhelming mass of beach-going humanity, and wondered which was the better: uncontrolled access that tarnished a natural aesthetic or exclusive access that preserved it. It was a question best left for another time, she decided.

Brandon pulled a key out of his pocket.

"Right," Maya said.

He opened the padlock, swung open the gate and they passed through it. The dirt path turned to sand as they arrived at a strip of pristine beach about a half-mile long, deserted but for a couple of people huddled together at one end, almost out of sight.

The vast Pacific Ocean stood before her, for the first time in her life. The sun, now a weak orange ball, hovered over it. Wind gusted off the water, whipping her hair around. She breathed deeply of the salty, invigorating air and watched the surf wash in just a few feet away.

Brandon kicked off his sneakers and waded barefoot into the shallows, engaging in what seemed to Maya a familiar ritual. Serge and Kira sat in the sand, as though waiting for something.

She shrugged, and followed Brandon's lead, taking off her tennis shoes and socks and rolling up her jeans. She followed him into the surf up to her calves. The water was stinging cold, but the pain quickly gave way to a numb sensation that wasn't all that unpleasant.

They walked south, weaving in and out of the sand and the surf, toward a jetty that jutted out past the breakers. When they reached it, Brandon rock-walked out to the end, and Maya, also sure-footed, followed behind him. They sat on the farthest boulder from the beach, dangling their feet down to where the waves could occasionally spray them.

Only sea and sky filled Maya's field of vision. Nothing else existed at that moment. She turned and saw Serge and Kira sitting at the base of the cliffs, shading their eyes with their hands. "Who are they?" she asked.

"Security," Brandon said, simply.

Maya turned to him, surprised. Brandon turned his gaze to the tops of the nearby cliffs. "You see that man up there?"

Maya gazed up at a lone figure standing at the top who appeared tiny from their vantage point. "Yes."

Brandon said, "That's your friend, Fiske."

"He's *here*?"

"Or one of his men."

"Spying on us?"

"Well, yes," Brandon said. "But don't worry, they can't hear us. The surf interferes with their equipment."

He turned to face the ocean, and she followed his lead.

"Georgia wanted me to fill you in on some details," he said. "It may answer some of your questions."

"It's about time."

"Have you ever heard of the Anderson Foundation?"

"It's a nonprofit organization, isn't it?"

"That's right," he said. "The Anderson Foundation is a philanthropy, an organization that exists solely for the purpose of giving away money to what they consider worthwhile causes. Do you know much about philanthropies?"

"Some," she said. "I did an internship at a public TV station. They had relationships with them."

"Many of the world's richest people pour millions, even billions, back into the community, into causes," Brandon said. "There are even foundations that spend money *to figure out* where to spend money. Now any organization with the right cause, grant proposal, PR or contacts can get that money. The lion's share goes to social programs, the arts and research.

"Back in the eighties, at the urging of one of its board members, the Anderson Foundation began to fund research on alternative cancer therapies. A man named Roger Anderson, one of the heirs to the family fortune, had lost his wife to cancer. As a result he became a fanatic about finding new treatments. But what made him different from the others in the field was that his primary interest was unconventional treatments. Anderson hated the traditional medical community. He saw them as ego-bound, slow and corrupt. Any idea they were loath to touch, Anderson gravitated toward.

"Some years earlier, two researchers, Carl and Stephanie Simonton, had made waves in the medical community by demonstrating that malignant cell growth could be slowed, even halted, using visualization techniques—employing the human imagination in a focused, directed way—for example, imagining the immune system's cells as killer sharks, Pac-men, and the like. So Anderson sponsored work that followed the Simonton's lead, funding similar studies that were also successful. He soon founded a clinic of his own.

"Over the years Anderson's successes in mind-body medicine enabled him to expand his clinic to encompass a wider range of disciplines, most notably the paranormal. His team of anthropologists, physicians and, yes, mystics, convinced him that the healing knowledge he sought already existed, in the past, with primitive cultures.

"His paranormal work, however, was far more controversial— and embarrassing to his conservative-minded family—than the mind-body medicine. They opposed it. To avoid a rift, he agreed to sponsor more conventional work and bury his research deep within the auspices of his clinic, hidden from public view. In return, the family agreed to leave him to indulge in his strange proclivities.

"Out of the way of scrutiny and with a lavish budget at his disposal, Roger Anderson quietly built a massive knowledge base on the subject of subtle energy and metaphysical healing. None of this has ever been made public, by the way."

Brandon paused, as a wave crashed against the rocks below them, sending up a spray that wet them both. As he wiped water from his face, he turned to her.

"I'm telling you this, Maya, because Roger Anderson is the main backer of the Mandala.

"Anderson, the man, is in his late sixties, eccentric, driven, charismatic. He met your father when David worked for Albert Fiske, and immediately understood David's gifts. He tried to lure him away. He didn't succeed at first, but David contacted Anderson after things fell apart with Fiske. Your father has worked for Roger Anderson ever since."

She asked, "What exactly happened between my father and Fiske?"

"Fiske falsified documents to give the impression that David had sold secrets to a foreign government. Fiske has many contacts. He did his job well; the frame-up was well-staged, elaborate, and screwed your father good. David ran, traveling for years, mostly in Asia and Africa, learning about energy and healing from native peoples. His psychic abilities always gave him an entré in certain circles. All these years—your whole life, in fact—Roger Anderson has protected him.

"The bottom line," Brandon said, "is that your father is wanted by the FBI for espionage. It's a phony charge but that's the reality. Running away, of course, only made it worse."

She said, "But he's innocent, right?"

"Everybody believes so."

"Do you?"

"Yes."

She nodded. A chill wind blasted them out of nowhere, and she tucked in her shirt.

"Look there," Brandon said, pointing out at the ocean.

"Yes, I see it."

The sun had sunk halfway down into the ocean horizon. Above it, a wake of crimson and gold filled the blue sky.

They watched in silence as the sun inched downward, its light so weak that Maya could almost focus on it without having to look away. Feelings stirred deep within her. She sensed a bridge form across time, connecting her with the thousands of generations of coastal dwellers who had watched sunsets exactly like this one, just as awestruck and respectful, feeling exactly what she felt. To the ancients, however, the far horizon into which the sun was about to disappear was far more mysterious than it was to Maya and Brandon. To them it was the edge of the world beyond which only void existed.

Now only a sliver of orange remained, floating on the edge of the world. Then it became a golden dot. Then there was only the fading blue sky, reflecting many beautiful colors. To the east, the sky had already turned indigo, pierced by the faint twinkling of a few stars.

Maya turned and looked up at the top of the cliff, but it was empty. The man was gone. The wind kicked up again, and Kira and Serge called out to them. Brandon waved back, and soon the group was together again, retracing their path back through the ravine. Maya swore she heard sounds along the trail, but when she turned there was only the quiet woods.

*   *   *

She sat alone on the expansive redwood deck, wrapped in a blanket that Brandon had given her. The temperature had dropped quickly after sunset.

Maya had been enjoying the deferential treatment accorded her by the Mandala, thanks to her relationship with a father she had never laid eyes on, whose status in this underground of spiritual adepts qualified her as a VIP.

The anxiety struck out of nowhere. Panic had the bad habit of showing up at the worst times, like when she was really excited about something. As if a warning switch got tripped every time she approached a heightened experience. The danger lay not with what might happen in the external world, but with the workings within the mind. The what-ifs. The culprit: that voracious devourer of her, the wolf. She had become too excited about meeting her father.

Doubt spread quickly, infectiously. What if. . . . What if he didn't want to meet her? What if he saw her as an intrusion from the past, a past from which he had escaped?

The wolf seized on these fears and ran with them. For weren't they true? Wasn't her existence a burden to those closest to her? Hadn't experience borne this out?

The train of negativity picked up speed. She was no longer just sitting innocently outside on a cool California night. Secret armies were swarming.

The descents were always like this, swift and surgical. The

wolf was busily manufacturing scenarios, blowing new life into the hoary terrors of the past, fanning whatever fear was nearest, creating a dark and hopeless future.

The counter-offensive seemed absurd to the rational mind, but as a strategy it worked. You couldn't argue with success. It had pulled her up from the deepest of depths. It would work again. It had to, or she was lost.

Taking a few deep, cleansing breaths, she gathered up all the resolve she could muster, even through the raging negativity; then, smack in the face of overwhelming evidence to the contrary, she forced herself—*forced* herself—with every ounce of will power . . . to affirm her goodness.

Even though she didn't believe a word of it.

She *was* a loser. She *was* a failure.

No! Not true. I am a good person.

You can't even get a job.

Yes, I can. I will work when the time is right. Things happen in their own time.

No one likes you. You have no friends.

I do. I am different, and so they are few. But they love me for who I am. I hold out for people who are good for me.

Your father left you. He doesn't care about you. He will reject you again.

He left me because he had to. Whatever happens is all right, because I have done my best. I cannot control what he, or anyone else, thinks. I can only be me—no more, no less. And that is fine.

Suddenly—which was the way it happened—the wolf's terrifying growl lost its teeth. It became a whimper, the dark reality a fantasy, the imminent nightmare an empty dream. Energy surged back into her. She'd done it, reclaimed herself.

The reversal was always astonishingly swift. She had halted a descent that two years earlier would have immobilized her for weeks. She breathed a satisfied sigh.

She had caged the wolf.

Self-destructive thinking, which always appeared to be such an awesome force, was just a house of cards that could be toppled with the slightest exhalation. The key was to deny it. It couldn't survive five seconds without a belief in it. She had found she could do this, no matter how convincing the beckoning voices seemed. It was hard, though, because while she was under the spell, denying the truth of what they said seemed as crazy as standing before a black wall and saying, "Look! A white wall!"

The trick, she knew, was to replace one self-created fantasy with another, a bad with a good, and *will* that it stick. When she did this, a white wall would materialize where the black wall had stood. Afterwards, looking at it, she would realize it had been white all along.

*   *   *

She reached over and opened the curtains of Brandon's guest room to see what the ocean looked like in the first light of day. But she was disappointed. It wasn't even there—everything, even the trees just a few feet across the street, had disappeared into a thick blanket of fog.

Never mind. She didn't care. It was a new day, and she felt good. Even before she brushed her teeth she determined how she would experience the day—not just the day, but the rest of the trip. Her strategy was simple: let it be. Let each moment take its course. Expect nothing, force nothing, interfere with nothing. Trust in the big U, the universe. Live that old saw: "There's God's way and your way—and your way doesn't count." How and when she would meet her father wasn't in her hands. Nothing was. This did not mean she would not fight the wolf when it came. Abiding the wolf and following the flow were two entirely different things.

She had fought the flow of the river of life all her life it seemed, each time getting beaten against the rocks or tossed onto shore. Only the ignorant fought that current. You *had* to go with it. What other choice was there? If she slipped, if she tried to push— *when* she slipped—she would recover quickly, detach, release any attempt at control. That was the plan. Stop trying to do what couldn't be done.

As the fog was lifting Georgia arrived, ruddy-cheeked and smiling, hugging everyone in sight. She was in jeans and a fringed cowboy jacket. She took a seat on the sofa beside Kira and Serge. Brandon and Maya settled into the chairs opposite.

Georgia glanced at Maya, and Maya met her eyes with enthusiasm. She was bursting with questions. "We're going to see him today, right?" she blurted out.

"Shh," Georgia said, waving her off. "I'm thinking."

Already pushing. *Let the day unfold.*

Georgia turned to Kira. "Are you ready?"

"Yes."

"Go, then," the old woman said, tossing her keys to Serge.

Serge and Kira said goodbye and left the house through the kitchen door, as Maya looked on, confused.

Maya wandered into the kitchen, frustration welling up inside her. She tried to quell it by focusing on her breathing but it was impossible. What was going on? It was infuriating, not knowing. Didn't these people talk?

She heard car doors slam shut outside. Then the engine started. She went to the window, just in time to see Georgia's car back out of the driveway. Serge was at the wheel, Kira in the passenger seat.

Maya returned to the living room.

"Where did they go?" she asked.

"Up the coast," Georgia said. "Did you notice anything about Kira?"

Maya shrugged. "No."

"Her hair? Her clothes?"

"No."

"Think."

She tried, but nothing came to her.

"She had on the same sweater, jeans and tennis shoes as you. Didn't you notice her hair?"

"No."

"It matched yours exactly."

"A wig?" Maya said.

"Yes, a wig," Georgia said, shaking her head.

Maya had been so preoccupied with trying to go with the flow that she hadn't managed to do it at all. All she had done was *try* to do it. She remembered nothing of Kira's appearance. She had missed it all.

"You need to pay more attention," Georgia said. "I'm serious."

"They're going up the coast," Brandon said, "to Oxnard."

"What's up there?"

"Nothing," he said.

Maya looked at them. Finally, she understood. "So, Kira was playing me?"

"A precaution, to lead away curious onlookers," Georgia said.

Maya nodded. "Will it work?"

"Hopefully," Georgia said. "I put out a call, too, saying we were going up there. Now get your things. We'll leave shortly."

CHAPTER 15

She lay down, as instructed, on the floor in the back of Brandon's car, on a stack of blankets. It was not uncomfortable. Georgia turned around and threw another blanket over her and told her to keep still as they drove into Los Angeles.

The road was windy and fast. She peeked out from the blanket at times and was able to look up through the back window. A constant wall of trees passed by, which soon gave way to buildings.

After a while they slowed in heavy traffic as they entered a noisier area with taller buildings. The air changed, becoming thicker, almost soupy. She could hardly make out the details of the buildings. Sometimes the lines of the walls seemed to undulate. Finally she realized what she was seeing: smog. The whole world had disappeared into a brownish haze.

Brandon took a few sharp turns, then stopped the car and reached up to the visor to click a small plastic card clipped to it. Maya heard a mechanical door open somewhere in front of them. She looked up at the balconies of an apartment building, when suddenly the front of the car angled down. They moved forward into a dark area, and Brandon cut the engine off to the sound of a gate closing behind them.

"Don't forget your backpack," Georgia said, opening the door. "We're going to have to move fast."

"I'm ready," Maya said.

She pulled herself up and out of the car. She was standing in a cement parking structure, lit by a few fluorescent lights. Dozens of parked cars surrounded them.

Brandon came around to her. "Do everything this great lady tells you and you'll be fine. All right?"

"I will," Maya promised.

Georgia kissed Brandon on the cheek. "I'll be in touch, my friend."

"God speed," he said. "Both of you."

Maya grabbed her backpack and followed Georgia through a door at the back of the garage. They emerged in a trash-strewn alley between several apartment buildings and hurried to the next street.

Georgia moved fast. Though Maya well knew how vibrant the old woman was, she continued to find her energy surprising. Georgia was toting a large shoulder bag as if it were full of feathers.

"Where are we going?" Maya asked, jogging to keep up.

"To that corner," Georgia said, pointing to a taxi idling in the street. They reached it and climbed in.

"Airport," she said to the driver.

Maya said, "You mean he's not here?"

Georgia turned quickly to her. "*Please*, Maya. Trust me, everything will work out for the best. I promise. Just be patient."

Georgia reached into her bag for a bottle of water and had a long drink. She offered it to Maya, who shook her head.

"Can I at least ask where we're going?"

"Look at the scenery, Maya. Take in the world. You've never seen Los Angeles, have you? It's interesting. That's Sunset Boulevard, there. Check it out."

"All right," Maya said with a pout.

Maya, who had forgotten the promise she had made to herself that morning, tried now to honor it, to release her attempt at trying to control situations that couldn't be controlled. She thought: I must accept what is—including being in a taxi going to the airport to, well, anywhere.

Georgia had told her she would see him. She trusted Georgia. Meeting her father could be dangerous. So they had to be careful. These were the facts. She had to accept them. She did accept them.

Sunset Boulevard was brimming with life. They passed vintage clothing stores, Internet cafes, script copying shops, night clubs, guitar stores, hot dog stands, purple-haired kids dressed all in black, low riders, and immigrants from many countries, all navigating, in cars or on foot, through the streets and the parking lots and the strip shopping malls. She saw little parks filled with the homeless, pushing shopping carts that overflowed with cans, containers, clothes and blankets. The area was far from the clean, breezy coastal neighborhood where Brandon lived, in so many ways.

A few minutes later they made the freeway, and soon were exiting the cab for the airport entrance. Again Maya struggled to keep up with Georgia, who strode quickly through the long hallways of the terminal.

Finally, they arrived at the departure gate. No wonder Georgia was rushing; they made the departure time by only ten minutes.

The destination: Albuquerque, New Mexico.

Before she could say anything, Georgia said, "The answer to your question is yes. Now let's board and speak no more of it."

*　　*　　*

Georgia closed her eyes and rested her head back on the seat during the entire flight. Maya couldn't tell if she was sleeping or just daydreaming. Only when the plane began to descend did she open her eyes.

The airport in Albuquerque was spacious and not the least bit as stressful as the one in Los Angeles, which had seemed to Maya like a bustling third world city. A tall, lanky man with a bouncy, sure-footed stride met them as they walked toward the exit doors. He had long sandy hair that flowed out of the back of a tattered fedora like a mane. He appeared to be in his forties, though as he approached she could see that his cracked, weathered face was probably older. Maya pegged him as an aging hippie. Georgia rushed over and embraced him.

"Maya Burke," Georgia said, "meet Keith Seputa."

Smiling warmly, Keith said, "Great to meet you at last."

"You, too," she said uncertainly.

"He's Mandala," Georgia said.

"Oh," Maya said, nodding. "So where are we going?"

Keith glanced quickly at Georgia, who said, "The impatience of youth. She's riddled with it."

"I remember that," Keith said. "It's when I made the most mistakes. And had the most fun. We can't afford too many mistakes now, Maya."

Why not? Maya wondered. But she said nothing.

Maya settled back comfortably in the back seat as he drove north on Route 25. It was late afternoon. Just out of Albuquerque the landscape changed dramatically, from highly developed to vast and empty. Maya rolled down the window and let the wind blast over her, pleasantly surprised to discover how good it felt just looking outside. For no reason that she could tell, she felt lighter, freer. Beyond the flat, windy plain, layer after layer of mountain receded into the distance.

Her sense of freedom intensified as they drove, as if it was okay to do anything she pleased in this place and suffer no consequences. She'd never felt that way before. Maybe Keith shared this feeling, expressing it in the speed at which he drove: a steady eighty-five miles an hour.

The boundlessness of the land, the warm colors, the empty highway, the speed—it was intoxicating. She felt weightless. If they had stopped, she might have bolted out into the nearest field and done cartwheels and handstands, giggling like a child. Maybe somersaults, too. A joyfulness overcame her, and she did not know why.

Afternoon melted into evening, and with it a patch of lights came into view, far up ahead, glittering like a multi-faceted jewel.

"What's that?" Maya asked.

"Sante Fe," Georgia said in a business-like tone of voice.

"No stops tonight," Keith said, as they drove past. The old West's trading capital receded behind them, as they continued northward.

Maya closed her eyes. Keith put some music on. Just as Maya was beginning to slump, Georgia piped up. "We're here."

"Where?"

"Taos."

"When you say 'here,' what exactly do you mean?"

"I mean we're stopping for the night."

"Good. I'm tired."

Maya had heard of Taos but knew little about it. Keith navigated through some residential streets and pulled up to a small adobe house in a neighborhood of many other small adobe houses, parking right on the front lawn, which was mostly dirt. He rushed around the front of the car to help Georgia out, but she waved him off.

"I'm not feeble yet," she said.

The air was dry and cool. Though it was dark, there was a moon, and Maya could see that fields of scrub grass and dirt surrounded the houses.

"Welcome to my home," Keith said.

Inside, the first thing Maya noticed was a hill of shoes and sandals in the foyer, piled up like a natural rock formation. Several were small, obviously children's. She wandered into the kitchen, where still-wet dishes dried on a rack in the sink. Space was tight but the interior of the house was cleverly designed, every inch maximized with shelves, racks and cabinets.

Keith scurried about trying to straighten up but Georgia squeezed his arm and told him to go and tend to his family. He said it was a long drive, and told them to make themselves at home.

After he'd gone, Georgia disappeared into a bedroom. Maya wandered around the house, feeling anxious in a place that abounded with the intimate energy of people she did not know.

She watched some TV in search of some comforting familiarity. Halfway through an old episode of *The Honeymooners* she heard loud snoring streaming in from the hallway. She went to look. Georgia was lying flat on her back in the master bedroom, her arms at her sides, fully clothed. Maya slipped her shoes off and pulled a blanket over the large figure.

Damn, Maya thought. She had been about to ask if they would see David Orr the next day. For all she knew, they were flying to a new town in the morning. She sure hoped not.

She sauntered out to the porch, wondering how she could possibly fall asleep. What she really wanted was to take a good long walk, as she liked to do in Plainfield in the late hours, air out her mind, relax. But she didn't dare. Who knew what the night held in this alien place? And what about Fiske? Had he found a way to follow them? Was he out here lurking in the shadows, eyeing the house through binoculars? To these questions there were no answers.

Her favorite way to get drowsy was television, and she switched it on once again, settling this time on a docudrama about the Native American chief Crazy Horse, the Sioux warrior who defeated General Custer and his troops at the battle of Little Big Horn in 1876. She enjoyed the reenactment because it was different: it presented the story from the Native American point of view. But something about it gnawed at her, though she couldn't quite put her finger on it.

Then it hit her. The show was inaccurate! The battle of Little Big Horn hadn't happened that way at all. This version contradicted what she already knew to be true, the one depicted in the movie *Little Big Man*. That was the more accurate one.

Suddenly a meta-truth dawned on her. It was a difficult one to stomach. Her reference for reality was movies and television. She shook her head. It was true. She had guzzled it all down, uncritically, believed whatever they had fed her. And who exactly was this *they*? She didn't even know. They were the people who were attached to the names that ran across the screen at the ends of the shows.

How much of her worldview was created by others? Was *any* of it accurate? What really happened at Little Big Horn?

Feeling like an idiot, she turned off the TV. Still she wasn't tired. But she had to get to sleep. The only available bedroom belonged to Keith's kids—two boys, she could tell by the toys. She crawled into the lower bunk bed, paged through *The Sword in the Stone*, which was hidden under the pillow, and after an hour of tossing and turning, fell into a fitful sleep.

*   *   *

Georgia was obviously a morning person, buzzing happily around the kitchen fixing breakfast, the optimism and energy glowing in her eyes. Maya, on the other hand, lifted her coffee cup to her lips as if she were elevating a bowling ball, and prayed for a caffeine jump-start. With all the sugar she'd dumped in, it was a guarantee.

It wasn't *that* early. Maybe seven. She'd gotten about six hours of sleep. Just enough to eke by. Sunshine poured through the kitchen window, lighting up Georgia's well-lined face, and making Maya squint. So far, Maya had managed to get only a few bites of toast and jam into her jittery stomach. Heavy-eyed, trying to focus on Georgia, she managed to nod at the appropriate times as the older woman waxed nostalgic about her years in Taos.

"I came here mainly because I wanted to live near the mountain."

"What mountain?"

"Taos Mountain," Georgia said, pointing out the window. "That one."

Maya leaned over and saw the area outside in daylight for the first time. The housing development was in a valley at the base of the mountains, the land between the homes wild and overgrown, vastly different from the geometric perfection of Plainfield's subdivisions.

"See it?" Georgia said.

"Yes," Maya said, looking up at the peaks outside. She sipped the coffee, felt herself come to life. "What's so special about it?"

Georgia clucked. "With that attitude I doubt you'd last long around here."

"What do you mean?"

"You can't live here unless the mountain accepts you."

Maya laughed, imagining a judgmental mountain—geology with attitude. Then her curiosity overtook over. What *would* a mountain's consciousness be like?

It would be slow. Slowest on the planet, most likely. Slower than her beloved trees. By comparison the trees would blaze through their lives. A mountain's changes would be measured by the centuries, the millennia. Hundreds of generations of humans would have to pass before it would even take notice.

Maya asked, "So how do you know if the mountain accepts you?"

"You know if it doesn't," Georgia said. "You start to notice your life isn't working. Little things go awry. You can't find work. You're moody. You've become accident prone. You have car problems. You can't make friends. The flow of your life is gone. If that happens, you'd better start packing."

Maya was listening intently. She had always been attracted to anthropomorphism, the idea that non-human life forms and even inanimate objects can have personalities. Yes, it was crazy, but it was also fun. Maybe intelligence was common. Maybe everything on the planet—people, cats, pin cushions, fleas—was conscious, only operating at different frequencies, making communication or even awareness of the others impossible, each consciousness like a radio receiver that could only pick up one station, though many others existed.

Maya's eyes lit up. Suddenly she knew the location of her father. She turned to Georgia. "He's in those mountains."

"Yes," Georgia said. "That is correct."

Finally.

"Where?"

Georgia took a bite of an apple she was holding, then set it on the table.

"There are networks of tunnels under the mountains," she said. "Nobody knows who built them. Some people believe it was the ancient ones, the Anasazis, the Indians who lived here centuries ago. The whole area is sacred to the Pueblos here, off-limits to whites. You can get into a lot of trouble messing around in there."

"Then how can he be in there?"

"He was invited. A group from a Pueblo have been in contact with your father for some time through the vortex communications network. As far as I know he's the only white man ever accepted into this very secretive part of their culture."

"What is he doing in there?"

"He's attempting to initiate the change."

The change—back to the journal. "But is that really real?" Maya said.

Georgia looked at her the way a preacher might stare down at an unrepentant nonbeliever sitting in the front row of his church. "I hope so," she said. "Because it's already begun."

"How do you know? I don't see anything."

"You haven't looked."

"Where?"

"Pick something."

"I don't know. Medicine?"

"All right," Georgia said. "Western culture views the human body from a mechanistic point of view, as a machine. Consciousness exists only in the brain. The body is just a system of moving parts, like an engine. So, decade after decade medical schools churn out doctors who treat the body exactly as a mechanic does a car.

"But things are changing. Deeper truth finds a way. The mechanistic view—an excellent foundation for setting broken bones, controlling blood sugar or clearing arteries—is beginning to evolve. Expand. In time, the body will come to be seen as possessing all of the healing powers it will ever need. Because it does. The conscious redirection of body energies will soon be discovered to render many of our current practices obsolete. In the coming years, procedures such as surgery will come to be seen as barbaric. Non-invasive energy healing will replace it. This is already beginning."

"That's just normal progress," Maya objected. "It happens in every field."

"That's where you're wrong. We helped to engineer it. We worked on that change for years. It could just as easily have not happened. After all, it hasn't happened for this long. Ask yourself: Why now? Why not fifty years from now? Or fifty years ago?"

Maya shook her head. "You're telling me a few people changed the way medicine has evolved?"

"Yes," Georgia said, ever patient. "That's exactly what I'm telling you."

"It's hard to believe."

"So was air travel a century ago," Georgia said. "Do you know what the collective unconscious is?"

"Yes," Maya said. "It's a theory that says that all of our minds are linked together on an unconscious level."

Georgia nodded. "The collective unconscious is a kind of psychic playroom, where the symbols we use to communicate with each other are lying around like children's blocks. We pick them up, build with them. We use them to create language, mathematics, music, myth. I'm telling you this because it's key to what the Mandala is doing.

"Concepts like soul, or god, exist in every culture on this planet. Why? Because they are drawn from this common area. They are there for the people of Africa and China to discover and use just as they were there for the people of Europe and the Americas.

"The glorious images painted on the ceiling of the Sistine Chapel originated in the collective unconscious, couched in the imagery of the time. The Bible's stories, savior myths, Mozart's symphonies, Shakespeare's plays, Rembrandt's paintings, Aesop's fables—were all pulled from the same well, translated along the aesthetic guidelines of each interpreter's culture."

Maya had no problem accepting this. "All right," she said. "But how do you change the medical field?"

"Take away the 'un' and make it the collective *conscious*. Do you see? It's much more efficient to manifest change consciously."

Maya nodded, digesting.

"That's the theory," Georgia said. "Now for the practice."

She took another bite of the apple, then put it back on the table. "Long ago," she began, "I learned how to meditate. Now what many Westerners don't realize is that meditation is not just a relaxation exercise or a religious ritual; it's an entryway into a powerful and practical state of mind. I practiced for many years, learning how to enter into very deep states of consciousness. Now anybody can do this. I'm not professing to be anything special. With the help of a Mandala teacher, however, I was opened to many secrets."

Georgia paused, searching. Suddenly her face lit up. "Imagine an onion, with its many layers of skin. Say the outermost layer represents normal waking consciousness, the state we know so well, from which we talk, drive, work, make love, and so forth. At this rather shallow level our thoughts ping-pong around incessantly, chaotically. You know the feeling. We all do. In meditation, your awareness dips below this level, passing through deeper and deeper layers towards the onion's core. And what is at this core? Pure being. Undifferentiated awareness. The land beyond 'I.' It is where thoughts originate before they worm their way up through all the layers of consciousness to the outermost level, where they go *pop!* This *pop!* is what we experience as a conscious thought. 'Oh!' we say. 'I have to go to the dentist,' or 'I'm cold,' and so on. Do you understand?"

"Yes."

"Now as I meditate, descending ever deeper through the onion's layers, I approach this core, this source, this most powerful level. It is here that we can employ reality creation. If one can focus on a desire *while maintaining awareness* at this level, it will begin to take shape, first in the pre-physical world and then, if backed by sufficiently strong emotion, it will 'thicken' into an event in the real world.

"Now the closer you come to the onion's core, the quicker this process happens—meaning the faster your intention manifests. Sounds easy, yes? Well, there's a catch. It's almost impossible to maintain consciousness at this level. You lose focus, drift, fall into dreams, fantasies, or simply fail to arrive there. Years of practice and discipline are required. The top people of the Mandala have met these requirements. So, Maya, to sum up, what I do is enter a state of supreme empowerment and then simply *ask for what I want.*"

Maya asked, "Do you get it? Do you get what you want?"

"Today, tomorrow, next week, next month, or next year—provided I harbor no conflicting desires. Another catch, and a big one. For example, if I were to ask for wealth yet believed I was not worthy of it, the intention would not manifest. If I ask for love but fear intimacy, I won't get it. Do you understand?"

Maya nodded.

"Now, in order to achieve a *collective* change rather than an individual one, you need many minds working in unison—"

She was interrupted by the sound of a car arriving at the front of the house. Maya frowned. She wanted to hear more. They walked out to the porch. Keith had pulled right up on the lawn, sending a cloud of dust in all directions.

"Get your things," Georgia said in a general's tone of voice.

Maya obediently ran inside to collect her backpack.

Within minutes they were on the road again, passing through the downtown of tiny Taos, with its town square of art galleries, restaurants, plazas and resurrected trading post.

They were soon back on the highway, passing through the open desert. Again Maya drank in the wide open terrain, exalting in the sense of freedom it brought. They didn't stay in the flatlands long. Keith shifted into a lower gear, and they started up a steep road into the mountains. Acacia trees sprung up on hillsides that sparkled with gold poppies, as they zigzagged up the switchbacks.

The higher they climbed the fewer signs of civilization they saw, until Maya felt certain they were totally alone in the world. Not a single car passed in either direction for some time. Her stomach churned with anticipation.

The landscape looked—no, *felt*—truly alien, as though they'd passed through a time warp into the distant past. She half-expected to glimpse pre-historic hunters carrying bows and arrows, their eyes alert for prey animals, striding through the woods on the sides of the road.

"This doesn't feel like the United States," she said. "This feels like *before* it."

Keith laughed. "That's exactly why I'm here. You summed it up, Maya. Who needs all that government crap?"

"I hate to tell you this," Georgia said, "but this state has been in the union since nineteen-twelve."

"Not in spirit," Keith said.

A rough dirt road appeared behind a rocky area and Keith slowed down to turn sharply onto it. They bumped along for five minutes before coming to a small village carved out of a hillside, invisible to anyone who did not know it was here, like the rest of this hidden world. A few aging trailers and ten or twelve adobe houses looked as though they hadn't seen any change in decades. One object, however, seemed very out of place: a satellite TV dish on the roof of one of the trailers.

Why live all the way up here? she wondered. Where did they get food, supplies? It was a long way down the mountain. The advantage, she decided, was the total freedom, if that's what you wanted. You could do whatever you pleased here. *They*—the authorities—didn't exist in this world. But the isolation was frightening, too. Anything could happen and no one would ever know about it.

Keith pulled up to a shiny Airstream trailer, and its metal door opened immediately. A beautiful brown-skinned woman with long hair and striking features greeted them.

Keith said, "This is my wife, Maria. Maria, this is Maya."

Maria smiled. "Welcome," she said in a soft voice.

"Thank you."

"Hello, Maria," Georgia said, and then hugged her.

"This is my sister's home," Maria explained to Maya.

"Come in," Keith said.

Maya had never been inside a trailer, and immediately fell in love with it. It seemed to have everything a house did—in miniature, arranged ingeniously.

Maria had prepared a lunch of corn tortillas and chili stew, which she served on the dining table. The travelers crowded together and ate hungrily. Maya guzzled two glasses of water to douse the burning of the chilis. Maria, looking on, smiled. She said almost nothing, though. Keith and Maria's two boys chased each other through the woods outside.

After lunch, the group filed outside, and Keith handed a sturdy branch of desert ironwood that had been leaning against the trailer to Georgia.

The travelers bid Maria and the boys goodbye and set off across the settlement, as curious onlookers peeked out from behind the

windows of the little houses and trailers they passed. Maya, spooked
by the furtive glances, turned quickly to catch the eye of a man
watching them, but he shut his curtains quickly. She made a face
at him anyway.

"People are shy up here," Keith said. "Best not to get them
angry."

They began down a trail that led into a pine forest, striding at
a good pace among the dense trees, ascending and descending
many times, until Maya found herself struggling to draw a deep,
satisfying breath.

"Hold on a minute," she said, panting. "Why can't I breathe?"

Keith said, "I'd guess it's because you're a city slicker hiking at
seven thousand feet altitude."

"When did we get up that high?"

"When we got off the plane," Georgia said. "This is the southern
end of the Rockies."

"I'll slow down some," Keith said, "but we have to keep
moving."

Maya pushed herself to keep up. Both of her companions were
far older than she, yet she was the only one gasping for air. It was
embarrassing. They slowed to wait for her many times, and always
after the steeper inclines. Georgia was bounding jauntily along,
using her walking stick with every step. It was clear she didn't
need it; she just liked it.

They came to a ridge which formed the outer edge of an
immense bowl-like gorge, and Maya looked down in wonder at
thousands upon thousands of treetops sweeping all the way down
to the bottom before sloping back up the opposite side. It looked
like a huge crater seeded with trees. Maybe that's what it was. She
didn't ask. Beyond it, the mountains rode one after another into
the distance.

They rested there, sitting on a fallen tree trunk. Keith passed
around a canteen, and Maya drank thirstily of the cool water. They
didn't stay long, though. Before she had fully caught her breath,
Keith led them back onto the trail, climbing again. Sighing, Maya
did her best to keep up.

The sun climbed high overhead, warming the air. Pine needles scattered all over the ground gave off a pleasant, toasty aroma. Feeling hypnotized by the scent, Maya yawned. She wanted so badly to lay down, just for a few minutes. It would have felt so good.

"Move it along," Keith called out, no doubt aware of the welcoming scent. And so Maya trudged on.

The next stretch was the most difficult of all. Thick, leafy branches and rutted, uneven ground made moving forward require more concentration than when the trail had been wide and easy to maneuver. Maya, exhausted, reaching the end of her endurance, was about to just stop when the trail abruptly came to an end.

A solid wall of forest stood before them, in every direction except backwards.

"What now?" Maya said, crouched over, hands on her thighs, catching her breath.

"This," Keith said.

He walked over to where the vegetation was thickest, where Maya couldn't see even two feet in, got down on all fours, lifted several branches out of his way with the back of his arm, and crept straight into the underbrush.

"You've got to be kidding," she said.

"Watch out for snakes," he called out.

"*Snakes?*"

"Think nice of them and they'll do the same for you," came the reply.

Georgia took her arm. "I'm afraid we can't waste time," she said. "It's the only way to get where we're going."

Maya wondered, Why are we in such a hurry?

The older woman, with her incredible stamina, followed Keith in, and having no other choice, Maya bent down and tentatively slid into the undergrowth, her eyes glued to the ground for any trace of slithering.

After ten interminably long minutes of creeping, which scratched her arms from wrist to elbow, she emerged, dirt-covered, in a sunlit grove of trees. Without knowing why, Maya felt a sense of total peace. She ran her hand along the delicate trunk of a sapling, overwhelmed with awe by the beauty of the undisturbed forest.

The trail started up again but the terrain changed markedly. The soft dirt of the forest gave way to hard rock, and Keith leaped sure-footed from boulder to boulder as Georgia and Maya followed. Maya rock-walked with ease, welcoming the concentration it required. It took her mind off her fatigue.

Then something changed, shifted, in her. With each step she felt her energy returning. At first she thought nothing of it but within a few minutes she was overflowing with stamina. She could hardly believe it. She had been bone tired just minutes earlier yet now she felt certain she could stuff several heavy boulders in her pack and haul them the rest of the way with no problem. It seemed somehow more than just a second wind. What had changed? Had gravity diminished?

They stopped in the shade of some trees, and Keith handed her a trail mix of nuts, raisins and chocolates along with the canteen. She ate and drank, and all was good.

Keith took off his hat, wiped sweat from his brow.

Georgia was grinning. Looking at Maya, she said, "Can you feel it?"

"Totally," Maya said. "What is it?"

"The vortex," Keith said.

"You can *feel* it?"

He nodded. "We can."

"Even an old bag like me can hike like a trooper here," Georgia said. "This is the very energy the ancients used to build the great structures that time could not destroy: the pyramids, Stonehenge, Easter Island, all of those things. All of those places are near vortexes. They use this exact energy."

"Yes, but how—"

"*Shh*," Keith hissed.

Maya froze. "What?"

"They're here," he whispered, nodding toward the woods.

"Who? Who's here?"

"*Look, there*," he said in a voice that held no trace of humor.

CHAPTER 16

The boy looked as though he was growing right out of the tree. Unblinking eyes locked onto her from between the leaves.

He emerged from the shadows, his face painted in scarlet and olive, his long black hair braided neatly, a breechcloth and leggings the only clothes on his slender, muscular body. He was young, perhaps in his mid-teens, and small.

Standing in the sunlight now, the painted boy inspected the group imperiously, his gaze settling on them one by one. Georgia and Keith didn't move. Maya followed their lead.

The boy pointed at Maya.

Maya's heart started to race.

Keith nodded.

Maya turned to Keith, panic in her eyes. Georgia whispered, "Don't be afraid, dear. It's what you've been waiting for."

The boy stood unmoving, staring at Maya.

"I don't *think* so," she said out of the corner of her mouth.

Georgia leaned in closer now, careful not to startle her, nudged her forward. "Go."

"With *him*?"

"Yes!"

Now Maya turned to Keith, hoping for a different response. But he just shook his head.

Horrified, she turned back to the painted boy.

"Come," he said.

Maya didn't move.

Now Georgia was insistent. "Listen to me. If you want to see your father, you'd better go with him."

Keith said, "Go!"

The boy waved his hand impatiently.

Still she didn't move.

"I'm not going to hurt you," he said in perfect American English. Then he smiled widely, displaying several crooked teeth.

Maya, baffled, couldn't help but smile back at him. "Okay," she said, stepping forward.

*   *   *

They didn't speak for some time. She followed a few paces behind as he led her up a trail that ran alongside a sheer face of solid rock, a gentle upward grade. As they climbed, the drop-off on the right grew longer, and she frequently reached out to touch the wall to her left to assure herself that something solid was at least on one side of her.

The trail narrowed, bringing her uncomfortably close to the drop-off in places. At these times she shuffled forward slowly, hardly lifting her tennis shoes off the rock. The boy moved along effortlessly, occasionally turning to check on her, sometimes calling out for her to be careful, his voice impatient.

They came to a two-foot break in the ledge that he easily stepped across. Maya approached it and hesitated, her gaze drawn to the treetops below. The terror of the long fall came alive in her mind, just as the plane crash had when she sat waiting for the flight to Chicago to take off, with all of its gory consequences. The thought was involuntary, and did not help matters at all.

"I can't do this," she said.

"Yes, you can."

"No. Really."

He stepped back toward her from the other side. "Walk across and I will catch you on this side."

Easy for you to say, she thought.

There was no other choice, of course, so she inhaled deeply, steeled herself, and with the boy urging her on, lifted her foot to cross—and caught her toe on a rock.

As she fell she grabbed desperately for the wall to the left but it was too smooth and yielded no catch. Her fingernails scraped white lines along the rock, as her body slid downwards into a hundred feet of empty air.

She opened her mouth to scream but no sound emerged. The bleak fantasy now exploded into her awareness: the terrifying fall, her form bouncing through the sharp branches below, the scrapes and punctures to her face and body . . .

Then, suddenly, she was hanging in midair, swinging like a pendulum from side to side, her body dangling over the great space of empty air above trees that seemed to be calling out to her.

Her wrist was burning. Something had latched itself onto it, was squeezing tightly. She craned her head up to look, straining against gravity and the leaden weight of her body. The boy's hands had welded themselves onto her wrist.

She grabbed at the ledge with her free hand, and found a catch for her foot in the rock. With remarkable strength, the boy pulled her up onto the trail as she pushed up with her foot.

She dropped thudding onto the ledge, suddenly drenched in sweat, and collapsed beside him, adrenaline shooting through her like an electrical current. She was trembling from head to toe. When she turned she saw that the boy's chest was rising and falling in powerful spasms, too, in perfect unison with hers. After a seeming eternity, her breaths began to slow. She turned to him, leaning against the wall beside her.

"You saved my life."

"I had to," he said, feigning calmness, his voice shaky. "If I didn't, I'd be in big trouble. Next time you should watch where you're going."

"What's your name?"

"José."

"Thank you, José."

"You're welcome, Maya."

"You know me."

"Of course," he said. "I just don't know what you're going to do."

With these cryptic words, he jumped up to his feet and began up the trail again, swiftly, as if he'd already forgotten the harrowing incident. She was loathe to continue but she knew she had no choice. To her relief, the path widened, so that she was able to lean far over to the left, a good distance from the cliff. José slowed for her, and she caught up to him.

"What did you mean back there?" she asked.

"You'll see."

"'You'll see'? That's it?"

"Yes. You'll see."

"Why does everyone have to be so secretive? What does that mean?"

"I don't know," he said, speeding up, as if to escape her questions.

"Yes, you do," she called out. "And you're going to tell me."

He didn't respond, just kept walking.

"I really appreciate what you did," she yelled out, "but I'm not moving until you tell me what's going on. Bye!" She stopped.

In seconds he was standing beside her, looking concerned. "We're almost there. Can't you wait a few minutes?"

She sighed. They started off again.

With each step she found herself becoming increasingly frightened. At one point, the urge to turn back was overwhelming. She had to fight to keep moving. She had no idea where she was, no clue what she was walking into, and her only friends in the area were far away now and growing ever more distant.

José walked the elevated trail as if it were a wide open field. Eventually, to her great relief, they began to descend. A long, easy downhill led them into a grassy clearing. At one point they practically had to duck as a flock of low-flying birds buzzed by overhead.

"Did you see that?" the boy said excitedly.

"What?"

"How many did you count?"

"How many what? Birds?"

"I saw four," he said. "Four different kinds. It's a sign."

"What are you talking about?"

"Different kinds of birds flocking together. It means we're near the source. Strange things happen at the source."

"Strange? How strange?"

"Strange."

She shook her head. Maybe it was best not to speak to José until they arrived at their destination.

They came to a rock outcropping at the far end of the clearing. "This is it," he said. "Are you ready?"

"For what?"

"For what you were curious about."

He held a finger across his lips for silence, and walking slowly, led her around to the other side of the outcropping.

The scene before them froze her in her tracks.

Many beautiful rock formations ringed a dirt clearing, its furthest wall formed by the side of the mountain. At the base of this wall stood a long flat ledge of rock, a natural platform about ten feet above the ground. Footholds had been chiseled in the rock below it as a way to climb up. A dark hole at the back led into the mountain. A cave, Maya presumed.

Halfway between the cave entrance and the spot where she stood with José, a dozen men sat cross-legged in the dirt, as silent as statues, forming a semi-circle that faced the cave. They were dressed in breechcloths like José, their heads wrapped in white shawls which glowed brightly against their dark skin.

The wind kicked up. Dust swept off the ground and into the eyes of several of the men, but they did not move. Even when tears began to stream down the cheeks of one of the men, he remained perfectly still. All of them seemed to be frozen in place. A tall man in the center, the only one not sitting, knelt on his knees, perfectly still, just like the others.

The sight that turned Maya's blood to ice water and made the hairs on the back of her neck stand on end wasn't the arc of still figures. It was the scene in front of them.

In between the cave and the men, a line of wolves were reared back on their hind legs, ready to spring, issuing throaty sounds so frightening that Maya's stomach squeezed into a knot.

The wolves' positions on the dirt exactly mirrored the arc of the men, one animal in front of every man.

Her only thought was *run*. To hell with New Mexico and Indians and the Mandala, and even her father . . .

Go!

Suddenly one of the wolves jerked its nose up and began to sniff the air, sweeping its head from left to right, back and forth, searching. Then the rest of the animals snapped to attention, sniffing loudly, moving off their positions, pacing in tight circles yet never breaching the invisible boundary formed by the line of men.

José touched her arm and she jumped, alarmed, and with that movement several wolves bucked their heads her way. Maya felt as if their eyes were reaching into her, probing at her insides. One of the wolves stepped toward her. She felt the muscles of her legs go soft, her knees become jelly. She couldn't run now—or walk—even if she had somewhere to run or walk to.

José, who seemed also on edge, put his arm around her waist, turned her around and carefully guided her back around the outcropping, out of sight of the animals and the men. Immediately the loud snarling on the other side quieted down.

Maya fell to the ground. José knelt beside her.

Almost in tears, she said, "What are we doing here?"

"Don't you remember what the old woman said?"

"No!"

"Your father is inside that cave."

"Why?"

"He's in the vortex."

She shook her head. Her eyes began to moisten.

No tears!

She couldn't let go, not now.

In a childlike voice, she said, "I have to go in that cave?"

He nodded.

"What about those—what are they, wolves?"

"Yes, of course."

Then the irony struck her: wolves! Had her inner wolf come to life in the real world, reproduced itself and found a way to really

stand her down? Had *she* created them somehow? Quickly she
shook off this thought.

She said, "Can you get rid of them?"

He shook his head.

"What am I supposed to do, just mosey on in?"

He smiled, the crooked teeth shining. "Then you understand."

"No, I don't!"

"You're supposed to get him out," he said impatiently.

She looked at him as if he were insane. "What?"

"Didn't they tell you?"

"You're the ones keeping him in there, you get him out."

"You don't understand," he said. "*He* is in control. *He* is moving
the wolves. And the birds, and everything else. We cannot pass
through. But you can."

"Listen, José, I've got an idea. Why don't we just get the hell
out of here?"

He shook his head, the frustration too much for him. "Wait
here."

"Where are you going?" she called out as he disappeared beyond
the outcropping. "Don't leave me here!"

But he was gone. Immediately the growling grew louder on
the other side.

She waited, confused, angry, absent-mindedly scraping lines
in the dirt with her fingers. Sarcastically, she thought: Was this
not funny? It was hilarious. It was absurd. She'd come so far, and
yes, she wanted to meet her father. But this, this was too much.

Wolves. Of all things.

Maybe her father wasn't really in there. How did she know
what the real truth was? And who was this coming toward her?

"I'm Walking Bear," said the tall man from the semi-circle, the
one who had been kneeling. He sat on the ground beside her.

"My son is a good boy," he said in a warm voice, "but sometimes
he talks too much. I will answer your questions, Maya."

"Good," she said.

"José says you are afraid," he said. "This I understand. The

wolves sound ferocious, do they not?" He made a growling face
and a gesture of outstretched claws.

"Are you joking?"

"If it were me I would be very scared."

"You've got it, brother."

"They could rip you to shreds."

"Duh."

"If I could go in for you, I would."

"Is he really in there?"

"Ah," he nodded. "You do not believe."

He looked into her eyes so deeply that she couldn't break out
of his stare.

"A good, strong soul, as I thought," he said. "Can I ask you
something? Did you almost have a car wreck recently?"

Her jaw dropped. "How did you know that?"

"And did someone help you put the brakes on?"

This statement stunned her so completely that she forgot where
she was. The wolves, the cave, her father—they all disappeared. It
was as though he had done a jujitsu move on her.

"Some*one*?"

She knew he was referring to the accident in Glendale, the
braking of the car that did not seem of her doing, that she had
assumed—with a ninety percent probability—was an act of body
consciousness. Now that figure was dropping fast. Another
explanation occurred to her.

No. It couldn't be.

When she looked up at him she could see he was absorbing
her reaction, watching her think. She turned away, toward the
outcropping.

"Don't worry about them," he said. "They are simple creatures.
Their orders are clear. Do you want to know what those orders
are?"

"No."

He smiled. "I'll tell you anyway: to allow no one in but you."

"Me?"

"Yes. And I think you owe it to your father, who saved your life, to go in and see him. If only to thank him."

"He did that? How? How do you know?"

Walking Bear nodded. "I know many things, Maya. You had help. You are lucky. Now it's your turn to repay this kindness."

"By getting eaten?"

"I want to be honest with you," he said. "We have a problem. Your father believes he can save the world all by himself. That's folly. He's been inside far too long. You must get him out. He will no longer listen to us. I promise, the wolves will not touch you. Sit and be with this. Take your time. We will wait. And when you are ready, come."

"I don't need any time. I can tell you right now—"

"No, you can't. Sit awhile. Don't worry, we're not going anywhere."

He walked off, leaving her alone.

For a moment she considered turning and leaving but she knew she couldn't. Not now. She was trapped. She had to be courageous. It felt lousy.

She sat. Time passed. She hardly moved. She'd had no idea she could sit so long. The solar disc coasted across the sky, its warmth disappearing as it got caught somewhere in the trees. Her stomach hurt. Her legs ached. She felt somehow different. Something had changed. No, snapped. Broke. Maybe her anxiety had reached such a fevered pitch that her nervous system had short-circuited.

Her life dispersed into a fog of unreality. She had trouble recalling the past. What did she care about? She didn't know. School and boys and friends and Muriel and the meaning of life—these things resembled words in a book she'd read years ago. She could only recall the broad strokes, not the details. The only real aspect of her life was the grassy clearing, the rock outcropping, and what lay beyond it. The wolves, the cave . . . they were real. And ultimately, her meeting with her father, if it were really going to happen. All else had receded into the background. Her whole life had been subsumed into a single, intense point.

It was almost dark when she rounded the outcropping, her face an expressionless mask. She was no longer Maya; not the old one, anyway. That skin had molted, without warning, seemingly in a tick of the clock. She had left it in the dirt on the other side of the rocks. She had deepened, become older. Even her gait had changed. It was slow, deliberate.

Had she been able to see herself she would have been shocked. The familiar, the stubborn, but the mostly agreeable Maya Burke had grown up, all the way. It was necessary, or the task could not have been done. Maybe there should have been more of a fight. The old had yielded so easily.

Still she couldn't find her memories. They didn't serve, didn't help the moment. The essence of her had been laid bare, to clear herself, to prepare. Her mind had become unclouded, receptive, tuned only to what was happening right now.

As she approached the arc of men from behind she felt new strength surge through her, perhaps borne of her inner self, maybe even of ancient origin. The burden of the past had slipped away. She had made peace with it. How? She didn't know.

She had seen her own death, again, only now it was the wolves, ripping her apart. Grotesque, yes. There was nothing to do but accept it.

No one in the circle moved; no one acknowledged her, save for Walking Bear, who came over holding a small pouch made of animal hide. He nodded to her, solemnly, and she felt his strength pass into her.

Fastening the bag to her belt, he said, "You are your father's daughter."

Yes, I am, she thought.

She turned around, stepped through his place in the circle, past the men-statues, into the unknown, her eyes focused straight ahead. She was past fear, caring, desire, liberated by the freedom of complete detachment.

The animals sprang to life, growling through yellow-stained teeth. She thought of what José had said, even through the intensity of the moment. He was right. The unbroken line before her did seem controlled.

Another step, and the din grew louder.

Forward.

Despite her newfound strength, intense fear overcame her. She did her best to push past it. So close was she to the animals she could smell their fetid breath. It didn't matter. They didn't matter. She had resolved to die, which meant to cherish the moment beyond all else.

Forward, she commanded herself through the resistance of her body.

Suddenly she was floating. Her body was gone, melted away like a block of ice in a furnace blast, a puddle on the ground. She was free. Free of the world. Weightless. She wanted to say—and maybe she did—"Thank you, thank you God, for everything, the whole trip, whatever it was about . . ."

She *had* done all right, hadn't she? If there was a celestial accounting to come, she'd fare well. Feelings of love as she'd never known filled her, for everyone she'd ever known, every experience she'd ever had. For the whole planet and all of its intense and wonderful life forms, for everyone whom she had touched or had touched her, even in the smallest way. It didn't matter what had happened or who was at fault. Regret didn't exist, not in this state.

I love everyone! Muriel, Josh, Brandon, Georgia, Fiske, myself . . . I love them all!

The wolf that had been standing in front of her lowered its head, turned, and walked away.

I love everyone!

Suddenly she realized what had happened. The animals had fallen silent. She could almost hear the breathing of the men behind her. She looked in front of her. The space was open. The wolves were all sitting, calmly watching her.

She turned toward the men. Still they wore blank looks; all but José, whose face was lit up in surprise. Walking Bear, kneeling in the center, implored her with his eyes: Move!

She stepped through the gap, and stood facing the entrance to the cave.

Immediately the gap closed and the wolves reassumed their defiant barrier, exactly as before, with all its terrifying sounds. Only now the Indians jumped up and erupted in cheers. The scene was surreal.

"Keep going!" shouted Walking Bear. "Don't look back!"

She hurried to the base of the cave and started up the footholds, climbing up to the platform where she knew she would be safe, for the wolves could not reach her there. Looking down, she grinned and waved at the men, sharing their excitement.

"Bring him out!" Walking Bear shouted.

"How—"

"The tunnel."

She crouched down and stepped through the cave entrance into a large anteroom lit by slants of sunlight that knifed in from cracks in ceiling. She saw a lightless hole at the back wall, the passageway in.

The pouch that Walking Bear had given her held a flashlight, some dried meat, bread in a container, a skin of water, candles, matches and extra batteries. She took the flashlight out, pulled the drawstring tight and fastened the pouch to her belt.

Squatting down at the passageway at the back wall, she switched on the flashlight. The beam illuminated a long, narrow tunnel which snaked out of sight. When she switched off the light it was as though she were looking into a cat's black eye.

Excitement stirred in her belly. *He's here.*

She glanced back at the main chamber a final time, then ducked into the tunnel, which was just barely wider than her body, so that she had to shuffle forward on her stomach to advance.

She crawled along for some time, the quiet broken only by the scraping of her jeans against the rock floor. The light shot around, throwing shadows on the bumpy walls, sometimes lighting the long corridor before her.

She had no idea how much time had passed—maybe twenty minutes, maybe an hour—when the tunnel opened into a cramped little room, perhaps as large as her car. Sitting down, she stretched her legs out as hard as she could to ease her cramped muscles.

Beneath her, in a crack in the floor, a stream washed over some colorful stones which shimmered in the flashlight's beam. She wanted to grab a few but decided against it. Better just to let things lie.

She shone the light into a dark space at the opposite end of the chamber, and seeing that it was a passageway, crawled into it. Again she scraped forward for some time before the tunnel brought her into another room, this one far larger than the last. She was amazed to find that it was as big as a classroom. Now, for the first time since she had entered the mountain she was able to stand up. The ceiling was high, too tall to touch. A group of large boulders had been arranged in a circle in the center of the room.

She shined the beam up at the ceiling, which was black with soot; then over to a wall where it illuminated several line drawings. Her eyes lit up. Was this prehistoric art in its natural state?

Excitedly she hurried over, brought her face up close to the petroglyphs and looked on in amazement at faded line drawings of animals and people. Then the beam settled on an image that chilled her: the webbed earth.

She looked closer. The earth had been drawn as round. Prehistoric peoples didn't know the shape of the planet. They didn't even know it *was* a planet. The images couldn't be that old then. Maybe the Mandala, or the Indians, or their ancestors, had drawn them. It made the most sense.

She sat on a boulder, pressing her palms against the cold stone, comforted by its solidity. She liked being in the cave. She was *inside* a mountain. This place was *old*. Her friends had often complained that her head was always up in the clouds, that she needed grounding. Well, here it was: the belly of a mountain. It didn't get any more grounding than that.

Sitting in this unusual place, her old life seemed so far away, beyond grasp. All of the world did, the whole of modern civilization. In fact—

Something moved.

"Hello?" she said, jumping to her feet, shining the flashlight around in every direction. "Anybody there? Who's here?"

The light ricocheted off the rocky walls, strobe-like, bringing the cave to life with movement, frightening her even more.

She heard a voice, soft, almost inaudible.

"Can you please turn that off?"

Startled, she dropped the flashlight. It hit the floor and rolled into a crevice, its beam stuck pointing up at the ceiling. Pale, indirect light shined in the direction of the voice.

There, on the far wall in the gray dimness, perched on a high ledge, sat her father, David Orr.

CHAPTER 17

Maya picked up the flashlight and switched it off, and the chamber was immediately swallowed up in darkness. Endless, absolute night.

His voice fluttered over to her through the invisible air, as though on gently beating wings: "Maya?"

"It's me," she said nervously. Though the cave was cool, her forehead had become moist with perspiration.

"I'm pleased," he said.

This is it, she thought. What she had so eagerly waited for, almost her entire life. She took a moment to acknowledge herself: she had done it. It hadn't come to her. But she was stuck. She'd sought, found, and now, face to face with the object of her search, she was unable to utter a single word.

Say something!

"Uh . . ."

The moment was so big, so heavy, she couldn't seem to manage it. She kept tripping over her own thoughts. What should her first words be? She had so many questions, she couldn't think of one.

Maybe he realized this, because more softly-spoken words drifted over. "I was the one holding you."

What? What was that? She didn't understand, didn't know how to respond.

"When you were a baby," he said. "You would fall asleep to that song, 'Country Girl.' Do you remember?"

She *did* remember—not being a baby listening to that song but watching a baby in the arms of a dark-haired man listening to a song, in her vortex vision.

It *was* him. And her.

"That was real?"

"Oh yes."

How did he know she had seen it?

"The answer to your next question, Maya, is that I can perceive the thoughts of others when we are both at vortexes. I saw your vision, too."

Hearing this she felt as though the air had been knocked out of her. She didn't feel that her privacy was invaded, though she was not sure why.

"I believe you," she said.

Breathe. Don't rush it. There's plenty of time. *Plenty* of time. She put her hand on her chest, felt it rise and fall.

I'm calm, she said to herself. Standing in the pitch black. I'm calm.

Slowly she came back to herself. A strong urge overtook her, the desire to shower him with information. Everything. Who she was, what she had done, growing up, school, the last weeks, Porter, Fiske . . . everything. The information wanted to spew forth in a torrent.

"How is your mother?" he asked.

At the mention of Muriel, Maya's feelings shifted in a way she could never have predicted. Something unwelcome had intruded on the reunion, something she hadn't planned on. To her surprise, what she felt was anguish, the pain of abandonment. What was happening? Why were Muriel's feelings suddenly so dominant in her? She wanted to lash out at him. He had left. He had abandoned them.

Yes, she knew why. He had to. But that didn't matter, not now, not in the grip of what was holding her.

Couldn't he have gotten a message to her all these years?

Stop it.

She couldn't stop it. The anger flowed. Why couldn't she just be happy to be there with him?

Of all emotions she could be experiencing, she felt close to Muriel, and with it came the urge to forgive her. She was stunned. She wanted to shout out to him, *You ruined her life! What have you to say for yourself?*

"Did she remarry?"

"No," Maya said through clenched teeth.

She wanted to walk, to pace, to throw off anxiety, to hit something, to do anything but stand still in blackness so complete it blotted out the whole world. For all she knew, nuclear winter covered the planet and the world's population had been irradiated into extinction.

Emotions pushed against the walls of her psyche, trying to break through. She was about to crack, she could feel it.

Get control!

She wanted to scream. Or cry. Or rage. No, she didn't want to do any of them. She simply wanted him to answer, to salve a grief of twenty years, to change the past, to repair it.

"Why didn't you ever contact me?" she asked.

An eternity seemed to pass without a word, the only sound in the black void her ever-quickening breaths. He did not answer, so she spoke again. Something easier, maybe.

"Georgia told me how you've had to live in hiding all these years."

"It was never safe for me," he said. "Not only for me, but for you and your mother."

She pushed; she had to know. "Georgia could have gotten me a message, just to let me know you existed."

"What did your mother tell you about me?" he said.

"She never talked about you."

"Nothing at all?"

"No."

"This is not easy."

He paused, then said, "Long ago Georgia and I decided it was best if you knew nothing of me. We wanted you to be free of the danger that had become an inseparable part of who I am, free of a desire that couldn't be satisfied. The truth is, I didn't know how long I'd last."

"Don't you see how wrong that is? Even one letter would have been enough. I've always wanted to know you."

She wanted to get closer. She didn't want to wait. Never mind the past. The past was dead. She said, "Can I see you?"

She had to wait for an answer. Finally he said, "All right. But be careful with that light."

She pointed it at the ground, switched it on, and the lower part of the chamber suddenly exploded in light. The walls looked sharper than before, undulating with every movement of the beam.

He was sitting on a high ledge, she could see, a shadowy figure set against the cave wall. She swallowed hard, toeing her way up, carefully shining the light downward, away from him. She reached the ledge and pulled herself up onto it, and there she was, right in front of him, her father. And she wanted to scream.

A thick fur coat covered his body. His head, poking out of the top, was mostly hair—awful, tangled hair—with a round pinkish area in the center, his face. Somewhere the beard stopped and the hair started, but it was impossible to tell where. Gaunt, pocked cheekbones pushed through the bird's nest. A pale protuberance stuck out of the middle: his nose. The eyes were all but invisible, lost at the bottom of dark wells, craters in sickly bone white skin.

Then he smiled, oblivious to her revulsion, and she melted. The nose seemed to shorten, the eyes became friendly, the beard shift away from his mouth to reveal straight white teeth.

"Maya," he said. His voice sounded so small, so weak, so, yes, innocent.

Whatever she thought, or felt, this was her father, her blood. The photo that Fiske had shown her was of a completely different being.

"I found your journal," she said.

"I wrote that for you."

"But how did you expect me to find it?"

He leaned back, thinking. Maybe this was hard for him, too. She said, "I thought you willed me to find it."

"I did," he said. "At first. Then I changed my mind. As time passed and the dangers increased, I decided you'd be better off not knowing what was in it. The truth is, I'm surprised you found it." He paused, then said: "I know Georgia wants me out of here. That's why she sent you. She's a good woman, Georgia."

"Yes, she is."

Maya moved in closer, leaned against the wall beside him. A pungent odor now hit her, and she resisted a grimace. Swallowing hard, she said, "Is this spot all right?"

He nodded, the great beard moving up and down.

Now she saw that his feet extended out past the bottom of the fur. No shoes. Long, crooked nails protruded from his toes like live roots. She also noticed a tunnel on the other side of him.

"How long have you been in here?" she said.

"I don't know."

"Georgia said six months."

"Maybe so."

"What do you eat?"

"I have supplies, but mostly the vortex sustains me." He pulled the fur sleeves up and lifted his emaciated arms into the air as if to prove his vitality, but he made the opposite point instead.

Looking at this pathetic, half-starved figure, her own flesh and blood, a primal urge took hold of her. She wanted to take him by the hand and rush him out, out of this dark, cold place into the clean air, nurse him back to health, care for him, shower him with attention.

She had never wanted to save anybody, but here it was. She needed time with him, needed to learn about him, to find out what had happened all the way back to the beginning, to her beginning; to Plainfield, and beyond.

"Come out with me," she said.

"I can't, not yet."

"When?"

"When the change is firmly in place."

"How will you know?"

"I will."

"How? What will happen?"

"It will start with little things. People's behavior. They will think and act differently, do things they would not have done otherwise. Good things."

"That's a nice goal."

"Yes, it is."

"Except one thing."

"What?"

"You're ill. You're weak. If you don't get out of here you may not make it until then."

He raised his hand dismissively. "The work is more important than one man."

"Yes, I know," she said, sensing an opening. "Can you show me?"

"Show you?"

"What you do. How you use the vortex. I've done it."

"No," he said, shaking his head. "What you did at Edgar Porter's is child's play compared to what happens here."

"Show me, then. Guide me," she insisted. "I have the ability. Everyone says so."

"No."

"It's my destiny," she said. "I'm like you."

He looked at her, then fell silent. He closed his eyes, disappeared inward. Finally, he turned to her.

"Are you sure you want to do this?" he said.

"Absolutely."

"Then turn off the light."

She did, and darkness engulfed them again. She leaned against the wall, waiting. For what, she did not know.

It happened fast. A buzzing sensation shot through her body, and then a numbness spread in her, starting at her fingertips and toes and advancing slowly toward her abdomen. It wasn't painful, just surprising. Her thoughts seemed to be disjointed, too, fluttering around like hummingbirds darting from tree to tree, never alighting anywhere.

Somehow she had moved. She was no longer in the cave. She was in a room, standing beside . . . Uncle Buddy! He was sitting on the edge of a bed, reading a magazine. Buddy! She wanted to speak to him, ask where he was, but before she could say anything he was gone. The scene had dissolved, just as in a dream, and she was back in darkness. Was she in the cave?

No. She was somewhere else, floating . . . *Oh my God!* . . . surrounded by stars, listening to the sound of her breathing coming from all around her. But it couldn't be. It was too loud, too pervasive. It gained in volume until it was deafening, as if the whole universe had suddenly come alive.

Then she saw where she was: the outer arm of a great galaxy. Long trails of bluish-white stars crept slowly in great curves around an invisible center point. She marveled at the beatific sight, which was clearer than anything she'd ever seen, as though a newer, sharper set of eyes had come to life.

She realized that somehow she had moved again, this time close to the swirling center. No, not close—directly over it. Below her, bright light poured out from the center point, and she could see that the closest stars were no longer points of light but violent, fiery suns shooting long, angry arms out into space. The suns were falling, like marbles, as if down a waterfall, one by one, disappearing into the spinning funnel at the galaxy's center.

She felt something pull at her, mildly at first and then insistently, and suddenly she was falling directly into the whirlpool among the bright suns.

"Let go!" she heard her father say, from somewhere.

Screaming all the way, she plunged downward.

"Keep going!" he yelled. "I'm with you."

Where? Where are you? Where am I?

Had she said it or thought it? She didn't know.

"You're in the inner medium! Follow your feelings!"

Shrieking soundlessly she sped into the bright tunnel. A clamor erupted around her, and then—

Quiet.

No. A sound. Crickets.

Crickets?

She looked at her body. It seemed solid. She squeezed her arms and legs. Yes, she was real. But where? Where was she real?

She then recognized the location, which should have shocked her, but she was beyond surprise.

She was sitting on a picnic table under a tree, beside a lake with rushes in the shallows, a bright blue sky overhead—and someone tapping her on the shoulder.

My God, she thought. *I'm awake in my dream.*

She turned, and yes, it was him, but this time he was not a hairy caveman. A healthy, vibrant David Orr, dressed in a flowing white robe smiled comfortingly at her. The ecstasy came, as it always had in the dream, only this time she was aware of it at the moment it occurred instead of after it was over.

He took her hand and led her away into the foothills, just as he always had. She felt so happy she was certain if she had let go of him she would have floated into the sky like a balloon.

They walked into the foothills, passing beyond the borders of her dream, and came to a settlement of old houses with porches and swings and big front yards. Children laughed and waved from perches in the trees. She wanted to go to them, to play, without knowing why, but her father urged her on, without speaking a word. She just *knew*.

They arrived at a house that was far different from the others, shaped like a pyramid and reaching up into the treetops. Windows opened out onto the surrounding woods. They walked inside.

The interior was unbroken by rooms, just a large space rising up to an open point at the top through which trees could be seen. The floor was smoothly polished wood. Several men and women dressed in white smocks just like David's sat on pillows arranged in a circle, their eyes open yet seeming to be focused on nothing at all.

A moon-faced woman with bright blue eyes looked at Maya and smiled, then stood up and walked toward the outside wall.

Follow your feelings.

Maya knew what to do. In this place, wherever it was, you just *knew* things. She glanced at her father, who nodded his assent. Then she took the woman's place on the floor.

The group—she counted six men and five other women—looked at her with strange, dreamy eyes that slowly began to close. Maya's eyelids grew heavy, too, and she allowed them to drop. Immediately she felt a warm sensation enter her from the direction of the man on her right and pass through her to the woman on her left. Waves of euphoria washed through her, and again she felt happy. No action was necessary. Just *being* was enough.

She opened her eyes, and to her surprise saw she was no longer sitting on the floor but floating in the air above the building, peering down through the opening at the people below. She gasped, looking at her own body with the others, but the happiness she felt overwhelmed her fear.

Think of the future, he had said, and she did.

The scene changed.

Skyscrapers rose out of an island city. She recognized it immediately: New York City.

But something was different. The streets were nearly empty. No crowds, no rushing taxis, no flashing neon, no billboards, no commotion. Just quiet. Eerie quiet.

Where was everyone? The few people she saw walked the sidewalks in a way that surprised her, many of them hand in hand, hugging, weeping, intensely conversing, not marching purposefully as the people of the city normally did. On one street, an old man fell down and a couple rushed to help him up. Afterwards, they all embraced.

Hovering over the green expanse of Central Park, she saw thousands of people stretched out on the grass lawns, on the hills, around the lakes, in groups of twenty or thirty. Always in groups. Why? What were they doing?

She moved laterally, to the East Side. Like silent bookends, the tall buildings girding the park were devoid of activity. She drifted over to them, hanging in the air like a ghost, confirming the paucity of activity. She approached a tavern, a restaurant, an apartment building. Doors were open but nobody was home. The electronics of the age, too, were silent.

She wondered about the rural areas of this world, this dream, this mystery, and suddenly she was far from the city, above a golden wheat field. Here, too, groups of people strolled together, basking in the warm sun, and singing. Singing!

Nowhere were the usual struggles apparent. She felt no weight, no burden, no *shoulds*. Amid all the strangeness, she felt herself to be home.

The scene shifted, again.

Now she was in an enormous office building, a labyrinthine maze of hallways and meeting rooms and work areas spread out under a ceiling so high that a layer of mist and clouds enshrouded it. Colorless cubicles stretched out in every direction, seemingly for miles, each populated by a single individual at a keyboard. The air was stagnant.

She thought *outside* and she was out of the building, on a crowded sidewalk, relieved. But the grimness was here, too, hovering like a dirty cloud over the sunless canyons. She looked up. Cars shot across the *sky* . . .

Someone approached. No, she saw, not a person but a synthetic, a humanoid. It didn't walk; it glided a few inches above the concrete. Through a vacant faceplate it asked where she was going.

An excellent question, she thought. Wish I knew.

Electric amber eyes blazed into her, awaiting a response. Before she could say anything, though, several sharp cracks rang out nearby, bullets ricocheted off cars, and a frenzied crowd began to stampede down the sidewalks and streets. The thing in front of her turned and buzzed off, yelling, "Order! Order!"

Maya looked around helplessly.

And she was gone.

Where now?

Nighttime. Cool air. A star-filled sky.

Relieved, she recognized her surroundings. She was outside of the cave, watching the arc of American Indians stare down a pack of equally determined wolves. She was back.

One of the wolves noticed her, turned her way. Maya felt no fear. She knelt down, extended her hand and said, "Come here, girl. Come on. Good girl," just as she would have done to an ordinary dog.

The wolf didn't budge. Instead, it began to shimmer and blur, and then melt away into nothingness.

Then Maya dissolved, too.

The great blue-white whirlpool of stars came into view, spinning above her now, rather than below. She readied herself for the dizzying trip through it.

The pressure of the ascent crushed her body . . . but did she even have a body? She looked at her arm. Was it there? No. Just empty space.

She shot out of the vortex like a rocket—and halted. In midair. In the dark. But not hovering as before. Sitting. Sitting on the ledge in the stillness of a pitch-black cave, pressing her hand into cold rock. The rock didn't move, she was happy to observe, didn't dissolve. It was real.

"Am I back?"

"You're back," came her father's voice from beside her. "You've done it."

She gulped down some air, felt the heaviness—the reality—of her body.

"I have? Done what?"

CHAPTER 18

"You've seen a future," he said.

"Really?"

"A *probable* future," he added, "shaped and peopled by your imagination."

"No kidding?"

It felt so strange to be experiencing exactly what he had written about so long ago, that she had learned about so recently. The probable future.

"How did you know about my dream?" she asked.

"If you mean how did I know about your projection, the answer is, I didn't. The trees, the lake, the mountains, the path, all these things were created by you, not me. They were your éntre into the experience."

"I never dreamed of a pyramid house."

"No," he said. "That's where the Mandala, or rather projections of them, meet. It's a mental construct. You see, Maya, the work isn't done on a physical level."

"Then where exactly were they?"

"At vortexes all over the world. The pyramid house is our gathering place. It exists in the vortex communications network. Georgia is often there, too."

"Why are they called the Mandala?"

"The name has been in use for a long time. The word means sacred circle. It's what we are."

Maya shook her head as if to wake up. "You know, if you told me that all that was really a dream—as in an I-fell-asleep dream— I'm pretty sure I'd believe you. Actually, it would be easier that way."

"Nonphysical work always feels dream-like. Without the

constraints of physical law, experience moves rapidly. There's no need to walk, run or drive; you're just there. All you have to do is think it.

"People have been doing this for millennia. The ancients projected their minds just as you did. They didn't build external technologies because they didn't need them. The physical world is just the outer crust of a multidimensional universe; the real action takes place at the deeper levels."

Intuitively she had always suspected something like this. Now she had, or seemed to have, an experience to go with the belief.

"Why did I see my uncle?"

"He's probably near a vortex."

"That would be a pretty big coincidence, wouldn't it?"

"They're everywhere. Most are minute. The world is punctured by literally millions of them. If you calm yourself sufficiently, you can feel them."

She shook her head. "I don't think I've ever been that calm." So much of the world was not as it seemed.

"So," she said, jokingly, "did I change the future?"

"Yes," he said, smiling. "But since you're not skilled in *consciously* directing the inner medium, you did it unconsciously. Look, there," he said, pointing down at the bottom of the chamber.

She aimed the flashlight toward the shadowy tunnel she had emerged from earlier, saw that it illuminated a lone wolf, nervously peering into the chamber, whimpering.

"You invited her in," he said.

"I did?" Maya said. "You mean I was really outside? I thought that was part of the dream thing."

"It *was* part of the dream thing. But you actually were there. Animals are more attuned than people to the nonphysical world. You changed the course of that wolf's life. Simple life forms are easier to influence than more complex ones, like humans. Still, it's no small feat."

"Now I feel guilty," she said. "Can it get out?"

"They take care of themselves."

As if on cue, the creature turned and disappeared back through the tunnel.

David turned to her. "Thoughts and desires are composed of energy which unceasingly forms into psychic structures in the inner medium. Whether or not they manifest in the physical world is a matter of whether or not they possess sufficient emotional intensity.

"Vortexes simply act as amplifiers, speeding up the process. At powerful vortexes like this one, reality creation is turned up to an unbelievably high degree. Harnessing it is difficult, but I must say, you held your own. I'm impressed."

"I did pretty well, didn't I?" she said, proudly.

"Don't get too full of yourself, though," he said, nudging her on the arm. "Developing the muscle for large-scale reality change can take a lifetime."

"And say you accomplish that, how does it work? How do you change reality?"

He paused. She could hear his raspy breathing. For a moment she thought he was wheezing. Then he turned to her and said, "In simple terms, you first visualize your intention. In the Mandala, we try for peace, health, cleaner technologies, new art forms, enlightened government and education . . . goals such as these, in every detail you can imagine. We then achieve a deep level of consciousness and give these intentions to the vortex. That's the basis of it."

As Maya listened to his words, she also scrutinized the speaker. Maybe what he was saying was true. Maybe it wasn't. But what about *him*? She was more interested in him than in reality change. How much had this utopian dream cost him? A normal life, yes. But what else?

"You've sacrificed a lot," she said.

Looking at him, a sadness overcame her. Maybe it was simple biology: grief for the fathering she had missed out on, the love she had been shortchanged. Or maybe it was an aftereffect of the mind-bending journey she had just taken. Whichever it was, emotions suddenly exploded in her. Her eyes grew heavy, the weight of all the stimulation bearing down on her at once.

"I don't think badly of you," she said, sniffing to hold back tears.

She shook her head. No, not now. Of all times.

He must have seen it coming for he reached out and gently patted her knee with the long, thin fingers and the crooked, uncut nails. The caring gesture proved to be too much for her. She burst out in tears. Within seconds her cheeks were soaked.

"It's been a long day," she mumbled, rocking back and forth, feeling waves of fear and pain.

He squeezed her hand. To her surprise, it was warm.

"I'll be all right in a minute," she said. She dug a towel out of the pack and wiped her face.

"Interesting," he said.

"What?"

"Shine the light on your shoes."

She did so, without thinking, just following along.

He leaned over, inspected the back of her tennis shoes. "That's a yin-yang you've got painted on there, isn't it?" he said.

She stared at him in disbelief. He looked back, confused. Suddenly she broke into a grin through her tear-soaked cheeks. He smiled, too, watching her. Then her grin turned into a laugh, and he laughed, too, without knowing why, rasping and coughing as he did. She howled so loudly that it echoed all through the cave, until a different sort of tears rolled down her cheeks, tears of happiness.

She had an idea. Maybe the time had arrived.

Go ahead. *Do it.*

"Dad?" she said. So strange, that word, coming out of her mouth.

He didn't reply. She wondered: Had she made a mistake?

She raised her eyes to meet his, saw that his pale eyelids were shut, his head tilted down.

She moved closer. She said, "Hello?"

She patted his arm. Nothing. Was he asleep? She shook him gently and watched in alarm as his head bobbed from side to side, the muscles of his neck gone flaccid. She began to panic. She grabbed him by the shoulders and yelled at him to wake up.

Slowly, with great effort, the eyelids crept open, as if pulling up the weight of the world with them. A drowsy stare turned her way.

Watching him, she remembered. She remembered why she was there, why Georgia had brought her to the mountain, why the universe had enlisted her on this mission. It was as clear as the New Mexican sky.

"It's time to go," she said. "We need to leave here now."

"No . . . not yet," he whispered.

"You're falling apart. If you could see yourself—"

" . . . not finished . . ."

"If you don't leave, that's exactly what you'll be—finished. I'm not going to let that happen, not in this life anyway."

She reached over and took him by the arm and began to pull him forward, away from the wall, to rouse him, maybe to let him know how serious she was.

The dark cloud appeared without warning, pouring forth from the tunnel beside him. She barely had time to cover her face.

The bats came at her in a long, steady stream. Without thinking she dropped down on her side and tucked herself in a fetal ball, wrapping her arms around her head. The clamor of flapping wings, the screeching, the pounding of furry bodies against her back and sides, made her shriek out in terror. The cave, which had been eerily quiet until then, erupted in violence.

David Orr emerged from his stupor, shouting. She could not separate his words from the din of the fight she was in, so she did not know what he said.

Whatever it was, it worked. Miraculously, within seconds the bats had re-formed into a cloud and returned flapping into their lair.

"What have I done?" he said frantically. "Maya, are you hurt?"

She unfolded her body slowly, sat up and looked at him, still trembling. She couldn't speak. Her eyes were blank. Her sweater was ripped in places, her hands scratched. She smoothed down her hair, tried to normalize.

"Are you hurt?" he said again. "If you are, I'll never forgive myself."

"I'm all right," she said slowly. "Just scared out of my mind."

"I'm losing control."

"You're right," she said. "You're going to hurt someone."

He shook his head ruefully. She opened up the pouch, pulled out the skin and drank some water. She offered him some but he refused. She wiped her face with the towel. When she had calmed down she turned to him, looked into his sorrowful eyes.

"Is there anything I can say to get you to come to your senses?"

He didn't respond.

"Listen," she said. "I'm pleading now. I'm sorry about this but the fact is, I need you. I need you to *be*. Alive. That's not too much to ask, is it? We don't have to see each other, or even stay in contact, but please just . . . exist. Out there, somewhere. Not in here, where you won't last. I'll stay on this rock if I have to, I've got nothing better to do until you change your mind.

"You *are* succeeding. It *is* changing out there. The change has begun, I've seen it. You should, too. It's time to take care of yourself. People are depending on you. Those men out there on the dirt, spending endless nights praying for your return. Georgia and Brandon. Stop hurting them."

She leaned over and hugged him, despite her revulsion at the way he looked and felt and smelled, and the dangers inherent in approaching him. And, to her surprise, he responded. He relaxed his head into the crook of her neck.

She'd done it. She *knew* it. The force upon him was too great— greater than ambition, greater than pride, greater than obsession. Greater than idealism. It was the pull of love. Many a strong soul had weakened before it. He released a tremendous sigh.

"Okay," he said.

She smiled victoriously. Not only might she have a father now, but she had found a strength in herself that complemented his, one that she had never known existed because she had never reached that far down.

She looked down at the chamber. Now what? He was weak. Could he even walk? How would she get him out?

The answer came from below.

"The wolves went home," Walking Bear called up from the chamber. "And let me tell you, they looked relieved."

"Is that you, Walking Bear?" Maya said.

"It's me," he said. "Are you ready to go?"

David couldn't answer. He had collapsed in his daughter's arms.

"We're ready," she said.

"You did well, young lady," Walking Bear said. "Now go get some air. I'd wager you need it."

She nodded. Yes, she did, she thought, as she made her way down.

A short time later, standing outside, in the area that had been vacated by the wolves, she stared up at the night sky. A veldt of stars filled the heavens. She'd never seen anything so beautiful. The stars looked like celestial sugar tossed down by God, illuminating the mountain in an otherworldly light, a gorgeous sight after the permanent midnight of the cave.

Soon the Indians emerged from the cave carrying a sling on which the still figure of David Orr lay. They handed him carefully down from the rocky ledge.

Maya immediately dashed over. José jumped down and blocked her way before she could reach her father.

"No, Maya," he said. "My father will tend to him. He wants you to rest. He said it is very important."

She stared at him defiantly. "Where are they taking him?"

"Please," he pleaded. "He is not going anywhere. I promise you."

She stood her ground, unsure of how to proceed. Then, the fact that she was brutally tired dawned on her. "Maybe you're right," she said. The boy nodded vigorously, relieved.

He led her back on the trail, shining a flashlight so she could see every step of the way. He kept close, even taking her hand at the difficult parts. After the long trail, they walked through the woods until they arrived at a site where Georgia had set up a camp.

The old woman was sitting on a blanket staring into a crackling campfire. When she saw Maya she rushed over and took her in her arms. Realizing that the younger woman was wobbling with fatigue, she took her straight into the tent and zipped her into a sleeping bag. Maya immediately fell into a deep sleep.

*   *   *

Dawn arrived with a symphony of birdsong flowing down from the trees. Maya's eyes slowly opened and she yawned so long and hard that she had to check to be sure she hadn't dislocated her jaw. Her bladder felt as though it was about to explode.

Weak green light lit the tent walls. Droplets of dew hung like stalactites from the canvas ceiling, occasionally dripping down onto the sleeping bags. Georgia lay snoring to one side, oblivious to the cacophony outside, a faint smile on her face.

Maya climbed out of the sleeping bag, unzipped the tent flap and poked her head outside. The fragrant scent of pine filled her nostrils. The grass was covered in dew. Her shoes were on the ground outside, and she pulled them on, stood up and stretched her arms out. Her bones pulled and creaked and groaned in ways she had never heard before.

She squatted behind a bush to relieve herself, and then found a log to sit on. Slowly the events of the cave returned to her, and she wondered: Where was her father? When would she see him? Where was José? Georgia was here but where was Keith? She saw no sign of him anywhere. Just the tent and a spent campfire.

Everything would have to be fathomed, in time. Patience, she told herself. The process of integration had already begun, for she'd had many intense dreams during the night, dreams which left her with the feeling of being anesthetized, as though some inner administrator was working hard to make sense of it all while the rest of her waited patiently for the outcome.

Georgia soon emerged from the tent, energetic and helpful, and within minutes was cooking breakfast over a new campfire. The scent of bacon sizzling on the skillet made Maya almost crazy with desire. She was famished. Georgia had stored the food in an ice chest which she hung from a nearby tree.

In between mouthfuls of bacon and eggs and coffee, Maya did

her best to recount everything that had happened in the cave. Her stomach, it seemed, had become a bottomless pit.

José arrived as she was swallowing the last of the coffee. He stood close to the woods, patiently waiting for her to finish.

Politely he said, "Are you ready to see him?"

"Yes," she said, wiping her mouth. "Although I've eaten so much you might have to carry me."

He looked at her nervously.

"I'm kidding, José."

"Ah, yes," he nodded.

"I'm coming too," Georgia said, kicking dirt over the fire.

The morning warmed up quickly. Sunlight pierced the canopy of trees, slicing to the ground in perfectly straight lines. Maya now knew the trail well enough for it not to frighten her. When they came to the familiar rock outcropping, she paused.

"This is it," she told Georgia. They stepped around it.

Maya stopped, stunned by what she saw just a few feet away at the cave, a scene as far different as possible from the one of the previous day. The same men were present, only now they weren't empty masks sitting in meditation. They were smoking, telling stories, eating, laughing. Maya saw no sign of concern whatsoever, only of celebration.

"There's Walking Bear," she said, excitedly. He jogged over to greet her and Georgia.

Maya then saw the reason for all the excitement: David Orr, standing tall under his own power, miraculously transformed. Bewildered, she could not believe her eyes. It was impossible. A man cannot change that fast.

The beard was gone, and the hair was long and clean, combed back in a ponytail—easy enough to do. The face, though still pale, had gained in color. The cheeks that were like sickly flaps had somehow filled out, and the unsightly nose, which may have been swollen, now appeared normal, in fact much like her own. His arms, though thin, moved about easily as he gestured to one of the men. Dressed in jeans and a summer shirt, wearing dark sunglasses that made him look like a movie star, he seemed on top of the world.

"How . . ." stuttered Maya. "He was just a mass of protoplasm yesterday."

"He used the vortex energy for regeneration," Georgia said. "With Walking Bear's help."

"In one night?"

"No, not exactly one night, dear," Georgia said.

"What do you mean?"

Georgia took her hand. Maya could sense a shock coming. She was afraid to ask, and braced for the answer.

"You were asleep for a day and a half," Georgia said.

Maya's legs suddenly became rubbery; she decided it was time to sit down on the ground for a spell.

David Orr walked toward her, laughing.

CHAPTER 19

He led her to a hillside a stone's throw from the cave and all of its festivities. It wasn't much of a private place because the men came around constantly to check on him.

Sitting on the grass beside him, she saw the phenomenal change firsthand. His appearance was far from completely healthy—the flesh of his face and arms was still pale and pocked, the muscle tone loose, the body still extremely thin—but he was close. Miraculously close.

"I have to wear these," he said of the dark sunglasses that rode high on the bridge of his nose.

"The sun's pretty strong," she said, shading her eyes. "Even if you weren't in a cave for half a year."

He smiled. They sat in silence. He seemed pensive, satisfied just to sit. Behind the big sunglasses, however, she sensed a current of strong emotion. His voice seemed a little shaky, uncomfortable.

His demeanor said: here we are.

"Not the reunion you expected, I'll bet," he said.

"Didn't even make the list of maybes. What about you?"

"Maybe I wasn't completely surprised."

She nodded. "Hmm."

"It feels so strange to be outside," he said. "Do you feel the energy here?"

"Yes," she said.

"So powerful." He smiled, enjoying the fresh air, drinking in the scenery.

"What are you going to do now?" she said. "I mean, after here."

He looked at her, knew what she was asking.

Before he could respond, she quickly said, "I mean, regarding the Mandala."

"Oh," he said.

Was he relieved? There was no way to know without seeing his eyes.

He shrugged. Maybe he hadn't thought that far ahead yet. "Continue the struggle," he said. "We're closing in on many fronts."

"That's good," she said.

An eternity seemed to pass before they spoke again. Why was it so hard to communicate?

She said, "What about . . ."

"Us?"

Yes.

She waited, looking down, nervously tapping her finger on her knee.

"Maya, I have to be honest," he said. "I don't know. We live our lives—but with a difference. A big one."

"A difference?"

"We know each other."

What did that mean?

"You said you needed to know that I exist, that I'm alive," he said. "You can see that I am. Thanks to you. You probably saved my life. That's quite a beginning, wouldn't you say?"

A beginning.

"Yes, but . . ."

She wanted more, an assurance, a guarantee, a declaration that he would be there, that they would be close, that they would have a real relationship. That he was her father. Maybe even that he loved her.

He didn't say any of it. He seemed, just as Muriel had said, removed, distant.

"This is difficult for me, Maya. We found each other. That's a start. We'll move forward from there. You know I'm in constant danger, and so are you if you remain with me. I can't have that."

"But we stay in touch, right?"

"Yes, of course."

"How?"

"Carefully. There are rules. I don't want you disappointed. Do you understand?"

"Rules? What rules?"

"Georgia will tell you. The Mandala are well practiced in these things."

He reached up and removed his sunglasses. Shielding his eyes from the sun, squinting painfully, his eyes met hers. It was the first time she had ever seen her father's eyes. They were blue.

"We'll be together, I promise you," he said. "For now, though, be with me, here, now. Don't worry. Let this moment be. Like you, I've waited a long time."

"Time," she said, as the emotions of the moment filled her.

Let it happen. Feel it.

She did feel it—the culmination of a lifetime of desire, the countless dreams, the months of searching, the days of travel. She felt it all. She sensed the possibility of a more complete life.

She leaned in, wrapped her arms around him and hugged him tightly—she was nervous but she didn't care—and only when she was sure the moment was branded in her memory, she released her grip. Maybe this was what a lifetime of yearning suddenly fulfilled felt like.

She heard a sound in the distance.

"What's that?" she said, searching the treetops.

He put his sunglasses on and looked up. His expression became intense, worried, and she imagined this look on him often, all the years he had been on the run.

"Oh no," he said.

"What?"

The sound steadily grew louder, then split into several tones, until their origin became all too clear. David craned his head to see how close they were, as did the men who now surrounded them and grabbed them roughly by the arms.

The helicopters hovered like birds of prey over the trees a hundred yards away, the clamor of the two machines roaring like an army of buzzsaws. Only through luck did they have to remain so far away; the area in front of the cave was too close to the mountain for a safe approach.

Frantically, the Indians scattered in all directions. Many took off into the woods. Cables dropped down from the helicopters and men in coveralls slid swiftly down them. As they hit the ground, a loudspeaker from above bellowed, "Stay where you are! Don't move! This is the FBI! Stay where you are!"

Maya, David and Georgia were pushed forcefully onto a path as a group of five Indians urgently implored them to run.

"Faster if you want to be free!"

David, in his weakened state, was carried by men on both sides of him. His feet hardly touched ground.

Maya, adrenaline surging through her body, sprinted along with everyone else, as trees and branches and bushes blazed past. At one point she stumbled and fell and scraped her hand, picked herself up again, and hesitating briefly, was suddenly pushed hard from behind.

"Faster!"

She heard dogs howling behind them, a frightening sound which grew louder as the animals gained on them. She wondered: Had the dogs been dropped from the helicopters, too? Obviously. Her spirits fell. All seemed hopeless. How could an emaciated man, an old woman, and a girl from Plainfield, Maryland outrun the FBI's tracking hounds?

The gap was closing, the barks growing louder. Within seconds she knew the escape attempt would be over. After all these years, the authorities would have David Orr. Her heart went out to him. She shuddered to think what kind of trouble the rest of them would be in.

She slowed for a moment to glance back and see how close their pursuers were, and was practically hit in the face by the man behind her, a stout Indian breathing heavily just like her, who shouted "No!"

Her heart racing, she turned and ran harder than ever. Her lungs struggled for air. Her legs ached. As the dogs closed in, the loudspeaker's staccato commands receded into the distance.

Something brushed by her leg, going in the opposite direction. What was that? She looked down but saw nothing.

Suddenly another missile blazed past underfoot. Then another. And another. This time she saw the color—gray—and knew what they were, these gray masses, these torpedoes disappearing behind her.

The wolves.

Within seconds a blood-curdling chorus of growls and barks and whelps filled the air, a wild collection of sounds that stopped the escaping party to listen.

They didn't linger long. The Indians pushed them on again and they surged ahead, almost beyond their endurance, distancing themselves from the ferocious battle behind them and the pursuit of their would-be captors.

No more dogs followed. Now they heard only silence, except for the crackling of the brush and branches underfoot.

They soon arrived at a cabin at the end of an unpaved dirt road; more of a trail than a road. Maya had no idea where it led, where they were, or if they were safe. The only thing she knew for sure, as did David and Georgia, was that they needed to rest.

"Where are we?" Maya asked.

"A safe house," Georgia said.

As darkness fell, they bid farewell to the Indians, who disappeared with hardly a word back into the woods.

*   *   *

The cabin was a large, dusty room overrun with spider webs, and furnished sparely with an old couch, a table, chairs, a rocker, a bed, and a fireplace. It was cold. Maya desperately wanted a shower, to wash the sticky sweat from her skin, but the cabin offered no bathroom or even running water. A lantern stood in a corner, but Georgia refused to light it for fear of being seen outside the cabin. The only illumination they had was the moonlight coming in through the back window. There was a well behind the cabin and an outhouse near the edge of the woods.

Georgia found a jug and filled it at the well. Maya located some glasses in a cabinet, and they all drank.

"Now we wait," Georgia said, setting her empty glass on the floor.

"For whom?"

"The Mandala," Georgia said. "They can't leave us here long. It's not safe."

David, sitting at the edge of the bed, said, "Are you okay, Maya?"

"Oh, fine. Having the time of my life."

He laughed mirthlessly, as if with his last ounce of energy.

"Sure," she said. "Don't worry about me."

Georgia lay down on the couch and closed her eyes. David, looking pale and shaky, fell heavily onto the bed. Within minutes both were asleep, breathing peacefully.

Which left Maya alone, exhausted but wide awake. She sat in the rocker and pushed herself gently with one foot. She wondered how David and Georgia could be calm enough to fall asleep when she was ready to jump out of her skin with anxiety. Yet there they were, sleeping.

When they awoke a half hour later, Maya, still rocking, was staring at the back door, waiting for the FBI to break it down.

Suddenly the curtains shielding the front window lit up, and Maya's heartbeat went into overdrive. A car engine whirred, then fell silent. Maya's fingers squeezed the armrest tightly. She turned to David and Georgia. Neither one moved. What could they do? A car door slammed and the footsteps she had been dreading sounded outside.

"Don't move," Georgia whispered.

"Don't worry."

The back door knob turned and the door creaked open—and Keith Seputa walked in.

"No time to waste," he said.

Maya exhaled a breath she'd been holding for almost a minute. They hurried outside and into the car.

"The FBI is all over town," Keith said, as he pulled the car out. They traveled the bumpy dirt road out to a main street. Maya had no idea where they were. "The pickup is out of town. It should be safe. We had to call Anderson."

"Good," Georgia said. "This is far too close for comfort."

They drove for an hour down a long, empty highway before Keith turned into the parking lot of a roadside diner. The lot was empty but for one car.

"This is mainly a lunch place," Keith said. "Nobody comes here late. You should be safe. I have to go back into town and deal with the rest of this. People are pretty upset about what happened."

"Be careful," David said.

"I always am."

They walked toward the restaurant, as Keith pulled away.

Only much later, after it was all over, as Maya was sifting through the memories, did she connect a portion of her father's text to the incident about to take place.

> *If events are learning experiences, and the Creator's mind*
> *is unknowable, then one can attempt to decipher the lessons*
> *until one's brain gives out in exhaustion, and still come up*
> *empty. There exist synchronicities that try and try to occur—*
> *and finally do.*

The lone car in the parking lot belonged to Albert Fiske.

*   *   *

Long ago, when David Orr had departed the everyday world of home and family and career to begin a new life of running from city to country to town, of shuttling from one hiding place to the next, of relying on people who shared his beliefs but who were strangers to him, he could not have predicted this. Not even with his well-honed precognitive skills could he have known that two decades after it had all begun, fate would place him face to face with Albert Fiske at a lonely diner in the desert Southwest. Opposing forces seek out their counterparts, and in their eventual joining are presented with an opportunity to crack the kernel of truth upon which their attraction rests. This was just such an opportunity.

Perhaps that is why Fiske swiveled around in his stool, away from the unfinished sandwich on the counter, at precisely the instant that David reached for the door. On some level he knew, just as David did, that their day had arrived. The knowing wasn't on a conscious level, though, for Fiske's face lit up in disbelief on seeing his man delivered to him as easily as the sandwich before him had come.

David, trailed by Maya and Georgia, was equally dumbstruck. The reality of the situation dawned on both men at the same instant, and they both moved involuntarily toward each other, as if an invisible string that bound them to each other had been tugged.

For the travelers there was no escape. No place to run, no helpful Indians, no friendly Mandala agent to assist them. Keith was long gone on the road to Taos. All that existed at this moment was the diner, the people inside it and the endless expanse of desert outside.

Two men occupied the stools on either side of Fiske, also with half-finished sandwiches before them. They turned to see what had drawn his attention.

Watching David enter, Fiske smiled. "Well, well," he said.

"Hello, Albert," David said.

"And my good friend Maya," Fiske said. "And the famous Georgia Roussey as well. Greetings, all. This is Agent Gaddis and Agent Andrelli."

The agents both stood up. The larger of the two, Gaddis, a thick-set man with the physique of a bull, strode past the group to the front door. He glanced out at the parking lot, and satisfied with what he saw, flipped the window sign over to read "Closed." He then planted himself in front of the entrance, hands on his hips, watching the group. Andrelli, a small, nervous man, remained beside Fiske, his hand hovering near a lump under his jacket which Maya guessed was a pistol.

Fiske stood up and spun the stool happily with his hand. Maya stepped closer to David, and Georgia remained near a booth, watching agent Gaddis at the door, who looked at her as if she were a gnat that needed swatting.

Fiske, relishing the moment, stared at David for a long time, nodding his head at his good fortune. Maya looked closely at him. Back in Washington, Fiske had seemed like a lot of bluster but not really a terrible guy; now his hostile demeanor seemed very real and threatening.

"I was so late getting here," Fiske said, "I was sure I'd miss you. I guess the god of flight delays was on my side."

Andrelli reached inside his jacket.

"No," Fiske said. "Not yet."

Not yet?

Maya became frightened. David showed no signs of panic, at least not outwardly.

Then Maya saw movement behind the counter. Feeling a surge of hopefulness, she watched closely. Had the rescue begun?

No such luck. A fry cook with scared, bulging eyes popped his head up, then dashed into the back room. A door slammed, and a moment later a car parked in the back started up and then sped away.

"How have you been, Albert?" David said. Still calm.

Fiske frowned, with great affect. "Not good, but I sense a sea change coming on." To Andrelli, he said, "What about you?"

"Yeah, me, too."

David shook his head. "Still holding a grudge after all these years?"

Fiske moved in close. "And why shouldn't I? Do you know what you did to me?"

"Yes, Albert, I do," David said. "And I know what you did to me. And the others."

"And what was that?"

"You disappeared."

"What the hell's that supposed to mean?"

"You were a man when I started working with you," David said in a voice that surprised Maya with its energy. "You turned into something else. I don't know what. Ambition. Ambition without conscience. You, the man I knew, left. We all paid for it.

Harris, Campbell, Prager, Poricelli. Everyone. I chose my path. But you made sure I couldn't walk it, didn't you?"

David moved forward and Fiske shifted back. Maya began to break through her fear, just as she had done with the wolves, by releasing her expectations, by being open to anything that might happen. She straightened her back, readied herself—for what, she didn't know.

Fiske's expression surprised her. He was confused, bubbling over with emotion, almost feral. Maya had never seen a look quite like it. "I thought you cared about the work," he said defensively.

"It was my life," David said.

"So?"

Maya didn't understand. Fiske's machismo, his swagger, was gone. Something had shifted in him. The two agents looked on uncertainly, as Fiske paced between tables.

"I would have given you anything," Fiske said.

"Yes," David said. "But in support of what?"

"Our mutual goals!" Fiske shouted. "What was it, the experiment with the politician? I agree that was over the line. That was a one time thing. The research is on the up and up now. It is, I swear."

David said, "I've never forgiven myself for going along with that."

"With what?" Maya asked.

"We tweaked a senator," David said. "Using active viewing. We got him to change his position on a bill that was up for a vote."

"Ancient history," Fiske said. "Besides, you knew what the greater goal was. National security. Maya here, you said it, remember? I want to protect the people. David, you know that's always been the goal."

"Albert," David said. "When you stepped over the line you never came back. Your goal was always the same. To control people. To have them do your bidding."

"It's your goal, too," Fiske shot back, pointing at Georgia. "Look at the Mandala. We're both doing exactly the same thing."

"No," Georgia said. "Our goal is to free people, not to control them. *Return* power to them. We're unshackling them. It's the opposite."

David said, "Do what you want with me, Albert. It's too late. The change is already happening. You can't stop it now."

"You're scared," Georgia said to Fiske.

"Hogwash," he said, now pacing furiously around the room. "Change doesn't scare me. The destruction of a country, a culture, does."

"The days of master and slave have ended," David said. "Once peoples' eyes are opened they'll do anything to avoid a return to that. The revolution has begun. You're too late, Albert."

The change in Fiske was jarring. He'd flip-flopped; he was reacting. David had pull with him. Fiske was awed. Maya had no idea that this would be the case. David's voice had become powerful, even hypnotic.

"The rule of might over right," David said, "which has dominated this planet for all of human history has only existed this long because people haven't understood their power to affect change. No longer. A new paradigm is being born, as we speak. Everyone will learn it. You will have to accept its inevitability. You can take me if you want, it won't make any difference. My job is done. Soon everything will be different."

Maya took a step closer to her father. Seeing Fiske flailing, and despite the arrest that she knew was coming, she felt emboldened. She said, "You're trying to keep a dying system alive."

Fiske turned to her, hostility raging in his eyes, and Maya immediately shrank back.

"That system," he said venomously, "has given you and your useless peers more advantages than any society in the history of the world. It's the only reason we don't live in pathetic wretched poverty like everyone else."

"How do you know?" Maya said.

Fiske had had enough. He turned to the man beside him. "Andrelli, are you ready?"

The agent, relieved to have something to do, reached into his jacket but Fiske abruptly grabbed his arm.

"Hold on a minute. There's one more thing."

He turned to David, looked hard into his eyes, then said, "You don't think *they're* going to let your little change take place, do you?"

Maya saw a look of recognition on David's face.

Fiske, arms crossed, gloated.

"What's he talking about?" Maya asked.

"Go ahead," Fiske said. "Tell her."

"Yes, tell me."

David shook his head. "It won't change a thing."

"Yes it will," Fiske said. Then to Maya, he said: "The people I'm talking about don't have a name. And if they did, we wouldn't know it. You see, Maya, the people who pull the strings don't actually exist."

Maya, puzzled, wanting to do anything to prolong the conversation and therefore her time with her father, said, "I don't understand."

"The rulers of this globe," Fiske said. "The real ones. Do you think the United States government controls anything? Think again. What you see on the news is only what's deemed fit for your consumption."

Maya suddenly felt as if she'd fallen into a deep hole.

"The global elite," Fiske said. "The extraordinarily rich and powerful—the ambitious, to use your father's word. Do you think world events just happen? Of course not. They are constructed. Architected. They turn on what these people decide. The global elite finance the wars, influence the alliances, control international banking and the markets, mold the careers of public figures who in turn do their bidding. Everything of import in this world happens behind the scenes. You think you know history? No, not really. You'll never hear about this. The media doesn't report it because these people own the media. Your father and I, we're tiny fish in a big ocean. If he hasn't changed over the years, he's probably still denying it. I don't blame him. I'd want to forget it if I could, too. It's difficult to accept that one isn't master of one's own fate."

Maya recalled some books she'd read by conspiracy theorists,
men who wove tales of secret societies, murky undergrounds, ancient
orders, private governments. She had once found their ideas
fascinating and even inspired, but mainly these writers appeared
to be crackpots consumed by paranoia.

"What do they want?" she asked anyway.

To her surprise, her father answered. "Servitude," he said.

David agreeing with Fiske and the conspiracy writers? Maya
was surprised. She turned to him. "You mean it's real?"

"Some," Georgia said.

David said, "History is often the story of these faceless rulers."

Now Maya was reeling.

Her father continued. "Why? you might ask. Why do they do
it? Why are they driven to control? It comes down to a twisted
attempt to be loved, if you want to know the truth, a sad and
distorted attempt for respect. Despots, no matter how heinous
their methods, believe they are making the world a better place. If
people *truly* understood them, they think, they would see this.
They would notice that they are working for the greater good of
humanity. The desire for acceptance underlies the most hideous of
acts."

"Thank you, professor," Fiske said. "Now I want to ask you
something before we have to go. Maybe we can clear up this whole
mess. If you play your cards right, who knows, things might work
out for all of us. Maybe, just maybe, you could return to the status
of a free man. New evidence in that old case could turn up, or old
evidence might disappear. Interested? Of course you are. You're
tired of running, of living the life, of not knowing whether you'll
be picked up on any given day, never having a place to call home.
That can all end right now. Are you with me?"

"Say your piece, Albert."

"It's simple," he said, "Come back. Work for me. We can work
all the rest out. I can take care of everything. Think about it—
everything forgiven."

Maya's jaw dropped. She couldn't believe it.

David, expressionless, stared at Fiske.

"You were the best," Fiske said. "Share what you've learned. Nobody is at your level. Some are good, but none are great. You were great. The past, as bad as it's been, can be forgiven. We can turn a new page, clear the deck. What do you say? Hell, I'm up for a whole new round of funding."

Say yes. You would be free, we could be together. Bend.

She looked into her father's eyes. She could not read him, could not see where he was going.

David turned to Fiske. "I've already been down that road, Albert. No thanks."

Maya's heart sank.

Fiske pointed to Maya. "What about her? She's not the type that will thrive in jail."

"If you harm her—"

"Yes?" Fiske said, stepping forward. "Then what?"

Maya's legs started to tremble.

Fiske turned to Georgia. "Now, that old crone, I believe she'd find a way to survive in the lock-up."

Maya, seething, moved toward Fiske.

David turned to her. "What are you doing?"

Maya lunged at Fiske. She had never committed a violent act in her life, did not even know how to fight, yet she threw herself at this powerful man with complete abandon. David put his arm out to block her approach but he was too late; she was already past him.

She didn't reach Fiske. Instead, she found herself in the powerful grip of agent Gaddis, who had grabbed her from behind. He laughed as he pinned her arms against her sides and lifted her up off the ground, her legs flailing about trying to kick him.

"Frisky little bugger," the agent said.

As Maya writhed, Fiske brought his face up to David's. "You're going away for a long, long time, Orr, and so is your little family here."

David said nothing.

"Andrelli," Fiske ordered.

"Right," Andrelli said. He grabbed David's arms and held them behind his back. David, still weak, didn't even bother to resist. Maya struggled but could not budge in agent Gaddis's grip. Georgia could do nothing but look on helplessly.

"Don't cuff him yet," Fiske said.

Staring at David, Fiske fumed with hatred. He took a deep breath, and then rolled up his sleeves, revealing tanned, muscular arms.

Maya yelled, "You can't do this! Stop!"

"Sure I can. It's easy," Fiske said. He flexed his right hand, extending his fingers out. Eyeing David's midsection, he made a fist. He held it in front of David's face for him to see. Georgia stepped forward, but Fiske said, "I'd advise you to stay where you are, woman."

"This is illegal."

"Call the cops."

He's really going to hit him, Maya thought. After all this, it comes down to macho male aggression.

Fiske reared back—and stopped.

Loud sounds were coming from the parking lot.

Crunch. Cruuuunch.

Everyone turned to the window. Several cars were arriving, scattering gravel beneath their tires.

CHAPTER 20

The long black sedans—Maya counted four—pulled in as regally as a presidential motorcade and halted, one after another. They waited silently beside Fiske's car. The back door of the last car opened.

Inside the restaurant, Fiske waved frantically at the agents. "Release them, quickly."

Maya immediately ran into her father's arms, as did Georgia.

Fiske had backed up against one of the walls and was rolling his sleeve down, trying to re-button it, but his hands were shaking so badly he couldn't do it. Nervously he looked around the room.

"What should we do?" one of the agents said.

"Finish your sandwich," Fiske said.

"What's happening?" Maya said.

The restaurant's front door opened, and two men dressed in dark suits lifted an old man in a wheelchair up the single step before setting him down. Dr. Porter reached for the lever in the armrest and the chair rolled to the center of the room. Agents Gaddis and Andrelli turned to one another, confused.

Dr. Porter spun the chair in a slow circle, surveying the room. "My, my, my," he said. "All of our players are here."

"My intrepid friend, congratulations," he said to Maya. "You found him. I'm impressed."

"Thank you," she said. Despite everything, she still liked the old man.

"With a little help from your friends," he added, turning to Georgia. "Georgia Roussey, I haven't had the pleasure."

"Your reputation precedes you," she said.

He bowed his head slightly, as much as he was able to.

One of the suited men flashed an ID badge at Gaddis and Andrelli, who registered a look of surprise on seeing it. "Wait outside," the man told them. Obediently, they ambled out through the front door.

Dr. Porter turned to Fiske, who wore the look of an animal writhing in pain. He couldn't meet the older man's gaze. Instead, he stared down at his feet.

"You did well, Albert," Porter said. "I'm going to relieve you now. I'll speak to you outside when I'm done here."

"But what about—"

"Now."

Maya, stupefied, looked at Dr. Porter with more curiosity than ever.

"This isn't right," Fiske said, standing his ground.

Dr. Porter sighed, then nodded impatiently to his men.

The two men grabbed Fiske by the arms. He didn't resist, as they ushered him toward the door. Craning his neck back, Fiske stared scowling at David until he disappeared out the door.

"Nasty business," Dr. Porter said. Quickly he regained his serene look and turned to David.

"How long has it been?"

"Twenty years, Edgar."

Maya attempted to gauge her father's feelings, but she couldn't. He sounded perfectly normal.

"Too long, if you ask me," the old man said. "Maybe it's age, or the regrets of spending life too conservatively, or the tedium of always winning, or just being an old fool, but I'm softening, David. I miss certain things. I miss you, and people like you. I miss our days at the university. Perhaps they were the best of all. That all began as a lark, a distraction, you know. I grew to love it. The experimenting, the theorizing, the arguing late into the night. I still work with the vortex, you know. I've had some good successes these last years. But, of course, I'm just a tinkerer. I don't have the talent that you and your daughter possess."

He smiled, his cheeks flush with color.

"Edgar," David said. "I don't understand. Why are you here?"

Dr. Porter laughed. "You may find this hard to believe."

"After everything that's happened, I doubt it."

Dr. Porter wheeled up close to his old friend. "Rank sentimentality, if you want to know the truth. It's possible, even from a hardened old trooper like me. You see, when your daughter showed up, I became nostalgic. I couldn't remember the last time I felt that way. I didn't even think it possible. Suddenly I wanted to get back into the game, as ridiculous as that may sound. I wanted to see you again. Maybe . . . maybe the end is approaching. My end. It's possible."

He turned to Maya. "I understand your father's mission, Maya. I know what he is trying to accomplish. He is trying to trick the world out of its present state of mindless servitude into a brave new world of unbridled freedom. Now, some people have the idea that even if this were possible it would mean chaos. The world couldn't handle it."

He paused to cough, and regaining his voice, continued: "And further, David has a notion that a cartel of men control the fate of all human affairs through their clandestine alliances and devious plots. Georgia, am I correct?"

She said nothing, just watched him.

"Yes, right," he said. He turned again to Maya: "Your father thinks he can change this deplorable situation by nudging humanity in a more 'positive' direction using the vortex energy as propulsion for social change. And who knows, perhaps he can. What do you think?"

"I don't know," Maya said.

"The wise, the cautious, point of view."

"Maya," David said. "You should know that Edgar here is talking about his own people. *He* is one of the global elite. Edgar owns chunks of *countries*. And he isn't always merciful when it comes to his enemies."

Porter looked at David, not with anger but with affection, the devotion of a father for a wayward son. "People like you think there is a great master plan for world domination," he said. "I'm here to tell you that there isn't. It would be intriguing, I admit, but who in the world is that organized? It's just not possible. Think of the unknowns. It's mind-boggling."

The old man laughed that same unnerving laugh that Maya had heard in the garden weeks ago. Again it made her cringe.

David took a step forward. "Why are you here, Edgar?"

"To see you."

"Am I to believe that?"

"You're a good egg," Porter said. "All of you. I admire what you're doing. I want to see it completed. I've been waiting a long time. And to prove my good faith I'm going to do you a favor. I've arranged to set you free, David. Fiske couldn't have done it, of course. Oh, don't look surprised, Maya, it's not that difficult a task. David, you are no longer a wanted man. How does it feel? You see, Maya, I have my connections. David, you'll be able to return to civilian life here in the states if you desire it. How is that for swift, corrective justice? You've done well, and I appreciate it."

He spun the chair around and started for the door.

"Wait," Georgia called out. "What do you mean? *What* have we done?"

Porter spun his chair back around, but before he could answer, David said, "What about Maya?"

"I adore her."

"Is she safe?"

"Yes, of course."

"Georgia?"

"Yes."

"And Fiske? What about Fiske?"

"A thorn in my side. I may send him somewhere. Don't concern yourself with him anymore."

David breathed a sigh of relief.

Again Georgia asked, "What did you mean, 'We've done what you wanted'?"

"Your plan," Porter said. "I wanted you to set it up, to see if it works. I'm curious."

"And if it does?"

"I may use it," he said, smiling. "In fact, it's what I'm living for. Now, can someone give me a hand with this step?"

Georgia and Maya looked at each other and shrugged. Then they walked over and grabbed the sides of the chair, lifted it up and set him down outside. He was surprisingly light. Georgia walked back inside as Porter waved for Maya to wait.

"Yes?"

"The ransacking of your house," he said quietly. "I am sorry about that. I truly am. Our friend over there is responsible," he said, pointing toward the car that held Albert Fiske. "But don't hold it against him. I hope you can forgive an unforgivable invasion. In light of your father's newfound freedom I would wager that you could. Yes?"

"Yes," she said. "Thanks for telling me."

"Good. Now goodbye." He pressed the lever and began to wheel off.

He'd only gotten a few feet away when Maya called out, "There's one more thing."

He stopped, turned back to her. "Yes?"

She walked up to him. "How did you know we were here?"

He smiled slyly. "I placed a tracking device in your backpack. I'm sorry about that, but I found it necessary."

"When?"

"When you were asleep, after the vortex."

She stared at him a long time. She didn't know how to react. There was so much to react to in general, she just decided to let it all go.

"Don't feel bad," he said. "I knew all of Fiske's moves, too."

He turned and wheeled across the parking lot, and was helped into one of the cars. He waved to her from the back seat, and she waved back. The headlights on all the cars came on and they started off, crunching the gravel under their tires. Fiske's car pulled out, too, driven by one of Porter's men. Maya watched the line of cars depart and make their way down the road until their red tail lights disappeared into the night.

Inside the restaurant, Georgia was standing behind the counter pouring coffee. Maya came in and picked up her backpack, dug around in it awhile and found a tiny rectangular device fastened between two seams of the fabric. She pulled it out, dropped it on the floor, and stomped on it with all her weight, until it had become a brown smudge on the floor.

"What are you doing?" Georgia said.

"Squashing a bug," Maya said. "It's dead now."

Georgia walked around the counter and handed cups of coffee to David and Maya.

Maya said, "Dr. Porter is really something, isn't he?"

David nodded. "Most men in his position have no interest in metaphysics. I've just never been sure what he wanted. Now I am."

They walked outside into the night. The desert was dark and quiet, the parking lot empty.

Maya suddenly felt sad. She stared at her father a long time, when he was looking away from her. She said, "How does it feel to be free and at home?"

He turned to her. "Home," he said, and then fell silent. He just stood there, gazing up at the star-filled sky. Then he took her hand and squeezed it.

"Don't look so glum," he said, wrapping his arm around her shoulder. "We're going to have plenty of time together."

"We are?"

"Sure. There's just one more project, one that our Dr. Porter didn't count on. He thinks Taos was our main play. It wasn't. After it's over I'll return home."

"What are you going to do?"

David remained silent. He just smiled at her. Then, behind her back, he winked at Georgia. Georgia, smiling, winked back.

CHAPTER 21

The late fall brought near-record snowfalls to the eastern seaboard. December arrived with a storm that buried the area between Baltimore and Washington under almost two feet of fresh powder, shutting down both cities and every town in between. The snow lingered, clogging up the flow of life for weeks, until a sixty-degree weekend late in the month melted much of it away. By Christmas, the last of the brown gutter slush had washed into the storm drains, and sidewalks and streets saw the light of day once again.

Maya hadn't minded the snow as much as the perpetually dreary sky, which, as usual, caused her to become somber and lethargic. She slogged through the days, wilting at the thought of exerting herself, and slept more than usual. But the truth was, she was doing better than she had in previous winters. Instead of complaining and whining about not being as energetic as other people, now she simply accepted the fact of her body chemistry and did what she could to compensate for it.

As often as possible she would pack her sweats and running shoes and drive to the gym to jog on the treadmill, do sit-ups, or lift weights. Afterwards, clean and showered, she'd sit at the coffee shop next door, pull out her notebook and do the cognitive therapy exercises Dr. Yanikowski had taught her, carefully writing down her self-criticisms and complaints and then figuring out the positive corollary to each. As usual, it worked.

Today, even though the weather was dismal, she felt good. It was a Sunday, a day for sleeping in and then walking up Connecticut Avenue to Dexter's International for pancakes and eggs and a look at the Sunday *Post*. She'd been living in D.C. for only a month and had already found routines that suited her.

The confidence she derived from living on her own manifested itself in practically every aspect of her life. Her apartment, though minuscule, was quiet and cozy, nestled at the back of a gargoyle-studded building just north of the zoo. On snow days she happily stayed in, reading or watching TV, or just gazing out of her apartment's third-floor window at the snow-laden trees or the cold-weather hikers who tromped past a stream that wound through the woods.

Her return from New Mexico had been fraught with sadness; it was unavoidable. For all of its terror and anxiety she missed the outlaw life, which had whetted her appetite for adventure. The reality of a job and a commute and rent and keeping a checking account was an anticlimax to be sure, but she accepted it. It was part of the package. Two months earlier she could never have guessed that any of this was even possible. Yet here she was. And the museums were just a few minutes away.

Muriel didn't like the apartment, of course. It was too small. It was too expensive. The kitchen was just a *nook*. The furniture was too spare. And on and on. Muriel's barbs were harmless, though, and Maya knew that in her mother's strange way they were meant as expressions of caring.

Maya didn't care what her mother thought. She knew she was doing fine. Nothing could put her off. The apartment was a small studio unit—what did Muriel expect?

She lazed around until one o'clock, then threw some clothes on. Muriel and Henry were meeting her at Saachi's, an Italian restaurant just a few blocks away, and she didn't want to be late. She put on her coat, locked the apartment, and headed outside for the short walk.

They were already inside, waving to her from a booth in the back. Henry's attitude, taste and approach, Maya had come to learn, was strictly classic American.

Maya slid in beside Muriel. Soon Henry had them raising their water glasses in a toast.

"To Maya's new life," he said. "May it be blessed with health, happiness and success."

"Hear, hear," Maya said, as they clinked glasses.

"All the best, kiddo," Muriel said. She leaned over to Henry. "Look at her, she looks kind of grown up, doesn't she?"

"That she does," he said.

Maya looked closely at her mother. In many ways, Muriel did not seem to be the same woman whom Maya had known all her life. The changes in her were phenomenal—especially since Maya had returned from her trip.

At first Maya figured it was just psychological projection: *she* had changed and was putting it on Muriel, who then seemed different. But that wasn't it. Muriel *had* changed, and although Maya had at first suspected some sort of mystical tampering on the part of her father, she had to give credit where it was due, to Henry Rossmore and the Alcoholics Anonymous program. Muriel had not only admitted her problem and joined up but had summoned the willingness to examine her life with a critical eye, something she had never been disposed to do. Ever since, much of the tension had been bled out of her relationship with Maya.

Although Muriel's transformation had not always been smooth, it was authentic, and Maya was happy to see it—from a distance. Her mother was discovering herself, probably for the first time in her life.

Maya had wanted to tell her about David Orr, and even came close once, but she decided against it. If such a disclosure were to happen, it would come naturally, in its own time, and not while Muriel was still on uncertain emotional footing.

Josh was around but only at the fringes of her life. He came by every couple of weeks and they would rent videos, see a band or go out for Indian food at Dupont Circle. He seemed to be the only person who liked her minimalist decorating scheme, which consisted of only the bare essentials with a few art objects thrown in.

One of the ironies of her new life was that Maya's father had lent a helping hand in kicking it off. The last of his money had gone for her move-in costs: first month's rent, security deposit, bed, desk, couch, stereo, CDs. The essentials. His journal sat securely in its original case, tucked in a desk drawer.

Hardly a day had passed when she did not think of her trip. When a letter from Gathering arrived, she immediately sent one off in return, inviting the girl to come for a visit. Her memories of Wilton, of Taos, of Los Angeles, and all the rest remained close, although life's mundane, everyday concerns were beginning to take up most of her thinking time.

"Maya," Henry said in his formal way—he was wearing a sports jacket and tie on a Sunday—"We have an announcement to make."

Muriel held her hand out, revealing an engagement ring.

Henry's face fell. "Honey, what about my announcement?"

"I know," Muriel said, "but we've already had a toast."

"That was for Maya."

Muriel looked at her fiancé, saw what she'd done, then said something that Maya had seemingly lived her whole life to hear.

"I'm sorry."

"Ah, it's okay," Henry said. "The point isn't how you say it, it's that it's going to happen."

Again the three clinked glasses.

*   *   *

Monday morning arrived with an icy norther—more cold weather. The wind was blistering, and Maya buried her face in her scarf and walked faster. She took the escalator down to the Metro station two steps at a time, speeding past the people on the right. She leapt the last few steps and dashed into a subway car just before the doors whooshed shut. Catching her breath, she gripped a pole as a few of the commuters glanced up briefly from their newspapers and paperbacks before resuming their downward stare.

Her life was different, but what about the change? In the time since her return she had wondered often about it, but the more time passed, the less real it seemed. Change was occurring, yes, but was it *the* change? How could she possibly know?

The cycle of life was turning, as always. The march of days, of seasons, brought constant change. The lives of the billions of people on the planet transformed, shifted, metamorphosed. If her father was right all this was powered by a phenomenon called the inner medium whose machinations ceaselessly spun new webs of events and experiences.

In a few months the cold of winter would pass, replaced by the warmth of spring. Pink blossoms would awaken on the cherry trees along the National Mall, and downtown would light up in bright pastels. The lawns around the Capitol and the memorials would dance with life, filled with people from all over the world. The sleeping grass would awaken with new shoots, and children would continue to wage the eternal battle against apathy and cynicism without ever knowing of its existence. Amid all this, Maya would happily pedal her bike along the forested path that ran the length of the city, listening to music on her headphones.

But that time had not arrived yet. Today, the sky was a concrete gray, the air frigid. Maya exited the train and walked the two blocks to the Lewiston Trust, an environmentalist think tank owned and operated by the Anderson Foundation. David and Georgia had had no trouble securing her a job. In fact, Roger Anderson was thrilled to hire the daughter of his favorite metaphysical researcher.

Maya strode into the lobby, performing her usual cold-weather ritual, opening her coat as fast as possible to revel in the burst of warm air that hits one squarely upon entering a heated building.

Today, a woman who had also just arrived greeted the warmth in exactly the same way. Her eyes met Maya's, and the two women smiled conspiratorially in recognition of a simple experience that is at the heart of the cold weather: everyone is in it together.

Maya rode the elevator to the third floor. She was the first in the office, as usual. She hung up her coat and made her way to the office kitchen.

Again her thoughts returned to her father. She'd had no trouble understanding his plan. She had even seen reality creation in action, if only on a small scale: the wolf that had wandered into the cave. Imagining reality creation on a worldwide scale was another matter. Who knew? Maybe it would work.

Stationed at the world's energy centers—its vortexes—the agents of the Mandala, those wraiths she had seen in the pyramid house, would attempt to initiate an enormous mass intention. If it succeeded, a powerful psychic impetus would be created in the inner medium. A wave would build that would eventually reach a critical mass of momentum and humanity's collective consciousness would be elevated, kicking off a large-scale manifestation of some kind.

The plan amounted to a tremendous group meditation backed by the power of the earth itself. That was the theory, anyway.

Maya poured the coffee grounds and water into the coffee maker and clicked it on. Soon people would be arriving and the office would buzz with activity.

Back at her desk, an e-mail was waiting for her.

Before she had left New Mexico, Georgia had instructed her in how to communicate with her father and the Mandala, which unfortunately meant *not* to communicate with them.

"Wait to be contacted," she had said sternly. Do not seek them out. Do not seek him out. That was the rule. Maya had no choice, so that's what she did.

An e-mail from him arrived at least once a week, to her satisfaction, and always from a new address. In the previous one he had written that he would help her to further develop her psychic abilities. The timing was perfect, for she had been noticing that her sense of knowing was growing more powerful than ever. Now there might be something to do with it.

Each e-mail also contained the promise of seeing each other again. She believed him. She had no reason not to.

Today's message read:

All on schedule. Pieces falling into place. Will jumpstart the new era through New Year's prayer. Have only to wait—too long, if you ask me.

Love you, Dad.

P.S. Remember: New Year's eve!

P.P.S. I will see you after.

What did he mean? New Year's eve was just a few days away.

All morning she tried to decipher the message, but she was stumped. Then, before lunch, she had it.

I know this.

She rifled through her drawer and yanked out a folder in which she stored newspaper and Internet articles. She pulled out a clipping: *World Peace Prayer.* She often had urges to save or buy or do something, without knowing why, and usually, at some point, she would find a need for it. Again, her special abilities at work.

Reading the article, she realized that her father was describing the annual tradition of spiritual and religiously minded people all over the world to pray for world peace at midnight December 31, Greenwich Mean Time. That way all of the prayers would be synchronized, going out at exactly the same moment.

She had never prayed in her life, at least not seriously. But the Mandala had opened her mind to the power of thought, and especially the influence of intense emotional desire. What was prayer if not these things? The intentions of both the Mandala and the world peace prayer were essentially the same.

The Mandala, poised at the globe's power centers in the Middle East, the Himalayas, Central America, the American Southwest, and all the other places, would make their demands for change at the exact moment that millions worldwide voiced the peace prayer. People who knew nothing of the Mandala's plan would amplify it beyond anything attempted by the Mandala alone.

What if it succeeded?

Maya knew right down to her cells that it was going to happen. And she was going to be a part of it.

EPILOGUE

January 1.

Halfway around the world, under the piercing heat of a tropical sun, a jailer unlocked a prisoner's cell door. A battered, bruised and haggard man peered up through blood-shot eyes. His crime? Writing magazine articles critical of his country's ruler. He had been tortured. His family had been harassed. He had been forced to confess to crimes he did not commit.

The guard, suddenly understanding the cruelty and injustice of the man's treatment, swung the door open.

"You are free to go."

"Why?" the prisoner asked through a haze of pain.

"It makes no sense to imprison you," the jailer said. "I can't bear it any longer. Please, go."

At that very moment, halfway around the world in a rural American state, a boy was chastised, diminished and punished—again—for being inattentive in school and aggressive toward his brothers and sisters.

"I can't help it," the boy protested.

"Can't you concentrate on anything?" his mother asked.

"Math," he said. The answer surprised him as much as her.

Suddenly, intuitively, without any idea why it was happening, the boy understood why the ancient Greeks saw mathematics as the language of the divine. His aggressiveness disappeared, never to return.

Thousands of miles away a young woman standing in a rice field in southern Asia, crushed with the grief at the loss of her brother, inexplicably found herself feeling hopeful about the future. She did not know why.

Farther to the east, a military dictator who had committed countless atrocities leaned over a map and fell into a momentary hallucination, visualizing the enemy general as his own brother. He continued his plotting but was noticeably slowed down.

In New York City an old man fell down on a sidewalk. A couple passing by helped him up, and then found themselves embracing him, much to their surprise.

And walking down Connecticut Avenue, Maya Burke was stopped in her tracks, overwhelmed by a sense of anticipation and excitement about the coming months. It was exactly the same feeling stirring in her father at that very moment on a remote mountaintop in South America.

The change was on.